# NO
# VACANCY

## STEPHANIE ROSE

# NO VACANCY

STEPHANIE ROSE

That's What She Said Publishing, Inc.

Cover Design: Najla Qamber Designs (www.najlaqamberdesigns.com)

Photography: Regina Wamba of reginawamba.com

Editing: Christine Allen Riley

Proofreading: Mitzi Pummer Carroll

*021622*

*To my son, who hogged my phone for most of our Jersey Shore vacation because his tablet couldn't pick up the spotty Wi-Fi, giving me no other choice but to take in the beautiful town and beach and sparking the idea that became this story.*

# SOUNDTRACK

Call You Mine - The Chainsmokers
All On My Mind - Anderson East
We Own Tonight - New Kids On the Block
Like I'm Gonna Lose You - Meghan Trainor (feat. John
Legend)
Endless Summer Nights - Richard Marx
Ice Cream - Sarah McLachlan
Love Me Anyway - Pink (feat. Chris Stapleton)
Takeaway - The Chainsmokers
Try - Pink
Summer Nights - John Travolta, Olivia Newton-John
Don't Give Up On Me - Andy Grammer
Lover - Taylor Swift

Playlist can be found on Spotify

# 1

## CATERINA

"I DON'T UNDERSTAND why you had to leave right now. Why couldn't you wait three more days and go with your friends? That's too long of a drive to make all by yourself."

My mother's worried voice flooded my car through the Bluetooth speakers. Why the hell had I answered the phone? I'd ignored every text and sent all calls to voice mail since I'd left, but my mother would be crazed with worry if I didn't pick up her call.

"Ma, I'm fine," I assured her as I tried to focus on the ding of the GPS signaling my next turn. The three hours I'd spent in my car trying to figure out where the hell I was going was oddly soothing. I was focused on something other than the reasons why I'd decided to start my vacation immediately.

"Did you and Trent have a fight?"

Any peace I'd found on my way down here dissipated in a rush at the sound of my boyfriend's name. Or, ex-boyfriend as the case was now.

"Something like that. I really don't want to talk about it, and I've had a long drive. Didn't you want me to relax and go on vacation?"

I pulled into a spot in the Anchor Motel parking lot, a few long beats of silence passing between my mother and me. Admitting that I'd been duped for God knew how long, stung like hell. The thought of what else had been going on right under my nose without me having one single clue was humiliating, and verbalizing it only made it more real.

"I did, Cat. But you sound anything but relaxed." I sniffed away the burning in my nose. Nope, I wasn't crying to my mother over this. "We'll talk tomorrow when you're ready."

I sucked in my bottom lip, biting the inside of my cheek as I nodded at no one, willing the tears pooling in my eyes back in the ducts. I would hold on to the tiny bit of dignity I'd left Brooklyn with.

I whispered a goodbye and ended the call, massaging the sore fingers I'd white-knuckled around my steering wheel since I'd left. The adrenaline had worn off, and exhaustion now flooded my veins in its place.

Somewhere between the Turnpike and the entrance to the Garden State Parkway, I'd figured out what had driven me to flee my own home. It wasn't the disintegration of a great love, although at one time, I'd thought Trent and I had something real. It was the time I'd wasted, forcing us into something we weren't anymore, or maybe never really were. But, after two years, I deserved a whole lot better. And, in the end, I'd never expected to come home early from work and catch another woman on her knees, blowing my boyfriend on the brand-new couch I'd just bought with my promotion bonus.

My phone screen lit up again, this time with my friend Megan's face. As much as I hated to, I pushed the button on my steering wheel to answer.

"I'm here. Just pulled up." I didn't even have a "hello" in me for one of my oldest friends because I had no desire to go into this horrible story—one I'd have to repeat over and over again once I'd finally let it out.

"Shit, Cat. What the hell happened? This isn't you."

"I can't go on vacation early?"

A long sigh echoing my mother's came through the speakers. "You can, but you don't. How long did it take us to convince you to take next week off? So, for you to escape to a town you've never been to, all alone? Yeah, you have us a touch concerned."

I let my head fall against the headrest. Megan was always the calm, voice of reason type of friend. Shocking her wasn't an easy feat.

Was this my fault? Had I become so obsessed with work that I'd missed all the signs that my relationship was falling apart? Or that I didn't really have one to begin with?

"I left Trent. And since his name is on our lease, I don't think I can throw him out. It was head to the shore for an early vacation, or stay home and ..." I wondered what I would have done had I stayed. I didn't even have it in me to really fight or consider what else around our apartment had been tainted. I had the strong feeling this wasn't a one-time occurrence, and, while finding out Trent had been unfaithful would have hurt one way or the other, he'd brought it into our home. *My* home. I ran because, at that moment, it felt like I didn't have a home anymore.

"You can still throw him out. If you'd called me, I would have happily stuffed his shit in garbage bags for you and thrown them off your terrace."

An unexpected laugh escaped me. "You're a good friend, Meg. I know this doesn't make sense, but it was something I had to do."

"Hey, as long as you're okay and safe. And I know you're

all twisted up, but maybe try to enjoy being away, just a little. Don't have the laptop stuck to you the entire time until we get there."

"I just need to work tomorrow since I left in such a rush—"

"I am confiscating it the second we get to the rental. Be warned."

I let a smile—a real smile—stretch my lips for the first time since I'd gotten into my car and headed for the highway.

"And Cat, I'm sorry. I don't know exactly what happened, but you always deserved better than Trent."

"I'm sorry, too. And thank you." I ended the call, sucking in a long breath before opening my car door to begin my lovely solo vacation.

I'd searched online for a hotel close to both the beach and where we'd be staying once my friends arrived. I'd found one with reasonable rates and decent reviews in less than five minutes. I was out the door the second the confirmation email came through.

The first thing that caught my eye about the Anchor Motel was an outside staircase leading to the rooms. This wasn't like the hotels I was used to, but when I booked the reservation, the only amenities I'd been looking for were a bed, Wi-Fi, and, after a quick online search, no noted visits from the Board of Health. The whole place had a gaudy, outdated feel to it that didn't come through on their website. Even at night, it was hard to miss the aqua trim on the windows and pink rails along the steps.

The hotel pool was huge and was chock-full of what looked like drunken college kids. It filled me with both nostalgia and despair since my days of bringing along a red Solo cup for a swim were so far behind me, I hardly remembered them.

As much as I tried to, I couldn't pinpoint when all the fun in my life had circled the drain. Or, as Trent pointed out before I shut the door behind me, when I'd become a cold fish who no one could get close to.

So far, my vacation was a pity party for one.

I made my way to what looked like the main office to check in and get my room key. The simple, old school feel of the Anchor reminded me of my childhood trips to Lake George. My extended family would make the pilgrimage from Bay Ridge, Brooklyn to the scenic upstate town every August. My cousins and I had loved staring at the pool through our window and making a game out of spotting the midnight swimmers. Now, I hoped my room had thick enough curtains and blinds to prevent others from seeing in.

"Hello, dear." A portly man with a full head of white hair greeted me with a warm smile after I tapped on the silver bell at the front desk. "Checking in?"

"Yes." It came out like a *"God, yes."* "Caterina Longo. I just made the reservation today." I jerked my chin toward the computer. I didn't want to seem unfriendly, but getting into my room and passing out on the queen-sized bed I'd reserved was my only priority.

"Ah, here you are." He nodded and reached over to the wall, grabbing a lime green keychain off one of the pegs.

A key? An actual key? I couldn't remember how long it had been since I had a real, metal hotel key. I always lost my key cards and had to get new ones programmed from the front desk every single vacation or business trip. If I lost this key, replacing it would involve a locksmith.

"Room 326, just up the stairs in the front." He grinned at me before pointing his finger toward the staircase.

"Thank you. Oh, and the Wi-Fi password?"

"Of course." He nodded with a grin. My clients usually

took Fridays off in the summer, allowing me a lovely and quiet day to catch up. Unless I wanted to work at the rental next week, and I had no doubt Megan hadn't been kidding about hiding my laptop, I'd need to get online tomorrow. And I hadn't seen a Starbucks for three exits prior to my arrival. I bristled at the thought of more hours in the car.

"Anchor is the login, password is anchor12345." He pulled a paper from the desk with the information printed on it. "Easy to remember, but we print these, anyway."

I nodded a thank you and tried to summon the energy to pull my large suitcase up three flights of stairs.

"Have a good evening, Ms. Longo. Oh, and just a warning. Sometimes, the Wi-Fi is spotty around the hotel, and guests complain about low signal in the rooms. The restaurant across the street, The Beach Pub, has a nice strong signal and is open late. I know how you young folk need your computers and phones."

I mouthed a "thank you" before leaving the office, chuckling to myself at being referred to as "young folk."

Before climbing the stairs to my room, my gaze again lingered a moment on the crowd around the pool. When was the last time I'd made time for my friends and had fun? I needed this.

A bright light in my periphery caught my gaze as I made my way to the staircase. My head swiveled toward a flashing "No Vacancy" sign in bright pink neon letters. It had the same effect as high-beam headlights would on my dried-up contact lenses. The Anchor was definitely a throwback to generations before me. I laughed to myself, thankful I'd made it under the wire and was able to secure a room before it was too late.

Rushing up the steps before any of the swimmers could call me "ma'am," I shoved my key in the door, jiggling it in the lock a few times before it would open.

I flicked on the light switch and dumped my suitcase and purse on the floor. Grabbing my phone, I finally read the plethora of texts that I'd muted on my way here. Despite my resolve, I paused when I spied Trent's name.

**Trent:** *I know you didn't really head to the shore. Point made. It's been hours.*

*Point made?* After bouncing the phone on my bed, I fell back and draped my hand over my eyes. How could I have been so blind for so damn long? There wasn't an ounce of concern in Trent's text. Not an "I'm sorry" or an "Are you okay?" He didn't even believe I'd really left. I tried to remember the last time we'd had sex or a time when affection had gone beyond a peck on the lips before heading out the door. I came up empty. Maybe Trent was right. I was too caught up in work and planning for my future that I forgot to pay attention to the present.

Rising up on my elbows, I scanned the tiny room as I worried a stray thread on the bedspread between my fingers. This was the most "in the moment" I'd been in a long time. With no buzz from my phone or ping from my computer signaling another email, the quiet lifted the fog I'd been under for so long. Maybe a weekend alone *would* help me figure things out—like what I wanted out of life. If all I cared about was my job, why did Trent's betrayal bother me so much? Maybe it was more bruised ego than broken heart that had pushed me out the door. When I thought of what kind of person that made me, a wave of nausea crawled up my throat.

"Ugh, you have to be kidding me," I groaned, spying the tiny lone signal bar in the corner of my phone screen. I could ignore it and climb into bed or venture across the street to the restaurant with the good Wi-Fi. My eyes darted from the bed to the door and back again. Grabbing my lime green keychain and my purse, I headed out the door and down the stairs.

If I wanted more out of life, maybe this crazy weekend all by myself could be the first step.

## 2

## CATERINA

My legs wobbled from either exhaustion or plummeting blood sugar when I pulled open the door to The Beach Pub. My body finally remembered needing silly things like food and sleep.

Until today, I'd never believed it was truly possible to forget to eat. Since I was a kid, I'd count the minutes until lunch, especially during those dark times when I'd attempt to diet. I could add not eating for an overextended period of time to my list of firsts today.

The place was empty. I supposed it wasn't surprising for this hour on a Thursday night, and, from the little I knew about Ocean Cove, New Jersey, it didn't exactly strike me as a party-all-night type of town. My friends had booked a rental here because it was an up-and-coming shore destination that had grown in popularity the past few summers. It was only a short distance from the main beach towns I'd vacationed in during my younger years, but I'd honestly never heard of it until Megan and Claire asked me to stay at the rental house they'd found. If my hotel was any indication, people had been vacationing here for years.

I found a seat at one of the empty booths and swept my gaze around the dining area. Despite its simple name, the place had a rustic yet modern feel to it. The walls were a rich, dark wood, dotted with scenic photos of the area and whom I assumed were locals. Large TV screens mounted on the walls captured the attention of the other two patrons inside. I searched the room for someone to take my order, my hunger getting the best of me as my leg bobbed under the table.

"I'm so sorry."

My head swiveled in the direction of a friendly, deep timbre.

"I was in the back and didn't realize you walked in. What can I get you?" The man attached to the voice made his way toward me. Even in my acutely pissy mood, I sucked in a short gasp. My weary gaze roamed upward as it swept over the trimmed sandy brown scruff covering a chiseled jaw, blue eyes that, even in the dim lighting, seemed translucent, tussled hair in that he-probably-made-no-effort-with-but-fell-into place-like-magic way. The whole package was so unnervingly perfect, I blinked and cleared my throat, positive I was caught gawking.

To be this attracted to a stranger after just breaking up with my boyfriend of two years, regardless of the circumstances, seemed wrong.

"Could I please see a menu?" The pathetic croak in my voice made my request seem like a plea.

My hollow belly sank at his apologetic wince.

"During the week, the kitchen closes at ten. I'm sorry—"

I cut him off with a groan before dropping my head into my hands.

"Of course, it does." I rubbed my eyes with the heels of my palms before I began digging into my purse in the hopes of finding a granola bar or something to have with a beer.

"You look like you've had a long day." He tilted his head, lifting an eyebrow as he searched my gaze.

"You could say that." I stifled a frustrated sigh.

"Tell you what. I could make you something small. What would you like?"

"I couldn't ask you to do that." I waved him off and continued to hunt for food inside my purse. I'd even have settled for a Life Saver at this point.

"Sure, you could. I have some pull." He grinned and rested his elbows on the top of the opposite seat of the booth. His easy smile made me forget my argument. I'd bet that smile made a lot of women forget a lot of things.

"If you could have one thing in the world right now, what would you want? Think bar food, though."

He grinned, and, despite my desperation, I grinned back. I was either that tired or that hungry or he was that gorgeous.

"Mozzarella sticks." I cringed when it came out *mutzadelle* sticks. Usually, I forced out *mozzarella, ricotta,* or *manicotti* the non-Italian way to avoid getting weird looks from non-Italian friends, but I guessed after the long day and night I'd had, putting a conscious effort into anything right now was an exercise in futility. "I mean, I'd like—"

A throaty chuckle fell from his lips before he nodded. "It's okay. I have two Italian grandmothers. Nice to hear someone say it right for a change. I'll be back in a few minutes. What would you like to drink?"

"Whatever beer is on tap would be great, thank you!"

My gaze fell to his black T-shirt and the threadbare jeans hugging his hips. Lucky jeans. He was built but not bulky, and I hoped he didn't catch me staring at his arms. My friends used to tease me for having a biceps fetish, and his were perfect, right down to the delicious way they stretched his sleeves.

"You got it." He made his way to the kitchen, my view of his back just as pleasing as the front.

I fell back in my seat, letting myself relax for the first time in hours. My phone finally stopped buzzing, I had a plate full of greasy calories headed my way, and I was somewhere where I knew no one, and no one knew me. That filled me with a confusing relief. I was one of those mysterious diners without a book or project to keep them company. It was just me and my thoughts as I waited for my food and beer.

"Feeling okay?" My waiter cast me a concerned glance as he placed the deep-fried goodness in front of me. I'd never been so happy to see food in my life and held myself back from shoving an entire stick into my mouth. My luck, I'd choke, and this new adventure I'd forced myself on would be for nothing.

"Thank you so much." I grabbed a stick and took a bite, my eyes fluttering as the melted cheese hit my tongue. "I'm fine, it's been a long day. I drove in from Brooklyn tonight. It was a spur-of-the-moment kind of thing." I washed the first stick down with a mouthful of ice-cold beer and whimpered in delight.

"You must really love *mutzadelle* sticks." The corners of his mouth lifted as he crossed his arms. *God, those arms.* Smooth, with a couple of veins trailing down to his wrists. My fingertips itched to find out if the dusting of hair over his forearms was as soft as it looked. Hunger was doing bad things to me.

"Tonight?" he asked after mulling over what I'd told him. "That's a long drive for a spur-of-the-moment."

"It's a long, sad story I won't bore you with. My friends are staying in a rental nearby starting on Sunday, so I figured why not start my vacation now?" I raised my beer glass in a salute.

"But, it's *Thursday*," he said slowly as if I wasn't aware.

"I'm staying at the Anchor until they get here. I'll work a little by the pool tomorrow and then...maybe sit on the beach, check out your daytime menu. Possibilities are endless."

He made a shrill, whistling sound through his teeth. "That must be some story."

"It's a terrible story you don't want to hear." I held my hand up, taking tiny bites of the last two sticks to make them last longer.

"Try me." He narrowed his gorgeous eyes.

"You don't even know my name."

"What if I told you mine? Joe." He extended a hand. I let it dangle between us for a couple of beats as I drew back in my seat. "Owner of The Beach Pub."

"Ah." I nodded. "That's why you had pull in the kitchen." I shot him a wry grin. I took his hand, and a foreign warmth spread through my chest. My tired mind was playing tricks on me. We held the handshake for just long enough to be awkward. "Caterina. My friends call me Cat."

"That's a beautiful name. Nice to meet you, Caterina."

I gulped as my gaze fell to his lips. There was something about the way my name rolled off his tongue as if his voice was caressing each syllable. When he took the empty seat across from me, I stiffened against the back of my seat. My attraction to this guy was as overpowering as it was confusing.

"So, talk to me." He leaned his elbows on the table and leveled his gaze at me. "Why the instant vacation? Did you rob a bank before you left?"

I rolled my eyes at the mirth in his baby blues.

"No, I did not. No need to call the local sheriff or whatever you guys have for cops out here."

His chest rumbled with a laugh, drawing my eyes to the way his T-shirt stretched across his broad torso.

"I came home from work early and caught my boyfriend, *ex*-boyfriend, cheating on me. On the new couch I'd just bought."

It was funny how *that* was the part I kept coming back to. Sure, the fact that my boyfriend of two years had his dick in another woman's mouth in our apartment stung, but the fact that it happened on my beautiful, brand-fucking-new, gray woven fabric couch twisted the proverbial knife. Dread filled me for all it would entail to go our separate ways along with the residue of shame at realizing that was probably the only reason we stayed together for so long.

"That sucks. I'm sorry that happened to you." Genuine empathy spread across Joe's gorgeous features.

"You're actually the first person I've told." I settled back in my seat, an odd relief relaxing my shoulders to let it out to someone. "I came home, found...that...and left. Shocked the shit out of everyone I know. See, I'm the sensible one. The one who doesn't go out on work nights, who dated one guy at a time in college, who never takes a vacation. The sensible one. The *boring* one." I shook my head as I dragged my nail along the drip of condensation down my beer glass, my eyes darting from the table to Joe. Why was I spilling my guts to a stranger? When my gaze met his, his eyes were kind without a hint of judgment, as if he was actually listening to me.

"Believe it or not, I know exactly how you feel." Joe draped his arm along the back of the booth. "When I wanted to buy this place, my family thought I was insane. I never expressed a big interest in business before, so where was this coming from?"

I laughed when he draped a dramatic hand over his chest.

"Not exactly the same, but I know how much it sucks when people underestimate you."

I blew out a long breath and nodded. "I left a mess that I'll have to clean up when I get back, but something in me... snapped. It sounds completely nuts now that I actually say it all out loud." I winced.

Joe gave me a warm smile. "Not nuts at all. I think it's brave to come out here all by yourself and sort things out. My family thought *I* was nuts for driving all the way here from Queens when I found out this place was for sale."

"You're not from around here?"

"Nope." He shook his head. "Transplanted local. Bars and restaurants are a dime a dozen in the city, but here, I thought I could really make it mine and not give into stupid trends that I didn't like. It's a cool little town, too, even if some streets are stuck in the 1950s." His smile stole a little air from my lungs. I sucked in a quick breath in a futile effort to compose myself.

"My friends say this is the new hot spot for vacation. Though, I honestly didn't even know the name of it until they told me they were booking it."

"It's like a big secret that everyone suddenly wants in on." Even his laugh was sexy—deep and gruff. "I could have tried for something closer to home or gone corporate after college like my brilliant sister, but it wasn't what I wanted." Joe leaned forward, squinting at me. "I'm not sure why I'm telling you my life story right now."

"I was wondering why I was telling you all my troubles, too." I laughed as my shoulders softened, my whole body less rigid as I locked eyes with Joe.

"But I'm guessing a lot of customers tell you their troubles. You have that kind of face."

"What kind of face is that?" The sudden heat in his stare made me tense up in a whole different way.

"The sweet smile and the crystal blue eyes. Like you don't have a mirror." I rolled my eyes, unable to hide the twitch of my lips.

"Like those big dark eyes don't make guys spill their guts all the time, at least that's what *I'm* blaming it on. Men probably trip over themselves to get to you."

"Trip?" I had to laugh. The man I lived with hardly spoke to me. The idea of guys tripping over themselves to get to me was as far from my real life as it could possibly get. "No, Joe. I lived with a guy for years who barely said a word to me the past few months. No one trips; trust me."

"Maybe you aren't looking hard enough." His voice dipped into a gravelly whisper, leaving me breathless at the sudden shift of energy between us. "Your ex was an asshole. We only just met, but a woman like you is pretty tough to ignore."

Ignored, dismissed, sadly dependable. That's how I'd describe myself until now. Catching the attention of a sexy stranger gave me a high I wasn't expecting.

"Good night, Joe," an older man called out to Joe before pushing the front door to leave.

"I guess we're the only ones here." Joe motioned behind him to the now empty restaurant. "Still hungry?"

I bit into my final mozzarella stick with a sheepish nod. "But I'll go, I don't want you to go to any more trouble." I reached for my purse and dug for my wallet when Joe grabbed my wrist.

"I'm hungry, too. I'll make you something else and sit with you if that's okay." My heart squeezed at the shy smile pulling at his lips.

I set down my purse and replied with a slow nod. "Sure, that sounds great. Thanks."

I glanced at the clock over the bar, it was midnight. Joe popped up and headed into the kitchen, leaving me alone with an odd twisting in my stomach. I wanted to stay but was uneasy. Although I harbored a ton of bad feelings at how we split, Trent and I were very much over, so it wasn't an unfaithful guilt nagging at me.

I may have been in my thirties, but I was much shorter on life experience than others my age due to a sheltered upbringing and overactive conscience. Sure, I had a senior level position at work and had a few long-term relationships before my last disaster. But the prospect of taking a chance on anything often left me in a cold sweat, even when I'd been a kid and was supposed to do crazy and stupid things. Letting down my guard and throwing caution to the wind never came this easily to me, and I worried my rash decisions wouldn't end with my impulsive drive here. Spying Joe though the pass-through window to the kitchen, I had the strong suspicion they were only beginning.

# 3

## JOE

"Tell me about you," I said to Caterina. "Any brothers or sisters?" I asked while trying to cover how flustered I was. Flustered over *her*. When I'd come over to take her order, I'd never expected to be entranced by some kind of spell. She'd peered up at me with those sad, chocolate eyes, and all I'd wanted to do was make her feel better. Once we'd begun talking, I hadn't wanted to stop. Her lush, pink lips had stretched into a smile, and I'd lost all sense of logic. The only thought that had been rumbling around in my head was if her mouth was as pillow soft as it looked. And don't get me started on her throaty laugh. I'd planted myself across the booth from her, and, other than the three times I'd reopened the kitchen—also a first for me—something about her pinned me to the seat.

"I'm an only child," she said after swallowing a mouthful of nachos. "I may not have the competition complex you have, but a lot of pressure, nonetheless. I'm my mother's only hope."

We shared a laugh before I shook my head.

"It's not that Bella and I are in a competition. My sister is beautiful and brilliant, so there *is* no competition when it comes to her. And I'm not saying my parents aren't proud, but I doubt I'll ever get the look of awe they give her. Of the two of us, she's more like my dad. He's a VP, and I expect her to be one any day now. Me, they probably hoped I'd get a steady job and get by." I shrugged—part of my act to cover how my family made me feel. They never showed me anything but love, but I still felt less than in their eyes. Opening my own restaurant was my dream, but it was a risk they never seemed to fully understand. Under this gorgeous woman's gaze, my mask was cracking—another thing I didn't get.

"Maybe *you* shouldn't underestimate yourself. It takes guts to open up your own place. I don't think I could do it."

I looked around with a wistful glance. We'd come a long way in two years, and I was nothing but proud. Keeping it moving in the right direction was the struggle that cost me sleep most nights. "It's nice to have something that's mine. Not having to answer to anyone, doing things my way. I'm not an asshole who won't take advice, but there's something freeing about doing it all yourself. My brother-in-law gave me a loan to buy this place. Though, he keeps calling himself a silent partner and won't let me pay him back. But he's also cool enough to never hold it over my head."

When I'd first bought this place—then an old dive bar called the Red Oak—I'd had big plans and dreams, with a limited budget. Owen had been a brother to me ever since I was eight years old, and my sister brought him home from college one weekend. Not to say my father wouldn't have helped me, but after I'd put all I had into my business, the very last thing I needed to hear were his doubts on whether it was a good idea or not. When I'd asked Owen for a loan, he hadn't hesitated a second before opening his checkbook.

"This is an odd place to want to open a business, though. I

know it's getting popular now, but wouldn't the main shore towns have been a safer bet?"

"My parents asked me the same question." I laughed, remembering how many times they actually did ask that very question after I'd told them my intentions.

Her gaze fell on my chest but quickly darted away. When I met her eyes, her olive skin reddened with a blush. I held in a laugh, not wanting to call her on checking me out.

"My dad took us here when we were kids. We'd rent a house, and it felt like we were in the country, far away from all the noise and the chaos. Although, now, the area is much more popular, so the chaos is finding me again, which leads to profit. So, it's not all bad. You know it's a hot spot when the college kids find you. Fake IDs have gotten a lot more creative since my day."

That was a big reason I didn't get involved with tourists. But Caterina wasn't an underage college girl flirting with me in the hopes that I'd forget how to do math when I glanced at her birthdate on her ID. She was a woman. A gorgeous woman I couldn't peel my eyes off of. I checked *her* out all night, too, but didn't waste energy on hiding it.

"Ah, yes." She nodded. "There were a group of what looked like college kids in the pool when I checked in."

"See? That means the place is gold." I raised my beer bottle before taking a long pull, noting her heated stare in my periphery. The air thinned between us at each pause in conversation.

"Enough about me, what do you do? Besides plan last-minute vacations."

She pursed her lips before leaning her elbows on the table. She hadn't stood yet, but the glimpses I'd gotten of her body were enough to make me squirm in my seat. Her full breasts stretched the thin fabric of her tank top, and I willed my eyes upward. There was a difference between checking her out and outright leering at her, and the more time I spent in her presence, the more I was teetering over that line.

"I'm an advertising account manager. We plan digital campaigns for clients. I work a lot of long hours. Coming here on a whim was a first." She dropped her gaze to the table, her eyes vacant and sad before she took another sip of beer.

"Hey," I whispered before giving her foot a gentle kick under the table. "Where'd you go?"

"Ever feel like the harder you try, the more you disappoint people?" She didn't meet my eyes as she flicked the last nacho crumb around her plate. "I work late all the time, sometimes a few hours on the weekend, trying to get...somewhere. A promotion, pride from my family and friends. I thought working hard now would mean good things down the line, but I was so lost in trying to make my mother happy, planning for my future, I never gave much thought to being happy *now*." Her sad eyes almost had me out of my seat and scooping her into my arms. Where the hell did that come from?

"Sorry. A full belly and too many drinks make me a little sappy. It's been a day, and you've been very patient. I'll be sure to tip nicely."

"Trust me, I know all about working to not be someone's disappointment and always feeling like you're coming up short. I followed the path I wanted, even if it didn't make a lot of sense to most people."

Constantly feeling like a disappointment fueled my drive to succeed, but exhausted me all the same. It was hard to make anyone understand why I obsessed over numbers and never took any time off, but when I met Caterina's gorgeous but weary eyes across the table, she nodded as if she did.

"I'd rather excel at what I wanted than fail at what *they* wanted for me. Or what my father wanted, anyway."

"Do you not get along with your father?"

"No, I do. That's the problem. He casts a huge shadow. I can never be like him, and, even though I don't want to be, part of me hates that." I fell back, shocked after letting something I'd never admitted to myself slip out. "I don't think I've ever said that out loud."

Confessing to her felt good. Why? It confused the shit out of me.

"Point is, I'm happy, but I get the constant need to prove yourself. Why I spend most of my time here, working, or trying to figure out how to make this place more successful. Maybe you could give me a hand in the off-season. I try to sponsor local events to keep the place alive, but I always wanted to try to advertise more." We did well in summer and okay in the early fall, but I was still searching for a way to keep up revenue all year long. Maybe this beautiful woman could help me. And if that gave me an excuse to see her again, even better.

"Sure, we could talk about what you need, once I get some sleep and can actually think enough to have a conversation."

"You've been doing okay so far; it's been three hours already, and I haven't tripped you up yet."

"Three hours?" She gasped and squinted at the clock over the bar. "It's almost three o'clock in the morning! How late do you stay open?"

"During the week, usually until one." I couldn't help but laugh as her eyes filled with panic.

"Oh, God, Joe. I'm so sorry. I didn't mean to—"

I reached across the table to grab her hand. "You didn't do anything. Come with me, I want to show you something."

Caterina's eyes darted from my face to my extended hand before she finally took it. After pulling her to standing, I led her to the floor-to-ceiling windows in the back of the restaurant.

"That's my favorite beach. What sold me on this place, actually—even though it needed a shit ton of work. Come look." I grasped her waist to pull her in front of me. Even her scent was intoxicating. My fingertips tingled with the need to touch her, but I forced my hand to rest at my side. "It's dark, but you can still see the waves crashing. When the sun sets, it's fucking beautiful." I fixed my gaze on Caterina's gorgeous profile—the delicate curve of her jaw, those perfect lips that had tortured me for the past few hours. The ocean had nothing on this woman. *She* was fucking beautiful and having her this close made the blood run hot in my veins. My control was slipping more and more with every second.

"Peace among the chaos. Reminds you that there are forces bigger than you, and you have no choice but to go with the flow, sometimes." I brought my hand to her lower back, her body leaning into my touch so slightly, barely a half of a centimeter, but enough to make me want more. Want closer. "But sometimes, you swim against the current and say screw it. *That's* what you did today."

"You mean when I ran away?" Her nervous laugh didn't hide the quiver in her voice.

"Ran away, escaped, depends on how you look at it. You have guts, Caterina." I slid my palm over hers and squeezed. The jolt from where our skin touched triggered a dozen fantasies. Was her skin this silky all over? What sounds would she make when I ran my hands all over her body? How would she taste? I knew she'd be sweet, and I wouldn't be able to stop once I started. As if she could hear my thoughts, she turned toward me, her lips parted as her chest rose and fell with her shallow breaths.

*Give me those lips, beautiful. Put me out of my misery.*

Before I could close the distance between us, she jerked away, slipping her hand from mine.

"Thank you," she told me in a breathy whisper. "I should go," she blurted before rushing back to the table. "It's so late, and I've kept you long enough."

"What did I just say? You aren't keeping me. I'll lock the door, and we can have some dessert before you go. I have a little chocolate ice cream left. Interested?" I inwardly cringed at my pathetic attempt to make her stay.

"Thank you, Joe. But I should get back. To the motel, I mean." She dug through her purse. "Thank you so much for bending the rules so I could eat. I think this should cover it—" She stilled when I dropped a hand on her forearm. That same spark between us ignited once again and stopped us both in our tracks.

"It's all on me. I'll close up and walk you back to the hotel. Don't run. Please," I pleaded in her ear, spying goose bumps trailing down her neck.

After everything was locked up, we walked across the street to the Anchor and into a time warp. It had been one of the first motels in the area and looked every bit its age.

"Joe, you don't need to walk me all the way up—" She laughed and held up her hands in defeat at my narrowed eyes. "You cook, and you're a gentleman; quite the enigma, Joe." She flashed a grin over her shoulder as I followed her, my eyes landing on those denim cutoffs barely covering the sweet curve of her ass. I was a gentleman with a dirty mind.

"You'd think they'd paint over the aqua or get rid of the neon anchor sign." I nodded toward the blinking atrocity next to Caterina's door. "But Lou is a good guy. You're safe here. Some of the hotels around the area are a little sketchy."

"Lou?" Her cute little nose crinkled at me.

"The manager. I've known him since I bought the pub. Always sends guests my way since his Wi-Fi sucks."

"That's exactly how I ended up at your place tonight. Not for the Wi-Fi, but he said you were open late." She wrapped her arms around her torso as her body rolled with a shiver. It was still eighty and sticky, common for July nights around here. I wanted to believe I gave her that chill.

"Really? Well, I'll have to thank him in the morning—or later *this* morning." I shoved my hands into my pockets, my fingertips still jonesing to touch her. "I'm really glad you came in, Caterina."

"Me too." Her voice was small as she came closer. "After... everything, today, thanks for renewing my faith that nice guys do exist." She brushed her soft, warm lips against my cheek, lingering a moment past polite.

"It was my pleasure." I kissed her forehead as my hand snaked around her waist. I'd battled with myself for hours, but having her this close to me finally made me crack.

My lips caught hers when she lifted her head. She froze but didn't pull away. I gave her a soft kiss and ran my thumb along her jaw, starting with sweet and tiny pecks before grazing my bottom lip across hers. A whimper escaped her as she fisted the collar of my shirt.

"If I'm being too forward," I threaded my fingers into her hair, smiling as her eyes fluttered, "tell me to stop."

She'd come in flustered and upset, and the last thing I wanted to do was take advantage. If she asked me to stop, I would. Although I wanted this woman so badly I couldn't see straight, I'd walk away if that's what I had to do.

Her eyes thinned as she glided her finger along the seam

of my lips. Now it was my turn to shiver. Parting my lips and holding her gaze, I sucked on the tip of her finger, drawing out another whimper.

"Not on your life," she murmured against my lips before her mouth was back on mine.

I'd only known this woman for three hours, but she was about to ruin me.

# 4

## CATERINA

When our lips met again, I expected a spark. Even fireworks from all the flirting and sneaky glances of longing over the last few hours, but I hadn't expected a kiss like this. An earth-shattering, senses-robbing kiss that literally made my knees give out as I grabbed Joe's biceps for purchase. My body melted against him as he ruined me with his lips. They were demanding yet sweet: seeking, tasting, and devouring. Regret and repercussions were so far from my mind, they weren't even on the same planet. When his tongue met mine, gently stroking with long sweeps as I mewled into his mouth, the only word echoing in my frazzled brain was *more*.

My head was spinning, yet I'd never known what I wanted so clearly in my life.

"Come inside," I pleaded against his lips.

What did I yearn for the most? The comfort I'd found in his presence tonight? The payoff from the chemistry simmering between us? Or just to prove to myself that I could *feel*? That I wasn't cold and hollow, but warm and beautiful. Joe made me believe I could be that—that I *was* that—and I didn't want it to end.

His gaze was pained as he pulled away, panting and flushed but shaking his head.

"I want to. Believe me, I want to—*so* fucking badly. But like you told me, you had a day." He grinned, cradling my face. "I don't know if you realize what you really want right now."

On the long drive up here, I thought of all the regrets I had—from the things I *didn't* do. Saying goodnight to Joe and heading into my hotel room alone was the right and sensible thing to do. But if I sent Joe away, the second I shut the door behind me, I'd know I'd made a mistake. Spending the night with him was most likely a different kind of mistake, but one I wanted to make. One I *needed* to make.

"I don't want you to leave. For once in my life, I don't want to put tomorrow before today."

I dug into my purse for my key, finally palming the scratchy lacquered keychain at the very bottom. Quivering and needy, I managed to unlock the door and pushed it open.

I glanced back at Joe. The heat in his eyes contrasted with the deep furrow of his brow.

"It's a good thing it's already tomorrow." He grabbed me by the waist and brought his lips back to mine before backing me into my hotel room and shutting the door behind him. I reached back to turn the locks before pulling at the hem of his shirt.

"I've wanted to kiss you since I first saw you," he whispered as he dragged open-mouthed kisses down my neck, grazing along a sweet spot no one else had ever found. I cried out as he cupped my breast through my tank top, teasing the nipple peaking against his thumb. "I need to taste all of you." He moved his mouth back to my neck, the silk of his tongue and scrape of his stubble driving me out of my mind.

"Please, I want everything, Joe," I begged. My voice was sandpaper, gravelly and rough with need. All the inhibitions I usually had during sex, especially with someone new, vanished as I sank my teeth into his swollen bottom lip and then ran my tongue along his jaw. He muttered a curse before dropping his head back.

"Be careful what you ask for," he warned. His moans vibrated against my lips as I licked a trail down his throat and over his Adam's apple. He was sweet all over, and my mouth watered for more.

I'd never been so ravenous for anyone before tonight, and I didn't care to figure out the whys of it all. If I thought about it too much, I might come to my senses, and it was way too late for that.

I tugged his shirt up and over his stomach, still nipping at his neck when he stepped back to peel it off.

My hands shook as they glided across his chest. My fingertips traced sculpted muscle, his skin hot and smooth as I made my way lower, halting at the thin trail tempting me inside his jeans.

"I want you..." I trailed off when his hands slipped down my torso, feeling for the hem of my tank top and raising it over my head.

I'd never been naked with someone I'd known for less than twenty-four hours. Hell, less than five hours. But, at the same time, I wasn't embarrassed or attempting to cover myself. Nothing had felt this right in years, maybe ever. Chills ran through me at the same time a sheen of sweat broke out across my skin.

"I've been thinking about this, too." He unhooked my bra and inched the straps down my arms before throwing it onto the floor next to his shirt. His cocky smile faded as his eyes roamed my body, starting at my shoulders until he cupped both my breasts. I gasped and arched my back forward on instinct.

"Do you have any idea how gorgeous you are?" My chest heaved as his thumbs traced circles around my rigid nipples. "I don't know where to go first." He grinned before burying his head into my neck and starting another trail of open-mouthed kisses across my collarbone. I lost the ability to speak, the only sounds now tumbling from my lips were tortured whimpers and shameless pleas to keep going and don't stop.

He pulled me toward the bed and sat on the edge, gazing up at me with the same crazy want in his eyes that made my head spin. He was mine for the taking, and I couldn't wait another second. I straddled his lap and crashed my lips to his, rocking against him as both of us wrestled to get closer. He was hard, huge, and almost right where I wanted him. I was so drenched I was sure he felt it through the layers of denim between us.

His hands traveling down my naked back sent a shock-wave down the fibers of my spine, making me squirm even more on top of him.

"You're killing me, Caterina," he murmured against my lips. His fingers threaded into my hair and weaved through a fistful.

"Is that a good or a bad thing?"

My body shuddered when his hand cupped the mound between my legs and squeezed. Blood soared through my veins as his touch sharpened the ache already pulsing there.

"You're soaked for me, aren't you? Right here?" He squeezed again with a feral gleam in his eyes. "You like that. Don't you, beautiful?"

I nodded a desperate yes before our mouths crashed together in another sloppy kiss. We were a tangled mess of lips and tongues. Every time his erection grazed my clit, a loud moan escaped me. My hips moved back and forth of their own accord. He pulled back on a tortured groan, peering up at me with hooded eyes as he sucked a nipple into his mouth. *Jesus.* He bit down hard before kissing it better, and I couldn't decide which I loved more.

Before I knew it, I was on my back with Joe settled between my legs.

"Joe, please," I pleaded as my hips bucked off the bed. His hands and mouth were everywhere, the urgency now slowing and his moves turning slow and deliberate. The tip of his tongue grazed the sensitive skin behind my ear, causing an inhuman cry to fall from my lips.

He laughed as he popped the button open on my shorts and dipped his hand inside my panties. "I need to teach you how to relax." His icy blue eyes darkened to almost black as his fingers found my drenched and swollen flesh.

"This is all for me, isn't it? Did I make you this wet?" His voice was a gruff whisper that ran right through me. "Tell me, Caterina." He slid a finger deep inside me and inched it out, shutting his eyes as he licked it clean.

"Yes," I croaked out. "I want you to...oh, God, Joe..." A wolfish grin spread over his lips as he slid two fingers back inside me, curving them before pulling out. My orgasm was right there, waiting to burst. He did it again, this time with three fingers and his thumb rubbing against my hard bundle of nerves. I was stretched so full, my eyes teared while the lower half of my body shook.

He brushed my lips, laughing and shaking his head when I leaned forward for more.

"Patience, baby." He nipped at my bottom lip. "I'm not rushing a second with you." He licked a trail across my collarbone and up my neck. I was a needy mess but too turned on to care. Joe was about to make me lose it with his torturous seduction.

He straightened to pull off my shorts, the wet skin between my legs chilling even though I still wore panties.

My body jerked when he pressed a kiss to the damp fabric between my legs. "Can I have a taste?" I met his eyes with a wordless nod before he pushed the material to the side and covered me with his mouth, alternating slow licks and tiny bites. My legs flailed back and forth until he anchored them with his forearms. I'd never had a build up like this and was starting to fear whether or not I could handle the release.

"So damn sweet," he murmured against my skin as he dragged his lips along the inside of my thighs. "You taste so fucking good, I could do this all night and never get enough." The throbbing between my legs was so intense, I could almost hear it beating. His lips came back to my clit, sucking it hard and grazing it with his teeth. The combination of the heat of his mouth, scratch of his stubble, and the sight of his head bobbing up and down finally made me lose it. I fell so hard over the edge, I shattered, screaming his name as I fisted his hair and bucked my hips against his mouth.

"I think you're trying to kill *me*," I breathed out, my voice mostly gone, my head falling back on the pillow.

He lifted his head and cupped my chin, running his thumb over my lips. "One more time; are you sure?"

I squinted at Joe, still trying to slow my rapid breathing. "Yes," I panted. "Very sure." I rolled up on my elbows. "You don't...want to...?" I couldn't figure out why Joe would back away now with my arousal still glistening off his lips.

He rolled his hips against me, his rock-hard erection pulsing against my sensitive core. "There is nothing more I want right now than to be deep inside you. *So* fucking deep," he growled as he thrust his hips against me, drawing out a needy whimper. "But I don't want you to regret it."

Grabbing the back of his head, I crushed my lips to his, moaning into his mouth as our tongues tangled and teeth scraped in a kiss of starvation. Joe dug his hand into my hair and gave it back to me with the same fervor. Want had already given way to guttural need, and neither of us could stop now.

He straightened and kicked off his pants and boxers. As I took in his naked body, my gaze zeroed in on his cock as it bobbed against his ribbed stomach. I had no words, salivating as he slid the condom down his length.

I'd seen a penis or two in my time, but I'd never gaped at one as if I were in a trance. He was long and smooth, and my tongue itched to lick up and down before I took all of him in my mouth.

He stilled at the end of the bed, my skin heating all over again as his eyes caressed my naked body.

"I'm the luckiest bastard in the world tonight," he whispered before he climbed on top of me, snaking his arm around my waist and lifting me off the bed.

"Ride me."

I squinted, my brain cells still recuperating from the mind melting climax I had not five minutes ago. "What?"

He flipped us over, so I was on top. "Ride me. I want to watch you come when I'm deep inside you."

My legs quivered as I lifted a thigh to straddle him, the sudden intimacy of watching him watch *me* stealing my breath. He cupped my cheek before skimming his thumb across my bottom lip like a lover would—not a stranger. This had morphed from amazing sex into something...else. Something I couldn't pinpoint and definitely something that didn't make a bit of sense with a man I'd just met. Strangely enough, in that moment, it was as if I'd never known anyone better.

I sank down on him, taking him in inch by glorious inch. Once he was fully seated inside me, I started to move. Up and down then in little circles until Joe groaned and sat up, his lips meeting mine in a ravenous kiss while he clutched my hips, meeting every thrust harder than the one before.

"That's it. Take all of me," he breathed, his body quivering just like mine was. "You're perfection, baby." He clutched the back of my neck as we moved faster in a perfect rhythm. "Fucking perfection. So good. You feel so good," he grunted. "Give me what's mine, Caterina. Come again for me, baby."

A second build-up started and burst at his request, this release coming faster and sharper as I sank my nails into Joe's back, whimpering into his mouth until the tremors finally faded. He stiffened under me, our mouths fused together in a kiss still desperate but somehow sweet as it slowed.

"That was..." His head fell against my chest as I raked my hand through his sweaty hair.

"Yes, it was," I agreed and pecked his lips when he lifted his head.

"Caterina, I need to—" He jerked his chin toward the bathroom.

"Oh, right. Sure." I climbed off of him without meeting his eyes.

"Hey." He cocked his head to the side with a laugh. "I just need to get rid of the condom. I'm not bolting. Not unless you want me to."

My cheeks heated as I shook my head. "No. I don't want you to," I admitted.

"Good." He kissed my forehead. "Stay right there."

I crawled under the covers, blissfully spent and refreshed at the same time, but wondering how I'd feel about it all when what I'd done sank in. What *we'd* done. Still, in this moment, it all seemed worth it.

He came over to the bed, naked except for his boxers, and sat on the edge. "Talk to me. What are you thinking?"

I rolled over and shrugged. "That I'm sore in places I didn't think you could be sore." I stretched my arms over my head. "It's actually nice."

He laughed and brushed the matted hair off of my forehead. "Nice to know I made a good impression." My heavy eyes fluttered shut as he caressed my furrowed brow with the tip of his finger.

"You probably didn't plan on staying, and I don't expect you to." He ran his thumb back and forth over my cheekbone, and I couldn't help leaning into his touch. Something about this man was soothing yet exhilarating. Joe was a high I already couldn't stop chasing.

"Doesn't it get exhausting assuming all the time?" He rested his forehead against mine. "I didn't plan on this, no, but that doesn't mean I want to go."

"This is crazy, don't you think?"

"This is the good kind of chaos, Caterina." His sweet smile melted me into a puddle.

"Cat," I said on a yawn. "Everyone calls me Cat."

Joe climbed under the sheets beside me and pulled me into his side. "Maybe I don't want to be like everyone else to you."

## 5

## CATERINA

My eyes adjusted to blurry new surroundings as they fluttered open, landing on the sailboat painting on the wall. At least it looked like the shape of a sailboat. I'd managed to pluck the contacts out of my eyes before I drifted off to sleep, so I couldn't say for sure. As I came to my hazy senses, the events of the past twenty-four hours barreled over me in a heavy rush. When I woke up yesterday morning, I'd been in my apartment with my now ex-boyfriend on what I thought was a regular Thursday. It took a split second to recall running like a madwoman from both, and a muffled moan beside me to remind me of something else.

I lifted Joe's hand from where it was draped around my waist and slipped out of his hold, grabbing my glasses and a T-shirt out of my suitcase at the foot of the bed. The more alert I became, the more the panic set in.

As morning light peeked through the cracks in the blinds, my shaky breathing filled the silence while Joe stirred under the sheets.

I took slow, deep breaths in an attempt to quell the twisting in my gut. People did this kind of thing every day.

Hell, my two best friends did it all through college. My night with Joe was one of those "things" but I wasn't one of those "people." I never had sex with anyone I didn't know for at least a couple of months. Yet, I pulled Joe inside, tore off his clothes, and rode him until we both saw stars without a second thought. Now, a delayed second thought echoed in my brain, and I wished I could jump right out of my skin.

Despite the worry of not knowing how to explain what happened to myself, much less anyone else, I couldn't deny how amazing last night was. More than amazing, our night together was everything I didn't know I needed. I hoped I had a few minutes until Joe woke up to figure out what the hell to say.

My head fell back on a groan when raindrops pelted the outside glass of my window. *Great*, I was stuck. The Wi-Fi in my hotel room wouldn't be enough to get any work done, and I didn't know if I could show my face at The Beach Pub today. Driving in the rain to search for a place to work was the exact opposite of a relaxing getaway to forget my troubles.

I turned toward where Joe still slept in my motel bed, an unexpected smile creeping across my lips. His hair was ruffled into sandy brown tufts, and my fingers itched to brush it off his forehead. He looked young and a bit innocent, nothing like a man who did and said all those deliciously dirty things, last night.

Of course, I didn't know his age or really anything about him. But I knew his lips, his tongue, how right before our kiss would ignite, he'd graze his teeth along my bottom lip. Joe had settled between my legs all night long as if we'd been doing this dance for years, not hours. He was a sweet man with amazing hands and a magical mouth. If only I didn't live three hours away, but I did. There was no other option than to think of what happened last night as a one-time thing.

I hated the light of day already.

"You hate the rain that much?" A deep timbre behind me made me jump.

"When I'm supposed to be on a beach vacation? Yes. I hate it *that* much."

Joe sat up on the bed, resting his elbows on his thighs with a sleepy grin. I awaited some kind of a reaction I couldn't pinpoint. I'd been surprised he'd wanted to stay last night, and I'd been too high on orgasms to consider why that may or may not have been a good idea.

After realizing how short my T-shirt was, I settled back into bed with the blanket up to my neck, as if we hadn't been naked and tangled up in the scratchy hotel sheets for hours. I glanced at the glowing red numbers on the alarm clock resting on the nightstand.

"How could it be six o'clock?" We dozed off after having sex, and then I woke to something poking at my back. Joe muttered a sleepy apology and backed away until I rolled on top of him; the need for him still fresh and raw, and my fuzzy brain still not registering consequences. I'd passed out again shortly after round two, so maybe I'd gotten a full half hour or so of sleep.

Why was it so easy between us? He was able, I was willing, and, while the flashbacks of all we did caused my cheeks to burn, they were exhilarating. I was a lover of lists, of clear cause and effect, and everything in its place. No matter what I tried to do, I couldn't figure out where to compartmentalize last night.

"Yeah, I'm an hour late."

He rose from the bed, still gloriously naked, and scooped his pants and boxers off the floor. Whereas I devoured the sight of him last night, my eyes darted around the room as I tried in vain to tear my gaze away. His biceps flexed when he lifted his shirt over his head, and his abs clenched right before they were hidden by the cotton. The thought of tracing each ridge and muscle with my tongue as I'd done only hours ago, popped into my head.

"We don't open until eleven, but I like to get there early to make sure it's all set up the way I want it. I'm a little bit of a control freak."

"Sorry," I breathed when I found my voice again. "I didn't mean to—"

"You didn't force me to come in or to stay. My apartment is right above the restaurant. I'll take a quick shower and change before I head in. Apologies are unnecessary."

He motioned to where I cocooned myself in the blanket before he pulled up his jeans.

"Just like covering up."

I returned his cheeky grin with a glare.

"Honestly, I don't know what to say. What do we do here?"

"What do we do?" His brows pinched as he slipped his feet into his sneakers. "I know what we *did* here." He cracked a sexy smile before settling into the small chair beside the bed. "But I'm not sure what you mean."

"I just got out of a long relationship. I need recovery time, and although we..." I rubbed my eyelids, hoping that would somehow make my words coherent. "Like I said, I've never done this before, so I'm unsure of how you ... part ways, I guess? What do you usually do?"

"What do I *usually* do?" He stilled before resting his elbows on his knees. "This may shock you, but I don't do this very often or at least not as often as you might think. Tourists can be a slippery slope, so I usually don't get involved. I work seven days a week and as many nights, so this," he motioned back and forth between us with his finger, "is not my norm. At least, it hasn't been for a long time."

"*I'm* a tourist. What made you get involved with me?" I blanched at insinuating we were involved past last night. For a woman my age, my experience in casual sex was less than nil, and I was making that all too clear. "I mean, not that you're involved with me now." I groaned, my face falling into my hands. "How about you just go to work, and we forget all about this? Thank you for everything."

*Thank you?* Did I really just thank Joe for having sex with me? Like, "thanks for the latte" or "thanks for filling up my gas tank."

The mattress dipped in front of me, but I wouldn't uncover my eyes.

"Because *Caterina*." He peeled my fingers away from my face and yanked me closer. My full name, a name I always hated, falling from his lips, made goose bumps prickle on my skin.

"Because I wanted to. In fact, I haven't wanted to do anything *that* much in a very long time. Whatever came over us last night to get us...here, was fucking amazing."

"Yeah." I nodded, a smile pulling at my lips despite my rising panic. "Pretty fucking amazing."

His hand cupped the nape of my neck, melting me into a puddle onto the mattress.

"Get some sleep, then come see me. I'll make you breakfast."

"Joe, you don't have to do that. I don't want to impose, or have you feel obligated."

"It's not obligation if I want to. Same as last night. You know, it's not a forgone conclusion we part ways and never see each other again, especially considering how small this town is. I can scramble an egg for you without it being some kind of long-term commitment."

A laugh bubbled up from my chest, both shocking me and relaxing me.

"Sure, I need a place to work. That would be a huge help, thank you."

Joe's lips tipped up into a smirk. "I'd like to see you again, and I'd like to think you want me for more than just my Wi-Fi." His brows shot up.

I may have run from my problems last night, but the distance hadn't made them disappear. But it was only breakfast, just like last night was only sex.

*Sure it was.*

"Okay." I nodded. "You have a deal."

His sleepy smile grew as he made his way to the door. "Get some sleep, beautiful. Keep the glasses on when you come by."

I crinkled my nose. "Why?"

"Because you're sexy as hell in glasses." His eyes traveled up and down my body, leaving more tingles in their path before he unlocked the door and closed it behind him.

Settling back into bed, I buried my head into the pillow, inhaling the spicy cologne, salty sweat, and blinding temptation that was all Joe. He'd said he didn't want to be like everyone else to me, and he already wasn't.

I'd lived a glorious fantasy for a night, but it was time to go back to reality.

Right after breakfast.

A HOT SHOWER and change of clothes had done nothing to zap me out of the haze I was in. I'd been known to put in late nights, but I usually afforded myself more than twenty minutes of sleep in order to function. Last night's events came back to me with every yawn, and I had to hide my smile each time.

"All right, what's with you today?" Dominic, my oldest friend and assistant manager, asked as he came up next to me. He was supposed to close last night but asked to switch at the last minute. I'd come into the pub this morning wanting to thank him, but kept my mouth shut.

"I'm tired. I worked last night like you were supposed to." I tried to glare at him before I cleared one of the tables, but even that was too strenuous for my weary eyes. Every move I made was as if I were in slow motion, and, for the first time, I considered napping on the couch in my office later in the afternoon.

"When I left, it was dead, I figured you'd close up early. Did you finally get laid? Here? Maybe I should check the cameras." He lifted an annoying brow before I threw a damp towel at his head.

"Why are you so damn nosy?" Jordan, one of my waitresses, asked from behind the bar. "What the boss does after we leave isn't our business." She nodded at me in some kind of solidarity.

"I see the suck-up wind shifted early." Dominic snickered, ignoring Jordan's icy glower before heading to the front of the restaurant.

"God, he's a pain in the ass, isn't he? Why did you hire him again?"

"True," I agreed. "But as annoying of a bastard that he is, I trust him more than anyone. You should've seen him in high school. He still gives everyone the same headache."

Dominic followed me here from Queens after I'd bought the building, applauding me for getting the hell out of the city and asking how he could help. He'd been looking for a new start after his mother passed away, although he'd never admitted it. I'd been more than happy to accept his help and have a friend close by I could depend on. It had taken a long time to get this place into shape, but without him, it would've taken a hell of a lot longer.

But to Jordan's point, he was a relentless ball-breaker who always needed to know everything, especially when it came to me and my life, or lack thereof, outside of The Beach Pub.

"So, did you?" Jordan's eyes lit up as she adjusted the apron on her waist. She was a college junior who'd worked for me since I opened the place two years ago. Her petite and curvy frame earned her loads of tips during our busy season. Jordan was a nice girl, even if she lacked a filter.

"Mr. Mullins looks like he wants more coffee." I motioned to the small cluster of occupied tables in the front. I used to freak out whenever we got slow but knew this weekend we would be so busy we wouldn't have time to stop or breathe. I learned to look forward to the short bursts of inactivity, as long as they stayed short.

I had a business to take care of and a loan to pay back. My father was going to find out about Owen's silent partnership sooner or later, and I dreaded that conversation. We had different opinions on what constituted an acceptable livelihood. He loved putting on a suit and tie every day and riding the subway an hour back and forth to work, and that was my idea of the seventh circle of hell.

I loved being an owner and making my own rules, but the added responsibility to this place and the ones who worked for me didn't allow me much free time. The Beach Pub was my first and only priority. I'd been so focused on making this place a success for what had felt like so long, I couldn't remember the last time anyone caught my eye to the point of knocking me on my ass.

Until last night.

My eyes had fallen on a beautiful woman, looking lost, tired, and so damn gorgeous, I couldn't get to her fast enough. Then, I planted myself at her table and wouldn't let her leave. I could've talked to Caterina all night, although *not* talking to Caterina for the rest of the night was well worth stumbling around my place of business all morning like a zombie.

My mind kept coming back to last night, well early this morning. Her dark hair sprawled out on her pillow as she writhed beneath me. The strangest thing about our night together was that it didn't seem like a one-time thing to me, and Caterina was definitely not a one-time woman. At least, I didn't want her to be.

The two busybodies who worked for me hadn't seemed to notice me glancing at the door since I'd come in, checking to see if she'd taken me up on my offer to make her breakfast.

Sure, I noticed women all the time, but they were a fun, very occasional pastime. I'd never laid eyes on a woman and dropped whatever I was doing just for the chance to talk to her. Something about us just clicked. The easy way I'd confessed things I'd never told a soul before made zero sense. I craved more of her and couldn't concentrate on anything else.

Could you really connect to someone you'd only just met? Or was that just a side effect of the unprecedented, mind-blowing sex we'd had? I glanced at the time on my watch—almost noon. I'd been obsessing about this woman for half the day and waiting for her not to show up.

"Hey, is Joe here?"

My head whipped around toward the sound of a familiar, sultry voice. Caterina was speaking to Dominic when she noticed me. A slow smile stretched her lips when her eyes locked with mine. It felt like we were the only two people in the room—just like last night. In cutoff denim shorts, a Yankees hoodie, and glasses, she was a fucking vision. Her chestnut hair cascaded down her back in long waves, and my hands twitched, my fingers wanting to sift through the strands and grab a fistful before I covered her mouth with mine again. I'd devoured her in every sense of the word last night and was still starved for more.

"Good morning, Caterina."

A pretty blush crept on her cheeks, and my chest swelled. Maybe she felt the same pull between us—the one that wouldn't let her out of my head since I'd left her motel room.

"I'll find her a table, Dom. Thank you." I glanced over her shoulder to his sly grin, knowing he'd break my balls until I explained who she was.

"I didn't realize the time." Her face crumpled into a frown after she glanced at her watch. "I understand if it's too late for breakfast."

My gaze fell to her lips, still swollen from last night—from me. She was here for me, and the notion made me purely happy. I had no clue what it was about this woman that grabbed me so intensely, but it wasn't letting go anytime soon.

Her chocolate eyes blazed a trail down my torso, darting up before they got to my waist. She lifted her gaze to mine and rubbed at her temples, probably realizing she was caught. She was so fucking adorable, I couldn't stand it.

"Even if it was too late, you have an in with the owner." I threw her a wink. "What can I get you? Eggs? Pancakes? The kitchen is at full capacity, so you can have whatever you want."

"How about both scrambled eggs and pancakes? I'm starving. Long night, you know?" She met my eyes with a cheeky but bashful grin.

"Yes, I do know." My gaze held hers for a long minute before I headed toward the kitchen.

"Okay, spill."

I grumbled at Dominic's demand as I made my way to the grill. Our cook wasn't that busy, but I'd told Caterina I'd make her breakfast, and, for more reasons I couldn't explain, I wanted to.

"She was here last night, and I told her I'd make her breakfast this morning if she came back." I didn't look up as I cracked two eggs into a bowl.

"You usually don't help with the grill unless it's packed. Why do I feel like you're leaving out a big part of the story?"

Ignoring the irritating weight of his stare, I poured the eggs on the griddle and reached for the bowl of pancake batter.

"You did get laid! That explains the vacant stare and nodding off at the counter. Good for you, man." Dominic jabbed my shoulder. "Finally."

"Finally? Dude, I'm not a virgin or a monk. Stop acting like it's a milestone."

"It *is* a milestone. All you do is work. I miss the days when we first moved here, and you were a little more relaxed. You're going to give yourself an ulcer before you turn thirty-five."

He had a point, even if I wouldn't admit it. When we'd first arrived, everything was new and full of hope, so I'd allowed myself a little fun here and there. Now, even though we were doing well, that light feeling I used to enjoy had become a brick on my chest. I bought this place to make my own rules and have my own idea of success, but the threat of failure loomed heavier over my head than I'd ever expected it to.

"Running a business isn't all fun and games. I have a loan to pay back, and, yeah, we're still making a good profit, but I need to make sure it stays that way."

"Owen doesn't *want* to be paid back. He hands you back every cent when you try. Take his advice and invest it back here. Advertise more, fix the outside tables, whatever. Loosen up, man."

I plated Caterina's breakfast before I looked up. Dominic was spot on again. I couldn't even remember the last night I'd spent the night away from this place.

"You're right. If I was going to make myself miserable, I could have worked for my father."

"You're admitting I'm right? You really must be tired." He stepped back, clutching his chest. "So, this girl is something else, huh?"

"She is, or, at least, she could be. I only just met her, but—"

"But nothing. Go with it. Who knows, maybe it's one of those love-at-first-sight things?"

I dropped the plate on the counter and leveled my gaze on

Dominic. "Love at first sight? Are you kidding me right now? Did you hit your head on the way in?"

He shrugged. "It happens. From what I hear. As long as I've known you, you've never been this twisted over a woman you'd only just met. I mean, back when you used to occasionally *see* women."

"I like her, but I'm not twisted, Dom." I didn't even buy my own wimpy denial.

"Really?" He cocked his head to the side. "You wouldn't even let me seat her and sprinted back here to cook her breakfast yourself. Jordan and I were cracking up at the googly eyes when you took her order."

"Googly eyes?" I squinted at Dom before I picked up the plate.

"I think anyone in this place who looked your way for more than five minutes noticed. See where it goes, live a little."

I said nothing as I followed Dominic back outside, not acknowledging the smug grin lifting his cheeks at my silence.

WHEN I ARRIVED at her table, Caterina was pounding on the keys to her laptop and didn't seem to notice me approach. Maybe we both had that in common—we were too easily sucked in by work to notice life happening around us.

"Here you go."

Her head jerked up when I set the food down in front of her.

"Sorry, I didn't mean to startle you."

"No, it's fine. Just trying to catch up on work while I can. Lou was right, I could barely get a signal in my room, but I know I can't stay here all day long." She pushed her glasses farther up the bridge of her nose, and my cock once again stirred to attention. She was sexy as hell in those frames and the thought of her wearing them because I asked her to excited me more than it should have.

"Stay here as long as you need to. No one will push you out, I promise."

Her shoulders slumped in relief. "Thank you." She closed her laptop and pulled her plate closer. "This looks really awesome."

"Can I get you anything else?" I cleared my throat, trying in vain to sound professional. The last thing I wanted was to make her uncomfortable. We had a good night—a great fucking night—but, as she'd mentioned, she wasn't looking to get involved with anyone. But she was here, and that made a spark of hope bloom in my chest anyway. Like I'd told Dom over and over again, I didn't have time for this.

*But I'd make time for her.*

I blinked away the odd thought. My sleep-deprived mind was playing tricks on me.

"No, the waitress got me coffee. Would you like to sit with me for a bit?" Her fingers traced the ridge of her coffee cup. "It's okay if you can't. It's not like the place is empty again—"

"Sure." My lips curved, my chest puffing out a bit when she beamed back at me. The spell that drew me to her didn't break in the daylight.

I sat down and called Jordan over.

"Can I get a cup of coffee, please?"

Jordan looked between Caterina and me with a sly grin and nodded. Ignoring her, I turned back to Caterina. She fiddled with the spoon on the table, gliding her finger up and down the silver stem as she studied me.

"I need you to indulge me for a moment. My name is Caterina Rose Longo. I'm sure you don't care about my full name, but you're the first man I've slept with that didn't know it beforehand, and, for reasons I can't explain, that bothered me. So, now you know."

I cracked up and nodded. "Well, it's nice to know you, Caterina Rose. I'm Joseph Kellan Hunter."

"Of course, that's your name." She shook her head and sliced into one of the pancakes.

"What's wrong with it? You'd hurt my mother's feelings if you didn't like my middle name."

"No, that's not what I mean."

Jordan placed a cup of coffee in front of me, and I nodded a thank you, ignoring her stare as she lingered before moving along to another table.

"Then, what?" I kept my eyes on hers as I reached for the sugar. This was already cup number four in as many hours.

"Your name drips sex, just like the rest of you. Women don't stand a chance, do they?"

I sputtered on a mouthful of coffee.

"I drip sex, and you don't stand a chance. Did I get all that right?"

"Pretty much." She nodded with a shrug. "You're impossibly sexy, and I lost myself a little last night. Well, a lot, to tell you the truth."

"Caterina, if you're asking me if I'm judging you in one way or another, I don't. I was right there with you."

I was all about easy and casual and would seek out only those on that same page. No one ever affected me like this, much less this fast, and last night seemed anything but casual.

She wasn't the only one with a first last night.

"I'm...there's a lot going on in my head. I'm getting used to being alone, even though I guess I was alone for a long time. Trent said some things that got to me yesterday, and I'm still working all of it out."

"What did he say?" Her defeated expression gave me the sudden urge to kick the ass of someone I'd never met.

She laughed to herself and crossed her arms.

"That I'm a cold fish who can't truly connect with anyone, and that he did what he did because I was too distracted with everything else to make him a priority. He's a jerk but has a point. My job was my focus more than he ever was." Her shoulders slumped as she pushed her eggs back and forth on her plate.

"The woman I was with last night was warm and passionate and ..." I stopped before I made an idiot of myself. "Blaming what he did on you is a dick move. Plain and simple."

"I agree. And thank you." She leaned over and draped her hand over mine. "You're a sweet guy, Joe. Did anyone ever tell you that?"

"Finish your breakfast." My voice was husky but stern as I motioned to her plate.

Caterina laughed before spearing a piece of pancake and popping it into her mouth. Her eyes fluttered shut, and her sexy little moan made my pants grow tight.

"Did you know your food noises are the same as your sex noises?"

"What?" Her nose crinkled up in confusion.

"Last night, when you took a bite of the mozzarella stick—"

"I was starving after a long drive." She scowled, but I caught the pull of a smile.

"And then later, when my head was between your—"

Her fork landed on her plate with a loud clank before her mouth dropped.

"Same noise. Although, the second time was more of a moan mixed with a scream."

She draped her hand over her eyes, her face beet red. "I think you have a dirty mouth, Joe."

"If you only *think* so, I need to up my game."

She balled her napkin and flung it at me, nailing me right in the chest.

"Hey, I'm not complaining. I like that in a woman."

Her brows shot up. "You like women who like to eat?"

"I like women who are hungry and not afraid to show it."

She cleared her throat and straightened in the seat. I was getting to her and loving every second of it.

"Another question, if that's okay."

"Shoot," I said, not able to hide the twitching of my lips at the blush still spreading on her cheeks.

"How old are you? I'm thirty-three."

"Just turned thirty. Are you okay with spending last night with a younger man?" I peered at her over my coffee cup.

"You just turned thirty, and you already own your own business? Wow. That's pretty damn impressive. Are *you* okay with spending last night with a woman in her almost *mid*-thirties?" She drained the rest of her coffee, her eyes still on me.

"I spent last night with a beautiful woman I couldn't get out of my head all morning. I'm *very* okay with that," I rasped, meaning every single word.

A shy grin curved her lips. "Like you said, it's a tiny town, and I don't want it to be awkward between us. But last night is as far as we can go. I've only known you for less than a day, but I can tell you're a good guy, it's not—"

I held up my hand. "No need for the 'it's not you; it's me' speech, I get it." I forced a smile to hide the confusing disappointment flooding my gut.

"I don't regret spending the night with you. At all. And I'd like to be friends while I'm here. You make a pretty awesome breakfast, it would be a shame to miss out on that this week." She grinned, her honest beauty hitting me right in the chest. I'd get to see her again but couldn't touch her again. No matter how I spun that in my head, it still sucked.

"Looks like it's clearing up," I noted, motioning to the sun peeking through the window. "You don't have to butter me up for my Wi-Fi anymore."

"I'm not," she whispered, her lips pursed as she met my gaze. "I wanted to see you again, too. The timing is just ..."

Her eyes darted everywhere before coming back to mine. "You deserve better than the woman I am right now."

A heavy silence fell over us. No matter how much of an anomaly Caterina was for me, she wasn't ready for anything beyond one night. Normally, I would have been relieved as hell. Even though she'd be here for the next week, she wouldn't pressure me for more than I had to give. My focus could stay on keeping this place in the black, without any silly distractions.

But Caterina was already the very distraction I'd managed to avoid, no matter what zone she pushed us into today. But she was a temporary one that I wouldn't have to worry about for too long.

I should've felt relief, but I didn't.

"What are your plans for the rest of the day?"

"Hmm, I haven't really thought about it." She scooped the rest of her eggs onto her fork. "I thought I'd work until the early afternoon and maybe walk down to the beach and get some sun, explore the town. Not used to all this free time—or being alone." She giggled, sounding a lot more relaxed than when she'd first sat down.

"There's a food festival tonight. All the businesses in town pitch tents along the beach, kind of like the street fairs back in the city. You should come."

"That sounds fun. Maybe. I'll see." Her eyes landed on my lips but darted away. Giving in to the attraction between us last night didn't work it out of our systems or even take the edge off it. If anything, it had doubled it. But, she wasn't ready for anything beyond that, and I wouldn't push.

"If you need to come back and work, you're more than welcome—anytime."

"Thank you. I appreciate that." Caterina packed up her laptop before pulling her wallet out of her purse.

"What are friends for? And keep your money." I shoved her hand away. "I offered to make you breakfast, so it's on me."

"Not again," she groaned. "I can't let you do that."

"I own the place, remember? It's not like I'm stealing." I stood and extended my hand. "I'll walk you out."

She stiffened, regarding me with caution as if I were offering her a bomb. When she finally grabbed it, her fingers quivered against my palm. Last night could've been the beginning of something great, and I believed we both knew that even if we couldn't understand it.

Too bad we couldn't do anything about it.

"This is so cute. He's holding her hand!" Jordan's loud whisper as we passed made Caterina's head jerk around.

I cast Jordan a cursory glance over my shoulder as I guided Caterina out the door.

"So, we don't have to complicate this, right?" Caterina took a shaky step toward me and planted a kiss on my cheek. Memories of last night exploded in my head at the feel of her soft lips on my skin. My hand fell on the small of her back in the long minute it took her to pull away. Touching her felt too natural and too good, making it that much more difficult to stop. "Friends?"

"Friends." I nodded, tucking a lock of hair behind her ear before I pressed my lips to her cheek. The scent of vanilla mixed with maple syrup flooded my senses. She was sweet all over, and my mouth watered to taste her again.

"See you around, Caterina Rose."

"Bad enough you won't call me Cat like everyone else." Her mouth twisted in a scowl, and my lips tingled to touch hers again. How could she be this beautiful and not have a single clue? "Using my middle name will make me drive one town over to eat, no matter how awesome your pancakes are."

"I told you, I didn't want to be like everyone else to you."

She flinched at my admission before I backed away.

I really didn't want to be just anyone else to her. It went against logic and everything I'd ever known to be true about myself, but she was already under my skin in a way no other woman ever had been.

And despite what she'd said, nothing about us felt finished.

## 8

## CATERINA

"I'll be home in a week. That's plenty of time for you to pack and get out." I paced around my hotel room, my hand balling into a fist at my side. Our conversation had been going around in circles for what seemed like hours, and I almost wished I was close enough to Trent to wrap my hands around his neck.

True vacation, where I could relax and regroup from the demise of my relationship, couldn't happen unless I knew Trent would be gone by the time I arrived back in Brooklyn. He hadn't stopped me from walking out the door, but, in an odd and aggravating-as-hell twist of events, he refused to leave our apartment.

After spending the day chasing some kind of peace, the closest I'd come was nursing a light beer next to the pool and almost forgetting the mess that was my life for a few sweet moments. Talking to Trent brought it all back. As my breathing quickened, I finally understood what brought me all the way out here alone. He wasn't even in the same room, and the rage and sour sting of betrayal suffocated me once again.

"When you get back, you'll be in a better mood to

straighten things out." The nonchalance in his voice had me seeing red.

Blood roared in my veins, giving me a headache. How often did Trent dismiss me? And why had I stuck around? My faded memory of the charming man I'd met years ago had clouded my judgment of the jerk he was now, but the misfortune of coming home early brought me unwelcome, but undeniable clarity.

"There's nothing to talk about or straighten out. You cheated. In our apartment. Where I could see. And you didn't care. After what you did, there's nothing to discuss. You have a week to pack your shit and get out." As tough as I attempted to sound, my voice quaked with a flood of emotion. Fury topped the list for sure. What kind of a man gets a blow job in the apartment he shared with his girlfriend and doesn't even say he's sorry?

As much as I'd thought about it, it was hard to pinpoint exactly when we became nothing more than roommates, but I still reeled from Trent's betrayal. No matter what we'd been or hadn't been to each other in recent months, his lack of respect for me hurt.

"I'm surprised you even noticed. Your head is always buried in your laptop or your phone. You're working when you aren't even *at* work. Maybe it wasn't my finest hour but—"

*"Not your finest hour?"* I screamed, wincing at the piercing pain caused by my own shrill voice. This had been his go-to since I'd caught him: I was a workaholic who neglected him and was to blame for it all.

"If you paid attention to me and the people around you once in a while, they'd stick around. I'm surprised you still have friends who invite you on vacation," he huffed. More than anything, I wanted to be home to clock him and obliterate the smug smile I knew was spreading his lips.

"You're right," I said in a scratchy whisper.

"I'm right? You're serious?"

"I must have been really distracted to not notice when you became a cold and heartless asshole. I'm not sure what's worse, if you set out to hurt me, or if you just didn't care that you did."

"Look, Cat." I almost heard a trace of contrition in his voice. "You have to admit, you're distracted all the time. No one can get close to you. You made this job your focus and don't see anyone else or anything around you. You can't blame people for moving on."

I took a sharp breath, willing back the angry tears. My friends hadn't cast me aside, even though I canceled plans with them all the time. My family loved me—though, they tended to hover along with my mother, worrying I pushed myself too hard.

Trent was playing dirty and trying to get to me, and I loathed how easily it worked. Even worse, as much as I'd fought against it, guilt rolled in my gut for how Trent and I ended. I didn't push his dick into that woman's mouth, but had my constant absence given him justification that it was okay? It was a ridiculous thought, but it wouldn't stop repeating in my head.

"No, I suppose you're right. Luckily, my friends and family care about me too much to cast me aside and disrespect me like I'm trash. You, by all means, can move on. Out by the tenth, or I call the cops to remove you."

I stabbed the red end button on my phone and threw it onto my hotel bed, trying to forget Trent's ugly words. I had a small circle of friends and family. I figured that was life as you grew up and started a career. Was I really missing some kind of connection gene? I'd never considered it before, and now it was all I could think about.

Rather than stew in my room, I threw on a tank top and cutoffs and headed out. Maybe I could sit by the beach and get lost in the sunset before drowning my sorrows in the homemade ice cream shop I'd spotted next to the hotel. In my teenaged years, ice cream after a breakup was a must. But it wasn't a broken heart I was nursing; it was a broken spirit.

I strode past the main office of the hotel, stopping when a colorful flyer caught my eye.

"You should stop by."

I jumped at Lou's voice behind me. He and his wife had made it a point to check on me each time they bumped into me today. *Was I okay? Did I need anything?* After the fight I'd had with Trent, kindness and consideration from strangers was a balm to the cracks in my self-esteem.

*Like last night.*

Giving Joe the brush-off was the right thing to do, but I wasn't expecting it to be so difficult to walk away from him. My head was still all kinds of fucked up from Trent, even before our last shitty conversation. As incredible as last night had been, I couldn't take it any further with Joe. I hated myself and my rotten conscience all day, especially after spotting the disappointment in his eyes this morning.

What did I expect? Or what did either of us expect, for that matter? We were two strangers who had amazing sex and nothing more—no matter how much it *seemed* like more. In fact, if I didn't know better, I'd think I missed him today. How do you miss someone you hardly know? You didn't—not really.

"The festival. Ocean Cove's first big event of the summer." Lou pointed across the street to the bustle of activity just behind The Beach Pub.

"I heard about that today." I took a second look at the flyer. "It's mostly food, right? No scary rides?"

"A few," he answered with a shrug. "My wife would never let our kids on one. She said if they put it together overnight, there was no way it could be safe."

"Your wife would get along very well with my mother. What else do they have? Typical fair junk food?" I prayed for Zeppoles, the deep-fried balls of dough smothered in powdered sugar that lured me to every local street feast. They probably called them something different here or made them into funnel cakes, which wasn't the same at all, but I'd take it. I was either eating or drinking my feelings tonight, and how much comfort could a light beer from the hotel offer? If I wanted anything harder, I'd have to go visit The Beach Pub and see Joe. The temptation to ask him for more than only a drink would be too great.

"The restaurants and some of the bakeries from the area have booths. It's a good way to get to know what's around town, and it's only two streets away." He nodded behind me with his chin.

"That actually sounds perfect. Thanks, Lou!"

He waved me off, and I headed down toward the lighted tents now coming into distant view.

I usually felt anxious about large crowds, but going alone and not worrying about separating from anyone was oddly liberating. I wouldn't stay very long, just enough to fill my belly then head back to the hotel.

All the different smells made my mouth water. I spotted pizza, burgers, fresh donuts, and cupcakes on the first line of tents. The festival stretched out almost the entire length of the beach and already beat any local street feast back in Brooklyn.

"I think the second tent on the right has *mutzadelle* sticks."

Startled by the familiar deep timbre in my ear, I jumped

and craned my head. My gaze met Joe's, and it was awkward how it *wasn't* awkward at all to see him again. His presence excited me as much as it soothed me, just like when I met him last night. He wore khaki shorts and a black T-shirt, with The Beach Pub embroidered on the front pocket. He never mentioned he'd be here, but of course, he would be. He was as much of a town staple as his restaurant was. I'd figured that out right away. What would it be like to be that purely happy with what you did for a living and where you lived?

Not that I hated Brooklyn, but it was all I'd ever known. And I did love my job.

*At the expense of everyone else.*

Shaking off the nasty sting of Trent's taunt in my head, I turned my focus back to Joe. Gorgeous, nice, too-good-for-my-baggage Joe. His shirt stretched across his torso, triggering a shiver at the memory of what he looked like without it ... or pants.

I raked my hands through my hair and shut my eyes. Infatuation and need for affection was what this was, all made that much worse, not having to wonder what Joe's affection felt like—what *he* felt like. Like he'd said, this was a small town, and I'd no doubt run into him a few times during my week here, so I needed to learn how to have a nice, *platonic*, conversation that wouldn't lead to me pulling him into my hotel room again.

"There's way too much here. I have no idea where to start." While my gaze kept shifting around to the action around us, his never wavered and stayed fixed on me. "What's at your booth?"

"Simple stuff. Sliders on the grill and some ears of corn. Dominic loves this and insists on running our tent himself. I'm just the eye candy." He winked before offering me the crook of his arm. "Come with me. I'll show you the good stuff.

Friends can show friends around a new place, right? No strings?"

The right thing to do would've been to say, "no, thanks," but I nodded and linked my arm with his. What harm would it do? While I had come here alone to process all the shit in my life, I supposed being alone today wouldn't be healthy. I enjoyed being around Joe, he seemed to want to be around me, why overthink? Keeping hold of him as he led me through the crowd, I was struck again with how natural being with Joe seemed. If I had to, I'd draw another line in the sand. Right now, I went along with what felt good, regardless of if it should or not.

"THIS IS the best sangria I ever had!" I gushed as I drained my third cup. I tried to pace myself since I hadn't had much to eat today aside from all the samples Joe and I had been gathering as we walked the length of the festival. But it was hot, and I was parched. It wasn't the amount of alcohol I was consuming going straight to my head, it was how fast I was inhaling it.

Joe pulled the cup down from my lips. "Emily soaks the fruit in booze before she mixes it in. Slow down, beautiful." He tapped my chin to make me look up. Maybe I wasn't drunk, but alcohol warmed my belly enough to melt away any denial or pretense. Why had I thought Joe and I were a bad idea? Because I'd only just met him? That it was too soon after a break up? I broke our gaze again, wobbling as I tried to hold on to my resolve.

"Is something wrong?" he asked, his hand moving to the damp nape of my neck. I zeroed in on his lips, wanting to taste them so badly. My body moved closer, almost powerless against the pull before I stepped back and almost tripped.

"No!" I answered too loudly to be convincing. "I'm having fun. With you. Well, maybe not as much fun as last night, but this festival is cool." I ignored the loud voice in my head yelling at me to close my damn mouth before I humiliated myself even more, but I kept going. "At least I had fun, did you have fun, Joe?" My question came out so pathetic and hopeful, like if a begging puppy could speak.

His eyes thinned to slits as he scrutinized my sloppy movements. He opened his mouth to say something before glancing over my shoulder to wave at someone.

"Excuse me, I need to say a quick hello to one of our vendors. Don't go in for another refill until I get back." He looped an arm around my waist and pulled me close, and I again resented my body's reaction at the spark from his touch. "Yes. I had fun. A *lot* of fun. Don't move, okay?"

My eyes stayed glued to Joe as he jogged away. I shook my head and pinched the bridge of my nose in an attempt to sober up.

Spotting an ice cream tent across the way, I held in a squeal of gratitude. I should have stuck to my original plan of stuffing my face with hot fudge covered goodness—alone.

Squinting at the flavor list in the back, I couldn't make out a thing. My eyes were tired and out of focus.

"Hi, there!" I greeted the sales girl in a louder-than-I-meant-to voice. "What do you recommend?"

"Our Pina Colada is usually popular." She shrugged when she met my gaze. "Can I see your ID?"

"My ID?" Not sure if she wanted to add me to a mailing list or something, I hesitated, but really wanted that damn ice cream, so I fished it out of my purse and handed it to her. She looked it over and nodded before handing it back to me.

"We only have one size, and it's $5.25."

I handed her the money, and she worked the ice cream into a beautiful swirl on top of a deep plastic cup. Taking it from her and digging my spoon in, my eyes fluttered when the sweet and tangy taste hit my tongue and tingled down my throat. It really did taste like a Pina Colada, even burning going down like one, too.

By the time Joe came back over, I was already three-quarters of the way down the bowl.

"I thought you left." It took a lot of effort to say only four slow and slurred words.

His eyes narrowed as he studied me, growing wide when they landed on the cup in my hand.

"Did you buy that from over there?" He pointed with his thumb over his shoulder to the girl who sold me the ice cream.

"Yeah, why?" I flinched at my loud voice.

Joe laughed before covering his mouth with his hands. "That has alcohol in it. More than the sangria. You didn't see it on the sign behind her?"

"It was dark." I stumbled as I tried to glance over to the tent and find where they noted the ice cream was full of booze. "I couldn't even see what flavors she had. That's why she wanted to see my ID? Hey, I got carded, Joe!" I slapped his chest so hard he fell back a step. "My thirty-three-year-old ass got carded. The poor girl must be nearsighted." I let out a loud cackle before almost tumbling over. Joe caught me and wrapped his arm around my waist.

"I'm not sure if you can make it up all three flights at the Anchor. Let me take you to my apartment and sober you up a little. No funny business, I promise."

As he led me away, I burrowed into his side. When he drew me toward him, I took the opportunity to nuzzle his neck, using my tipsy condition as an excuse to indulge. *God, he smelled good.* I remembered how smooth and sweet the skin on his neck was, and I sank my teeth into my bottom lip so I wouldn't be tempted to take another taste.

"Joe," I whispered into his ear. "I'm sorry."

What was I sorry for? Sorry for leading him on tonight, unintentionally-intentionally because I liked him and wanted to be near him? Sorry we couldn't go further than we already had, and couldn't go back? Or sorry that from the moment he met me, I was an unglued damsel in distress?

Joe stopped and cupped my cheek, turning my face toward his.

"Don't be sorry." His lips brushed my forehead. "Friends take care of friends, right?"

As loopy as I was, I didn't miss the sad glint in his eye, confirming what I already knew.

We weren't really friends and never would be.

# 9

## JOE

I LED Caterina up the short flight of stairs to my apartment, keeping one arm around her waist as I unlocked the door. I'd had a blast showing her all the different tents and filling her in on Ocean Cove, and just being with her in general, but I couldn't shake my worry. She'd gotten tipsy by accident, but I wondered what was bothering her tonight to drink so much so fast. Even when she laughed at my dumb jokes, there was a sad gloss to her dark eyes. I suspected it had something to do with her ex, but I wouldn't press. I'd give her a few bottles of water before taking her back to her motel room, then try to forget I'd ever met her—just like I'd been trying to do all afternoon.

I sat her down on my couch and handed her a bottle. She shook her head and swatted it away.

"Thank you, but I'm really fine," she slurred before I put the bottle in her hand again, raising a brow until she finally took a drink. "It's okay. I can handle my ice cream."

"I'm sure you can, sweetheart." I laughed as she lifted the bottle to her lips again. Those soft, sweet lips that tasted as good as they looked. Forgetting I met her would've been a hell of a lot easier if she was more forgettable. Unfortunately, she was the exact opposite.

She wore a tight tank top and tiny shorts that showed enough smooth olive skin to make my mouth water. It was all I could do not to ogle her amazing body, as I'd caught countless guys doing as she walked past them tonight. I couldn't blame them. I couldn't take my eyes off of her, either. Those beautiful, sad eyes got to me most of all, and, although I shouldn't have made it my concern, it was. I was worried about a woman I'd only just met. Worse, the fantasy of being her hero and making it all better both confused and overwhelmed me.

I tucked a stray lock of hair behind her ear and traced the delicate curve of her jaw. Her watery gaze shot to mine, that now familiar current pulsing between us at my slip of endearment. "Just drink for me, okay?"

I cupped her neck, and her head fell back as she leaned into my touch. The alcohol must've lifted her inhibitions and the wall she'd tried to erect between us earlier. Either I was soothing her, exciting her, or both. My chest swelled at either possibility.

Caterina grabbed my forearms and pulled me toward her. I crouched down in front of her and lifted the bottle to her lips. Her pained eyes got to me in a way I wasn't expecting, and before I could stop myself, my hand cupped her cheek.

She turned her head and nuzzled my palm. With very little effort, this woman was killing me after only a day.

"You really are adorable. And sweet and kind." She pressed a kiss to my cheek, lingering long enough for my eyes to clench shut and my cock to thicken in my shorts. I was stone-cold sober, so my own inhibitions needed to stay put. No matter how tempting it would be to kiss those lips, to lick inside her mouth and feel her melt against me again, my job was to take care of her—not take advantage. After only one night, I'd gotten to know her body too well, and all I wanted to do was push all those buttons I had the pleasure of discovering last night.

"No one can get close to me. I'm cold." She sniffled as she downed the last of the first bottle.

"Whoever told you that," I cradled her face and turned it toward me, "was an asshole."

She shook her head. "You've only known me for a day."

"I know enough."

Her eyes shot to mine, her shoulders slumping before breaking our connection. "I loved being with you last night, Joe. I'm sorry my shitty baggage ruins everything."

"Nothing is ruined. I loved it, too. Stop acting like it was a hardship on my part. I don't regret a single second of being with you."

Her hands fell to her thighs, her breaths coming quick as her head drooped.

"I'm...dizzy. And woozy."

My lips curved up as I smoothed the hair off her forehead. This girl was beautiful, and, even in this depleted condition, took my damn breath away.

"You have about seven different types of liquor in your system, and I'll take a wild guess that you didn't eat much today since I made you breakfast." I lifted a brow.

She shrugged before replying with a reluctant nod, fixing her eyes on the last drops at the bottom of the water bottle she swirled in her hand. "Can I lay down, Joe?"

"Sure." I squeezed her shoulder. "Come with me."

The only women I'd ever had in my apartment were my mother and sister. I'd told Caterina the truth about not having many one-nighters, even before my business drained all the fun from my life. But I'd made it a point to never bring one back here, even just for a stop. I liked the ease of controlling how and when I wanted to leave. But for reasons I couldn't explain, I wanted Caterina here. Maybe it was knowing once she sobered up, she wouldn't be back. And I wanted to steal as much time with her as I could before my next brush-off. Did that make me romantic or pathetic?

I grabbed her hand and pulled her to standing, leading her to my bedroom at the end of the hall. My apartment was small but had a decent-sized kitchen and living room—not that I entertained much. Friends came to the pub rather than my apartment when we did hang out together, which I realized as I settled Caterina onto my bed, hadn't happened in a long time. In the midst of running from her own life, Caterina made me see what was missing in mine.

"Stay with me, Joe." She took hold of my arm as I tried to pull my hand away.

Straightening, and purposely not answering her, I gently slipped from her hold and headed back to my kitchen to fish another bottle of water from the fridge.

Even if sex didn't happen, getting that close to her now wouldn't be right, no matter how fucking good her body would feel against mine. Whether or not she was aware of it, the mixed signals she was sending me messed with my head.

Returning, and sitting on the very edge of the bed next to her, I unscrewed the bottle cap and tipped the bottle to her lips, her hand draping over mine as she gulped. She had a gorgeous neck. Last night, the soft slope beckoned my lips to trail down her collarbone to that tiny patch of skin that had pulled a sexy-as-hell moan out of her when I'd traced it with my tongue. Caterina stirred an immediate need in me, and I needed to remove myself from the temptation.

"See?" She hiccuped a sad laugh. "You don't want to be near me, either."

Her pleading chocolate eyes could become my downfall if

I wasn't careful. "The exact opposite, but you're not in a condition to tell me what you want."

"You said that last night, and I knew exactly what I wanted. Please." She placed my arm around her waist. My hand rested on the small of her back, and I was somehow unable to refuse her, for anything.

"For a little while." I crawled in behind her and snaked my arm around her torso. My chin dipped into the crook of her shoulder, but I wouldn't pull her too close. I fought to keep control of my big head, but my little one didn't give a shit what was right or wrong. The proximity of her perfect ass and knowledge of how it had felt under my fingertips and lips was enough to make me hard as a rock.

"You aren't cold," I whispered into her ear. "Any man would be out of his mind to not want to get close to you."

She swiveled her head to brush my lips, muttering "thank you" before falling asleep. I pressed a kiss to her temple and began to pull away before she cinched her arm around my stomach. For a slim woman, she had a strong hold. Not wanting to wake her or upset her again, I settled onto the mattress and felt my eyes grow heavy. I was already dreading another morning we'd have to part ways and forget anything happened.

When she rolled over and cuddled her head into my chest, I realized I couldn't do that. I thought of Dominic's comment about love at first sight. I'd never believed in any of that, but no woman had ever had this much of a hold on me, and definitely not this fast. It made absolutely no sense, but there was no denying there was *something* between us.

Maybe she could ignore it in the morning, but I couldn't.

# 10

## CATERINA

"Good morning." A whisper in my ear jolted me awake.

Perhaps *jolted* was the wrong word, as my limbs felt twenty pounds heavier when I attempted to roll over. I sank my head into the pillow, noting how soft and smooth the fabric was against my cheek. These weren't the scratchy hotel sheets I'd slept in the night before. My eyes flew open as I sat up, panic filtering through me as I realized I had no clue where I was.

"Hey, relax." Joe squeezed my shoulder. I winced before turning toward his voice, blinking a few times before he came into focus. How did he look that damn good first thing in the morning? I cringed, pretty sure I looked as awful as I felt.

"You're in my apartment. You had a little too much alcohol, and I brought you back here to give you some water, but you wanted to lay down, and we both fell asleep. That was it, I promise."

I nodded and raked a hand through my tangled hair.

"Even though this is only our third day of knowing each other, you don't have to explain. I know you wouldn't do anything while I was like that. I haven't exactly showed you my best self since we met, have I?"

"That's not true. But, if you don't mind me asking, did something happen yesterday? You don't strike me as someone who drinks that much very often."

I cocked my head from side to side, then cringed from moving too fast.

"The sangrias were partly because I was thirsty, partly because I was a little upset. I had an argument with my ex, and it's been playing in my head for most of the day."

"You walked in on him cheating. Why isn't he begging for your forgiveness instead of picking a fight with you?"

"That's a great question." I rubbed at my eyes, my dried contacts almost gluing them shut. "I neglected him because I was so sucked into work. It's all my fault he had to look elsewhere."

"If, for argument's sake, he felt neglected or whatever, he should have told you instead of bringing someone else home. Don't give that jerkoff, or the bullshit he told you, a second thought."

I burst out laughing at Joe's clenched jaw. "I should have said something, too. We'd been nothing but distant roommates to each other lately, but I'd written it off as a rut." I pushed off the bed, stumbling back from the headrush. "I guess I ignored a lot because I didn't want to deal with the inconvenience of parting ways. Now, of course, it's a mess. But I can move on. Maybe he is right; I am cold."

I forced my gaze back to Joe's. I was ashamed, embarrassed, and so sick of showing nothing but the most unglued parts of me to this man from the second I met him. "I should feel a little sad about ending things, shouldn't I? I'm hurt about the way he did it, and I'm mad, and, like you said, guilty. But saying goodbye to my boyfriend of two years, who I *lived* with?" I shrugged and lifted my hands up. "As my baby cousin says, I got nothin'."

"Getting cheated on, in your own apartment, was *not* your fault. From what you've told me about this guy, he's the cold one, not you." Joe edged closer to where I sat on his bed. "And I happen to have firsthand experience that you're the complete opposite of cold." A hot shiver swarmed over my skin as he searched my gaze.

"Thank you, Joe." I picked up his hand and squeezed. "You're a pretty great guy."

"Thank you." I pulled my hand back, but he wouldn't let go. "I think you're pretty great, too. Even though I feel another brush-off coming on."

I grimaced and shook my head. "It's not that I'm brushing you off, it's just, well, right now..." I stilled when he tightened his grip on my hand. His thumb glided over my wrist, leaving tingles along its path.

"Maybe the timing is bad, and the logistics are a little messed up, but I'm not the only one feeling this, am I?"

"No...you're not," I stammered. "But—" a lump in the back of my throat caught me by surprise. "I'm not in a good place right now. I'd say I'd made that abundantly clear." I grabbed Joe's other hand, dreading lifting my head to look him in the eye. "You're sexy and kind and I'm sure there are a ton of women waiting who are more deserving of your time."

"*You* deserve my time, Caterina." His mouth flattened to a hard line. "I'd love to give you more of it, but I get it. Just promise me you'll forget this asshole and what he said."

"That's why I'm here." I grinned and kissed his cheek, enjoying the feel of his stubble against my lips a little too much, remembering the delicious scratch it left on the inside of my thighs. No, he was definitely not the only one feeling this. How amazing would it be to have a real chance with Joe?

The only thing we could have was a fling with an expiration date, and that was unfair to both of us.

"I'll walk you back to the Anchor." He patted my thigh and stood.

"You don't have to do that, Joe. It's daylight, and it's close."

"I don't have to, but maybe I want to." He quirked an eyebrow and made his way out of the bedroom, leaving me with a headache and sour gut. I knew I'd done the right thing, but why did it feel so awful?

I woke up on Sunday morning on the wrong side of the bed, agitated for a reason I didn't want to pinpoint, so I tried my hardest to ignore it. Whatever I'd had with Caterina, if it was actually anything, was over. Yet, I couldn't stop thinking about her and rewound the past few days over and over in my head, searching for a reason for my insane, but unshakable fixation on a woman I hardly knew. It was driving me batshit crazy as I tried to stay as busy as possible behind the bar.

"If it isn't my little bro."

I turned toward a familiar Southern twang. My brother-in-law strolled through the door, scanning the area around the bar before mimicking a whistle. "Nice to see my investment doing well!" He strode up to me and slapped my back. "*You're* doing well, Joseph."

"Thanks, Owen." I smiled before he scooped me into a hug. Owen had always had a booming presence that couldn't be ignored, whether he tried to be noticed or not. Under all that swagger, he was full of heart.

"Financials look great, too, even though you don't have to

send them. I believe I told you that." He frowned and slid onto a seat at the bar.

"You won't let me pay you back. If you really want to be a silent partner, then yes, you need to look. I'd appreciate you not sharing with my sister, but—"

"Joe, come on now." He frowned and shoved my shoulder. "Your father and your sister are nothing but proud of you. They like the financial side of life. It's not for everyone. Fuck knows it's not for me." His mouth twisted in disgust. "And, I hate to break it to you, but judging by the way you handle the books, your dad's numbers gene didn't miss you completely."

"The great OT is here!" Dominic grinned before marching up to where Owen sat and extending his hand. "Good to see you."

Owen rolled his eyes before he took it. "Dom, like I always tell you, I haven't been OT for a very long time. Good to see you, too."

"What does OT mean?" Jordan fluttered out of the kitchen, crinkling her nose at all of us.

"His name is Owen Thompson, but back when he was a college hockey star, he'd always force games into overtime. Then he became OT, the legend."

"Why does this fascinate him so much?" Owen asked me as he nodded in Dominic's direction.

"Because you're the closest he'll ever get to being friends with a famous athlete." I shook my head. "If anyone brings up hockey in here, he mentions how he knows an NHL scouting agent in two-point-five seconds."

"I'm better known for finding great hockey players than being one for a hot minute once upon a time," he explained to Jordan as she hung on his every word. Women of all ages fell at his feet, but he only had eyes for my sister. "Could one of y'all get me a cup of coffee?" He cupped his forehead and pressed his temples. "I drove straight through from Manhattan early this morning, and I'm running out of conversation."

Jordan darted into the kitchen with Dominic snickering at her exit.

"You still got it, OT." He jerked his head to Jordan's quick departure.

"Is that why you name-drop me? To get laid? Does it work?"

"Maybe once or twice. So, what brings you to the shore? Trailing a potential new sign on vacation again?"

"I went on a run with a new prospect on the beach this morning a couple of towns over in Wildwood. I thought when I quit sports, I'd be able to stop training like an athlete. This was the only free time this prospect had on vacation. With the numbers this kid has, I had to meet with him on his terms. It's the fun of scouting. Tell me," Owen dropped a hand on my shoulder, "do you name-drop me in front of women, too?"

"He doesn't need to," Dom answered for me. "One has him pretty riled up at the moment."

"What's this?" Owen's brow jumped. "You holding out on me? Nice to hear you're stepping away from the spreadsheets every once in a while."

"Nothing to tell." I grabbed a towel and wiped down the top of the bar and feigned interest in anything I found to be out of place.

I caught Owen shooting Dominic a puzzled glance.

"Ask your brother-in-law on that one," Dom said. "I know the highlights, but he's not exactly the sharing type."

"What's going on?" Owen rested his elbows on the bar as he studied me.

"Nothing. Absolutely nothing." I crossed my arms and leaned against the register. "I met a woman. She came in one night, and she was..." How did I explain Caterina? She was gorgeous, sexy, smart, and didn't want anything to do with me. I tried to give Owen the shortened version of what had been eating away at me the past few days. "We...had something. I can't explain it. She said she's coming off a breakup and didn't want to start anything, but it feels unfinished. Which is totally insane. I've only known her for three days. That's not enough time to have any actual feelings. Besides, I don't have time for that shit. You know that."

And I didn't, yet Caterina still raced through my brain since I'd dropped her off at the Anchor yesterday. We hadn't exchanged any information. No phone numbers or addresses. Running into her was a good possibility, but I doubted she'd come looking for me. Clean break—as if we'd never met.

But we had, and, as hard as I tried, I couldn't forget her.

"You seem pissed off enough about it for some kind of feelings, though. What's eating you about this woman?"

"We spent the night together, and I wasn't planning on taking it further than that, but I couldn't stay away from her. I ran into her the next day and thought maybe we had a chance, but she told me she's not ready for any of that. In fact, she told me twice. But I can't get her out of my head, and it makes no goddamn sense."

He nodded a thank you to Jordan after she set his coffee cup down on the counter. "When you get hit, it usually doesn't." He grinned before taking a sip.

"Hit?" I squinted at Owen. "What do you mean hit?"

"I knew the second I met your sister she was the one. Maybe it wasn't totally crystal clear at first but, from the time I met her, I couldn't leave her alone. Sometimes, connections are immediate, and there's nothing you can do to stop it. I'm guessing she's a tourist or not from around here."

"She was staying at the Anchor. She drove in alone from Brooklyn and wound up here."

"A one-nighter with a tourist isn't like you. Didn't you say you've steered clear since the stage-five clinger Dominic couldn't shake from Pennsylvania?"

A laugh slipped out. "I did, but there was something about her. And I—"

"Couldn't stay away." He chortled and shook his head. "So you keep saying. Sorry, dude. I think you may be fucked."

I laughed and shook my head. "I can't be fucked. I don't even really know her or how to get in touch with her."

"But you know enough to be this twisted from having to walk away. I get the feeling this isn't over. You aren't going to be able to let it sit." His shoulders shook with a laugh as he drained the cup.

"She'll be staying in a rental with her friends. She probably won't even come in here."

"I bet she does. And I bet she'll brush you off a couple more times before she gives in. You just need to decide on your approach."

"I don't have an approach." Talking about Caterina was as ridiculous as thinking about her. "It's not like I can text her or ask her to tutor me in accounting." We'd all heard the story too many times. My sister was brainy and had been burned by a jock, so, for the longest time, she wouldn't give Owen the time of day until he got creative.

"She's going to come to you. Call it a hunch. And when she does, step back a bit. Don't be an asshole, but also not so accommodating."

"I wasn't accommodating."

Jordan cleared her throat behind us before pouring Owen more coffee. "When she came in yesterday morning, he wouldn't let any of us seat her and made her breakfast himself. It was beyond adorable."

"Oh, Joseph." Owen cracked up. "You're so fucked. And whatever happens with this girl, I'm glad you put yourself out there for a night. We're all a little worried about you being alone all the time."

"Trust me, I'm never alone." I nodded to where Jordan was taking another order with a new waitress shadowing her. Business was heating up, and two more waitresses were set to start this week. That was the kind of thing that filled me with joy when I wasn't so damn distracted.

"Dominic is relentless enough. He doesn't need help."

"He's a good friend who's looking out for you, not just busting your balls. Life is more than work." He peered at the clock over my shoulder. "I better head back."

"You came all the way out here to drive back the same day?"

He shrugged. "Gotta do what you gotta do, right? I don't like spending a night away from Bella if I can help it. We'll be back out to visit soon."

He rose from the chair and pulled me into a goodbye hug. "Remember what I said," he whispered in my ear before slapping me on the back.

I always remembered what he said. Only this time, I had no idea what to do with it.

## 12

## CATERINA

I sat at the breakfast nook—yes, this swanky rental had a breakfast nook—nursing an iced coffee as I waited for my friends to arrive. I was able to pick up the keys and settle into the house on Saturday and check out of the Anchor early, promising Lou I'd let him or his wife know if I needed anything.

After catching up on some work emails and letting my mother know I wasn't in a strange hotel anymore, I had a relaxing day to myself, stocking the kitchen with plenty of food for the week for all three of us. I even tested out the grill with a hamburger last night, pairing it with the red wine I grabbed at the liquor store on the way back from the supermarket, relishing my last moments of solitude and trying to get my head screwed back on straight from the past four days.

The whole point of coming out here alone was to have time to myself to figure things out, but now it was getting lonely. I'd had a few moments of clarity last night before I dozed off on the couch after polishing off a pint of ice cream, non-alcoholic this time.

By tying all of my self-worth into my career, I let everything else in my life fall to the wayside: my friends, my family, and my relationship. Trent had been looking for an excuse to cheat—I realized that now. But I'd made it far too easy. Even though what he'd done was deplorable, he forced me to open my eyes and finally see the crappy path my life had taken.

The rental had already given me a little peace. At the very least, it prevented me from peeking across the street at Joe's restaurant, trying to *not* try to spot him.

A sting of disappointment washed over me last night when I realized I wouldn't be able to smell Joe on these sheets. He was a blip: a beautiful, sexy, wonderful blip and my friends would get me through this limbo I'd fallen into. The memory of blue eyes, a sweet smile, and the best sex of my life would become more and more distant. The attraction between us had been palpable, but the timing was off, and I had nothing to offer him now. No matter how real our connection seemed, in real life, we lived three hours away from each other. Working out a plan on how to extract Trent from my life *and* my apartment in the quickest and most painless way possible—if that way even existed—would take up most of my time upon my return.

But, I was supposed to be on vacation. I'd deal with Trent when I had to and not let him ruin one more second of my time while I was here.

"Anybody home?" Claire's voice boomed through the open windows as she banged on the door.

I popped off the stool and headed for the door. The second I opened it, my best friends tackled me with a hug.

"We are so glad you're here!" Claire gushed. Megan let go, but Claire still had me in a death grip. I sputtered a cough as I pushed back from her embrace.

"I'm glad I'm here, too. Kitchen cabinets are stocked, we all have our own bedrooms, and the backyard is *sick*. This is an awesome house." They set down their bags and beamed at me. Another one of Trent's taunts echoed in my head as guilt poked at me. I *was* lucky to still have friends that wanted me around after neglecting them for all these months.

"Thank you for including me." My voice cracked as I looked between them. "I know I've been sucked into work, but all of that is going to change. I promise to never take you for granted ever again. The single life is good for me, so far." I hoped they'd miss my watery eyes. Epiphanies were taxing.

Claire *pff*ted before lifting the handle of her suitcase. "Life without that asshole will be great, and we're going to have a blast this week!" She kissed my cheek before heading upstairs.

"Now that whatever you had with Trent is over, Claire unburdened herself and told you her true feelings." Megan squeezed my arm before lifting her own bag. "And I agree, life without that douche will be spectacular, and, tonight, we celebrate! Give us some time to freshen up, and we'll head out."

"You just drove for three hours, and you want to head out already? Don't you want to relax tonight and go out tomorrow?"

"Hell, no! We're going to celebrate being young and being alive this week. Thirties are the new twenties. Claire found this cool bar-restaurant on Yelp, not too far from where you were staying. The Beach Pub, I think it's called? The food and the night life are supposed to be great. Come on, Cat. Let's go out and live a little."

*Fuck.* I was going to tell them about Joe, once I did the whole breakup information dump, but I wasn't ready to talk about him yet. I missed him. There. I finally admitted it. I missed a man I hardly knew and already had regrets for pushing him away. I thought once my friends came, they'd provide me the distraction I needed, not lead me right back to him.

I trudged up the stairs and headed to my bedroom, pulling out the silky black off-the-shoulder blouse I'd bought months ago in hopes of a fancy date night that never happened. I pulled my ankle length skinny jeans up my legs and stepped into a pair of high heeled sandals. After I fixed my hair and makeup, I gazed at my reflection and rolled my eyes. I was dressing up for Joe, and that wasn't right. I'd said goodbye—twice—but fate was once again putting me back into his path. Maybe staying home and faking an illness would be the noble thing to do, but Megan and Claire would never let that fly. Plus, despite pushing him away, I wanted to see him. And even though I acted as if I wanted him to move on and forget me, I took my appearance up a notch tonight so he'd remember. A disgusted groan erupted from my throat. I was ashamed of my actions and the mixed signals I sent to this nice man who'd done nothing but help me since I'd met him.

As I waited for my friends, I looked up The Beach Pub on my phone, feeling an odd surge of pride when I stumbled across an article.

*Joe Hunter, 30, is the sole owner of The Beach Pub. Renovating the former Red Oak and introducing a brand-new menu, the establishment has quickly become a local seasonal favorite in the two years since its opening. Calling ahead for dinner reservations is recommended, especially in late July and August.*

Maybe Joe wouldn't notice me in the crowd. I could pretend and try to ignore all I wanted, but there would be no way I wouldn't notice *him*. This was going to be a long night.

When we were seated at a table after a fifteen-minute wait, I was relieved when a waitress I didn't recognize sauntered up to the table.

"I'm Maureen. Are you getting food and drinks or just drinks?"

"Both," all three of us answered at once. Maureen giggled at us before handing out menus.

"We have three kinds of sliders, and the macaroni and cheese bites are my favorite. There's a sampler with all of that plus chicken fingers and mozzarella sticks to share. Usually works in a smaller group, but depends on how hungry you are."

"How about a bottle of red for us to share? And all that stuff, too." Megan glanced across the table as Claire and I nodded in agreement, ignoring the wave of sadness at having mozzarella sticks not specially made for me like the last time. I was so pathetic, I was getting on my own nerves.

"We can work all of it off on the beach. We're close enough to go for a run in the morning." Claire was the pain-in-the-ass fitness nut of all of us, but I'd been doing enough stress eating since Thursday to let her push me out the door at the ungodly hour she would awaken and drag me to run with her.

"So, tell me, Kit-Cat, what have you been doing since Thursday?" Megan's brows shot up as Claire shifted in her seat, both awaiting my answer.

"Not much, really. I worked a little on Friday, sat by the pool, went to this food festival for a bit." I shrugged, omitting the mind-melting sex I'd had with Joe on Thursday night and falling into Joe's bed, tipsy off my ass, on Friday night.

Megan fell back in her chair, narrowing her eyes at me.

"She's hiding something from us," she whispered to Claire with her suspicious gaze still centered on me.

"She's totally hiding something," Claire agreed before Maureen came over with our wine and set the glasses in front of us.

I glared at the both of them while Maureen poured.

"*She* is sitting right here, guys." I pursed my lips and tapped my finger against the side of my glass. "There is nothing to—" My mouth went dry when I spotted the man I'd hoped in vain I'd be able to avoid. Joe was behind the bar with Dominic, laughing and leaning over to whisper in a beautiful redhead's ear. At least, I thought it was a redhead. The lighting was dim, but there was no mistaking Joe's easy smile. *God, he was beautiful.* Instead of a T-shirt, he wore a button-down with the sleeves rolled up to his forearms. I wasn't sure if it was regret or jealousy nauseating me: regret at walking away from what could've been a great thing because of circumstance, jealousy for the lucky woman who basked in Joe's attention and could allow herself to enjoy it.

I exhaled a long breath and brought my wineglass to my lips for a long pull. It was easy to gravitate toward Joe, and I was sure this woman was one of many in this town who vied for his attention, but it stung like a bitch to watch.

"What are we looking at?" Claire's head swiveled around to where my eyes remained glued. "Ooh, he's hot." She tapped my hand. "You look amazing tonight. Go talk to him. Start the Trent cleanse." She shoved my shoulder.

I scanned the room for a quick exit. My mouth was dry, and I swallowed to mask my gasp for air. The beach behind the restaurant was now open for customers, and I needed to sneak outside to regroup before I spilled what I'd really been doing since I'd arrived.

"I need a little air. I'll be right back."

I shot up from my chair and rushed over to the back door, inhaling deeply as I clasped my hands behind my neck.

My gaze drifted toward the waves crashing onto the sand in the distance. The ebb and flow of the water was soothing, yet sad, bringing back memories of Joe's anecdote about chaos and swimming against the current. He'd called me brave, but I was the exact opposite. Becoming involved with Joe was as messy and chaotic as it could possibly get, but it would be the good kind of chaos. The best kind.

Sure, we could just enjoy things for now, but that wasn't how I was wired, no matter how hard I'd been fighting to go against the grain and be different and daring. More time with Joe meant more certainty of getting hurt when it inevitably ended. And, as much as I wanted to take a chance, that fear paralyzed me from acting on it.

"Why didn't you come over to say hello when you came in?" Joe's voice startled me out of my thoughts. His beautiful blue eyes shot me an icy glare, and I could only shrug in response.

"You were speaking to someone. I didn't think you noticed me, honestly." The clipped edge of my voice surprised me.

"I *always* notice you. I was talking to a friend of mine. Just like *we're* friends, right?" He motioned between us with his finger, taunting me.

"You don't need to explain. None of my business—"

"You weren't jealous, were you?"

I didn't know whether to kiss or slap the smirk off of his face.

"No. Of course not."

"There's no shame in admitting it. I sure as hell didn't like all these guys gawking at you when you walked out here." He crossed his arms, a hint of a smile contradicting the feral gleam in his eye.

"No one was gawking—"

"I didn't like it."

The husky, possessive dip in his voice made me shiver. He had no right to sound like that, and I shouldn't have liked it so much. But I did. My eyes fell to his lips as I avoided the singe of his heated stare. The fantasy of him claiming me with his mouth in front of everyone like he had in my motel room played out so vividly in my brain I took a step back on instinct, terrified I'd want it bad enough to let it play out in real life.

Fantasy was where it needed to stay.

"I know why we can't … go back there." He ate up the distance I'd attempted to put between us in one step. "But I can't deny wanting to. And neither can you. At least you can't very well." He choked out a laugh before heading back.

My heels sank in the sand, Joe's words pinning me to where I stood. I wanted to call him back, but when my mouth opened, I couldn't find the words.

"And Caterina?" Joe called to me before pushing the door open.

"Yeah?" My voice was a shaky whisper from all the adrenaline coursing through my veins.

"You're gorgeous tonight." My breath caught from the electricity pulsing between us. "*Fucking* gorgeous." His blue eyes darkened as they caressed my body, my skin tingling along the path of his gaze before he disappeared inside.

I bent over, clutching my knees in an attempt to even out my breathing.

I couldn't run from something that kept finding me every time.

# 13

## JOE

I NEVER DOUBTED that Caterina and I would cross paths again while she was here. The main attractions of Ocean Cove were too close together, and the restaurant was in the middle of it all. I wasn't sure if she'd ever come back here, but I'd run into her somewhere, that much I'd known. My plan was to be cordial but not attach myself to her side—the exact opposite of what I'd done since the moment I met her because I couldn't help my damn self. When I'd spotted her, looking so goddamn gorgeous, I couldn't stand it, my plan had flown right out the window. There was no way I couldn't notice her, with her perfect ass poured into those skin-tight jeans and her bare shoulder teasing and torturing me. She'd stalked outside on fuck me heels, and, once again, my need for this woman trumped any sense of reason or self-preservation. Unable to fight against this ridiculous pull between us, I'd followed her.

But now, the rest was up to her. She was just another customer tonight, and I'd ignore her and the countless guys I'd caught staring in her direction. I had a business to run. While I couldn't deny I still wanted her and had to fight every cell in my body not to grab her by the neck and kiss her until she gave in, I wouldn't. The restaurant was too busy for me to waste time pining over a woman who was afraid to want me back. The struggle to shift my priorities to where they'd always been was new. Eventually, I'd be able to peel my eyes from her table and pretend she wasn't even there. That would take some work, but the frustration building since Friday morning fueled my incentive to at least try.

"Joe?" Jordan asked, tearing me away from my thoughts and reminding me I was the boss around here. "Can we put three tables together? The guys in the back are asking."

"No, not when it's this busy. If they give you a hassle, let me know."

I glanced toward the crowd Jordan was referring to and recognized one of the guys at the far end of the table. When Caterina had walked outside, he'd openly eye fucked her. The possessive idiot in me hoped he'd get rowdy, so I'd have an excuse to throw him out.

"Are you all right, Joe?" Jill asked me from where she sat at the bar, studying me with a confused gaze. We'd dated for a couple of months before we decided we were better off as friends. She managed one of the newer hotels along the beach, and we had a mutually beneficial business relationship that I was thankful I hadn't fucked up. She was a good friend, but, every once in a while, I'd catch a flash of regret in her green eyes.

"I'm fine." I turned my gaze back to hers. "Busy, new staff starting tonight. It's a good stressful, but you know how it is."

"I do." She nodded, her fingers drumming on the bar. "But you thrive on busy. Ever since you rushed outside, you've been like a different person."

"I'm not ..." I started but trailed off. Jill knew me well

enough to see through my hollow denial. "It's stupid. I'm a big boy." I shot her a grin. "I'll get over it."

"For as long as I've known you, you've never looked at anyone the way you're looking at that brunette over there." She regarded me with a wistful smile that never made it to her eyes. "She's lucky."

"She's not interested." I attempted to cover my disappointment with a shrug. "What we had was short if it was even anything. She's only here on vacation."

"Seriously? The poor thing is going to give herself neck cramps if she keeps turning her head this way. I don't know her, but I'd bet she's very interested. The kind of tension I'm sensing between the two of you doesn't come from indifference."

I stilled and grabbed the edge of the bar, hating the defeated tone in her words. This was why I didn't date. I didn't have much in me to give, and I always ended up disappointing someone. Jill was a good person, and she deserved better than what I had to offer, which was nothing at the time. But with Caterina, it was already different. I was already different. She wasn't an afterthought. Hell, lately, she was my *only* thought. But right now, I had no choice but to walk away.

"Joe?" Maureen, one of the new waitresses, asked me from behind Jill, "do we have the right to cut customers off? They're on their fifth bottle of wine, and they're getting a little loud, but they're insisting on more." She grimaced and motioned to another loud table near the back door.

Jill laughed at my defeated sigh.

"I'll be right there."

Maureen exhaled in relief before heading to the kitchen.

"Gotta love tourists. Bake in the sun all day, and drink all night." Jill turned to the drunken table in question and shook her head.

"I should take care of this." I leaned over the bar to kiss her cheek. "I'm sor—"

"Stop. We were always better off as friends. There's no need for sorry. I'm happy." She dropped a hand to my forearm. "And I really hope you are, too. Or that you will be."

## 14

## CATERINA

"Talk. Now." Megan pointed to my chair when I came back to the table.

I didn't want to go through it all and become upset in front of Joe, but I knew when I returned to two sets of saucer-wide eyes, I wouldn't have a choice.

I sucked in a long breath before I unloaded it all, starting with the welcome home I'd gotten on Thursday.

"Are you fucking kidding me?" The heads of everyone at the table next to us whipped around to Claire's outburst. "In your apartment, knowing you were coming home?"

"Ah, but he didn't know *when* I was getting home." I picked up my wineglass, zoning out at the whirl of red liquid as I swished my glass around. "I've been averaging getting home between eight and eight-thirty during the week, and this was just before seven." I coughed out a sad laugh. At least Trent had paid enough attention to me and my schedule to learn to work around it.

"So, *that's* what made you leave in such a rush." Megan squeezed my arm. "I'm sorry, Cat. I totally get why you couldn't wait to get the hell out of there."

"Me too," Claire agreed, her voice much softer. "I hope you got here and jumped into bed with the first hot guy you saw." She elbowed Megan's side, and they both shared a "like that would ever happen" laugh. Their smiles faded quickly when I shrugged in response.

"You did *not*," Megan whispered before her jaw dropped.

"Oh, I did." I took a bite out of one of the sliders while searching their gazes for a reaction. Their strong surprise, or, more accurately, the utter shock, triggered an unexpected laugh to slip out of me. This entire trip had been an adventure outside of my comfort zone, and sleeping with a gorgeous stranger was about as far outside of my normal as you could get.

Despite myself, I looked back toward the bar and caught Joe's gaze. His eyes locked with mine as if he were issuing a challenge. Too bad I was too much of a coward to accept.

"Wait, was it sex-on-a-stick back at the bar who keeps staring over here?" Claire's eyes sparkled as she looked over my shoulder.

"Joe is the name of sex-on-a-stick at the bar, the owner of this place, and yes, he's the one."

"Wow," Megan gasped. "Good for you! So, I guess you guys have been," she motioned between me and the bar behind me, "ever since?"

"No, just the one night. Long story short, I ended up here my first night to get something to eat. One thing led to another, and—it doesn't matter. I can't start up anything with anyone now." I smoothed the stray waves off my damp forehead. "Whatever it was, is done. It's better this way."

"Really?" Megan giggled and shook her head. "Judging by how flustered you are when he's only across the room, it doesn't seem *done* at all."

"I'm not flustered," I snapped, the denial not even believable to my own ears. Megan and Claire could always see right through me. Although it didn't take a detective to decode how I felt about Joe. They cast each other a side-glance before bringing their gazes back to mine.

"Okay, yes. We had incredible chemistry, and it was the best sex of my life, but it can't happen again."

"You can't say 'best sex of your life' and let it dangle like that." Claire narrowed her eyes at me. "He looks...intense. Like he'd be really *thorough*." Her eyebrows jumped. "Am I right?"

"Yes," I admitted. He was so thorough I couldn't stop thinking about it. Every kiss, every touch, the sex hadn't been just fantastic, it had been life changing. He knew my body better than anyone I'd ever known, including myself. "And he's sweet. So damn sweet." I held in the story of dopey, tipsy me and how Joe took care of me like a perfect gentleman. I didn't want him to be a gentleman anymore. I wanted the insatiable, dirty-talking animal he'd been the night we met, but I feared I'd pushed him too far away.

"Would you believe he's only thirty and built this place up himself after only a couple of years? But, I shouldn't be getting involved with anyone now, much less have a fling with someone who lives over three hours away." I lifted a shoulder and reached for a chicken finger, breaking it apart until it was nothing but greasy white strands on my plate.

"Cat, I'm just going to say it." Megan fell back in her seat and leveled her gaze on mine. "And I promise you, this comes from a lot of love. Stop fucking up your life."

I dropped the meat onto my plate and squinted at Megan. "Fucking up my life?" My nose burned, and something scratched at my throat, probably more of that pain-in-the-ass clarity. I came here with the full knowledge that I screwed up somewhere, but hearing a close friend say it aloud took it to another crushing level.

"Since I've known you, you've always been too busy working toward something to actually enjoy anything. We had to push you to go out—even back in college. You were always afraid of screwing up that one test or project, convinced it would mess up your plans for the future. You were too busy planning your life to actually let yourself have one, babe." Her lips pursed as she drew back into her chair.

"So, you guys agree with Trent that I'm a cold fish?" I huffed to hide the crack in my voice.

"First of all, don't compare us to that douche." Claire scooted her chair closer to mine. "But I hate to say that he had a point. He was doing whatever for God knows how long, and if you hadn't come home early that day, you never would have known. It's easy for you to get sucked in, overwork yourself and not see anything else. That being said, he took advantage of that fact. And if you working too much really bothered him, he would have said something or tried to salvage whatever you guys had. My guess is that he's being petty because he doesn't want to leave the apartment."

"Exactly. And stupid me put his name on the lease." I lifted my hair off of my sweaty neck, trying to cool down from all the tension and frustration.

"There are ways around that. Don't worry about that now. Now," Megan motioned over my shoulder toward Joe, "you need to figure out what kind of regret do you want to live with? The kind from jumping into a passionate *fling*."

My lips twitched when her voice dropped on fling as if it were a dirty word.

"Right after you ended a passion-*less* relationship," she continued, "or steering clear because it's too complicated?"

Steering clear wasn't working. From the time I pulled Joe inside my motel room, things were already complicated. I'd foolishly thought putting a stop to whatever was brewing between us would be the easy thing to do. But all it had done was exhaust me and upset us both.

"I'll go out on a limb, judging by how miserable you look at the moment, you wouldn't be able to live with yourself if you don't at least give it a try."

"I can hardly live with myself now," I finally admitted. "This doesn't make any sense. We just met. And what happens—"

"Stop that." Claire swatted my hand. "Best sex of your life, remember? Don't worry the whys or about what happens just yet. Right now, just take a chance and enjoy the ride."

"I may not even have a chance. I've done nothing but give him mixed signals, and I think he's had enough." I exhaled, now feeling every ounce of the disappointment and regret I'd been trying to push away.

"Do you mean the same guy who is *still* stealing heated glances over here and looked like he was ready to take that guy's head off just for staring at you? I think if you straighten it out, you'll still have a good chance." Megan patted my arm. "Go over and talk to him."

"No, not tonight. The mornings here are quieter, not as many people around." I swiveled my head and spotted another crowd around Joe, charismatic bastard that he was. Nope, I couldn't confess anything to him tonight.

"Where do I begin?" I rubbed at my temples, feeling not a little terrified but oddly relieved. Whatever happened, I wouldn't have to wonder what could've been. And Megan was right, that would torture me. It *already* tortured me.

"That's our girl!" Claire shoved my shoulder, and a laugh escaped me.

"I think you already know," Megan said. "Telling the truth is always a good place to start."

## 15

## CATERINA

AFTER TOSSING and turning most of the night, I headed to The Beach Pub while Claire and Megan were still asleep. On the too short walk there, I'd tried to figure out what the hell to say to Joe while bracing myself for rejection. My first boss always said to do the hardest task first, and the rest of your day would be cake. A "no thanks" from Joe would more or less ruin my entire day, but no matter how we resolved things I could move on—eventually—after I spent however long I needed to beat myself up for ruining what could have been something great.

Opening the door, I searched for Joe. Sucking in a breath before I lost my nerve, I made my way up to the front counter of the restaurant on shaky legs.

"Oh, hey, I remember you!" Jordan chirped when she came up to me. "Caterina, right?"

"Right." I nodded. "And you're Jordan."

"Guilty as charged. Would you like me to find you a table?"

"I got it, J. Thank you." Joe was so close behind me, his breath fanned the shell of my ear.

She looked between us before giggling to herself and scurrying away.

"I didn't expect to see you here again." Joe's eyes raked over me before he motioned to follow him. "Are your friends here for breakfast, too?" Gone was the easy rapport we'd had from the beginning. This Joe didn't even smile. I had an uphill, if not pointless, battle ahead of me.

"No. I came to talk to you. Are you busy?" My stomach sank when he stilled.

"I have to stay by the bar this morning, but I could find you a seat there. Come."

Okay, he was willing to talk. That was a good sign. Maybe. I followed him to the bar and climbed onto a stool.

"What can I do for you, Caterina?" Joe fiddled with the glasses behind the bar, his short sleeves revealing the flex of biceps, offering a brief moment of torturous distraction. I was nervous and flustered on so many different levels, my head spun.

"I need you to hear me out."

Joe stopped and lifted his gaze to mine, but didn't reply.

Taking that as some kind of 'okay,' I went on. "First, I want to say that I'm sorry. I've thrown a lot of mixed signals at you, and it's not fair. You've been nothing but wonderful, and I've been nothing but taxing. Again, I'm sorry."

His nonchalant shrug didn't help my nerves. "You don't need to keep apologizing. It's fine. I get it—"

"I'm not done." I held my hand up. "That was only the first part."

"The first part?" He squinted at me as he drew his head back. I thought I caught a tiny smile playing on his lips but wasn't sure if that was wishful thinking.

"Yes. I like you. A lot. Too much, in fact. And it's confusing as hell. I feel more of a connection to you than I did to the man I spent two years of my life with. I'm not going to lie—that scares me a little." I blew out a shaky gust of air and dropped my chin to my chest before lifting my gaze to continue. "I just broke up with someone, no matter if I felt anything for him or not, and my home is three hours away from yours. What I'm feeling shouldn't be real, but I can't help but think that maybe it is. I've been miserable since Saturday morning. What I'm trying to say is that I want to take a chance. Explore whatever this is between us while I'm here." I studied Joe for a reaction, a twitch, or even a breath. Nothing. Was this working? Was he about to throw me out? I had no clue.

"And like I told you, I never spent the night with someone I'd only just met, but I couldn't *not* be with you that night. I wanted you that much. How crazy is that? For me, and the sad little life I've led, that's borderline insanity." My words were coming out faster now, his non-reaction compounding my anxiety. "Even if this turns out to be a clusterfuck that ends badly, I can't walk away. At least, not again."

I plopped my elbows on the counter and leveled my eyes at Joe. "Could you, I don't know, blink or something for good-ness sake?"

His tongue darted out and swept over his bottom lip before he set his hands on the counter on either side of me, boxing me in, his eyes boring into mine.

"So, you're saying you want to take me out?" A slow grin spread over his lips.

He laughed when I jabbed his arm.

"Enjoy that, did you?" I glared at him, but the relief coursing through me finally let me breathe again.

"Maybe a little." A smile pulled at the corners of his mouth before he held out his hand. "Give me your phone."

I fished it out of my purse and handed it to him after punching in my password.

After grabbing it from me, he jabbed the screen a few times before a faint ringing sounded from his pocket.

"Dom?" He called out while his gaze stayed fixed on me.

"I'm right here, oh, hey!" Dominic nodded a hello in my periphery. "What's up?"

"I need you to close tonight. I'm leaving at seven."

"I can definitely do that." I heard the smile in Dominic's voice before he moved away. My eyes were just as glued to Joe's.

"Text me the address of the rental. I'll pick you up about eight."

"Didn't you tell Dominic seven?" I leaned in closer, my heart hammering against my rib cage when Joe ran the tip of his finger along my jaw. Having had sex with Joe should have taken the power out of his touches, but it did the exact opposite. I knew his lips and his fingers and...other places. A tiny touch, even accidental, only made me want it all, all over again. Butterflies took flight in my stomach at the prospect of actually getting it, not talking myself out of it as I'd done for the past few days.

"I have a few things to do first." His lips grazed my cheek, trailing a hot path to my ear. "If you want to take me out, Caterina, I'm all yours." My breath hitched when he took my earlobe between his teeth and gave it a nip. Joe saying he was mine, however he'd meant it, made the tiny hairs on the back of my neck stand up as a chill rushed through me.

"While I have you here now, want some breakfast?" I relaxed at his easy smile. We were back. Only this time, I wasn't putting anymore walls between us.

"Are you going to make it for me?" I leaned my elbow on

the counter, resting my chin on my hand. His head fell as his shoulders shook with a laugh.

"Sure, if that's what you want." The heat in his eyes triggered a cold shiver down my spine.

"Yes," I answered, without a drop of uncertainty. "It's what I want."

*Along with you.*

How this would end up, I didn't know, but I had no choice but to go along for the ride.

"Is that a takeout order? That's huge!" Maureen mused from behind me.

"Not exactly." I flashed her and Jordan a smile over my shoulder. "I'm planning a picnic on the beach."

I'd agonized over this all day long and was confident I'd picked a good menu for tonight. I included almost one of all the entree specials, but I owned this place and all the food in it, so I had all the means to go overboard. I remembered what she seemed to love the most from the festival and tried my best to build off of that.

Caterina had given me the impression that no one ever made a big deal over her. Even if this feast was overkill, I hoped she'd love it. My cheeks still ached from the huge grin planted on my face ever since her "confession" this morning. She'd shaken like a leaf but pulled no punches about what she wanted, and her bravery was sexy as hell. I had to summon a lot of restraint not to pull her over the counter by the waist and kiss the hell out of her. We actually had the chance I didn't think she'd let us have, and there was no way I wasn't pulling out every stop tonight.

"Special delivery from Maria's!" Dominic sang as he came into the kitchen with a large white paper bag. The grease spotting the paper confirmed they'd sent over exactly what I ordered.

"Maria's?" Jordan crinkled her nose. "Now? The bakery doesn't deliver until tomorrow morning. I didn't think they were even open after three."

"Usually," I said, stifling a smile. "And they aren't; I made a special request."

"Special request? How the hell did you do that?" Dominic's jaw dropped. "I'm impressed, man."

I shrugged as I stuffed the steaming hot paper bag into the thermal carrier. "I have a daily order and give them plenty of business and promotion. I called in a small favor. No big deal."

"No big deal? You've *never* called in any favors, especially over a woman. Ladies," He glanced at Maureen and Jordan and jerked his head in my direction, "what you're seeing right now is unprecedented and epic."

"So dramatic." I shook my head but wouldn't look up, in too great of a mood to let anything get to me today. I peeked at my watch, noting I still had a little time to run to my apartment to change. Between the influx of customers and planning this picnic for Caterina tonight, adrenaline had kept me running non-stop. But, I wasn't tired at all. Every part of me felt alive as if everything was falling into place exactly where I wanted it to.

I ambled back into the dining area to dig my buzzing phone out of my pocket.

**Caterina:** *Can I ask where we're going?*

**Joe:** *Nope.*

**Caterina:** *Seriously? Can I at least get a hint so I know how to dress?*

**Joe:** *Nope.*

**Caterina:** *Okay, but when I embarrass you for being dressed inappropriately, remember, it's your fault.*

**Joe:** *In a potato sack, you'd be the most beautiful woman in the room. In ANY room. So relax, and enjoy the surprise.*

**Joe:** *Wait, relax. You may not know what that means, let me think how to explain...*

**Caterina:** *Very funny. Is there food involved? I'm starving.*

**Joe:** *Nice try for a hint. See you at eight.*

**Caterina:** *Grr. Fine.*

**Joe:** *Did you just growl at me? That's fucking hot.*

**Joe:** *Still not telling you.*

"I'm not used to you smiling this much." Dom laughed as he regarded me through thinned eyes. "You had us all worried you'd be married to this place for the rest of your life."

"I *am* married to this place. It's still my first priority, but, like you said, time to get the stick out of my ass and have a little fun."

"You packed enough for more than just fun. You like this girl. I'm glad, but are you guys on the same page? I mean, she still lives in New York City, right?" He leaned against the wall next to the bar with his arms crossed.

"Brooklyn, yes. She told me this morning she wants to give whatever it is between us a chance. Honestly, I have no clue what's going to happen. But, I need to see where it goes, anyway. I know it makes no sense—"

"Nothing has to make sense. Just go with it." He slapped my shoulder. "I'll open tomorrow. That way, there's no excuse to cut the night short. Get out of here. I got this all handled."

"You always do. And thanks."

"Running this place with you is my job. No need to thank me." He slapped my arm.

"I mean, thanks for being a ball-breaker who forces me to see things I don't want to, sometimes."

A tiny smile played on his lips. "You'd do the same for me. You did. By letting me come out here with you in the first place."

I nodded, turning to go back into the kitchen and collect everything I'd prepped for tonight. It still felt like our time was running out, but, at least, she was willing to give us a chance. For right now, that was enough for me.

I parked outside of the address Caterina had texted and climbed the front stairs. I'd only been to the rentals in Ocean Cove a handful of times but always left in awe. Some of the houses were mini-mansions, but Caterina's rental was on a street with the more modest houses. Before I could ring the bell, one of her friends appeared in the doorway and almost made me jump out of my skin.

"Hi, Joe. I'm Claire. Very nice to meet you." She held out her hand for me to shake as she shut the door behind her.

"Nice to meet you, too." I took her hand. Claire held it for a long beat as she studied my gaze.

She beamed at me before she gave me another once-over. "You are *just* what she needs, I can already tell. I love that you didn't tell her where you were going. She's a planner, and she's been going nuts."

"I had a feeling she would." I chuckled and shook my head. "I hope I didn't make her *that* crazy."

"Nah. She needs it. She never lets herself have fun. Well, she didn't until this week."

Her eyes met mine and darted away. I sucked in my bottom lip to hide my smile, realizing Caterina probably spilled about that first night we met.

"Show her a good time and don't hurt her and you and I will be good." She leveled her eyes at me in warning.

"Understood." I held my hands up in surrender. Claire was tall and slim, but I could tell she would have no problem trying to kick my ass. "The last thing I'd ever do is hurt her; I promise you that."

At least, not on purpose. I already knew one night with her wouldn't be enough, and things would get messy when we got closer.

When, not if, because I already hated the thought of letting her go.

"All right." Caterina's exaggerated sigh made it outside before she did. She strutted up to me in a short denim skirt and an off-the-shoulder top, twirling around before her hands fell to her sides. I gave her body a shameless perusal, my mouth watering to taste the silky olive skin right above her collarbone. She said I dripped sex, but this woman basked in it, and she had no clue.

"If I have to change, tell me now."

She met my gaze with a scowl until I pulled her flush to me and looped my arm around her waist.

"Don't you dare. You're perfect." I planted a kiss right behind her ear. Her body stiffened then slumped against me.

"Hi," she whispered and kissed my cheek.

"Hi, yourself."

She giggled and lifted her head. "You look pretty perfect, too. But when don't you, right?"

We both turned toward Claire clearing her throat behind us.

"You kids have fun. Don't bring her back until sunrise." Her brows shot up before she stepped back in the house and shut the door.

"Okay, so I won't embarrass you. Ready?"

"I told you, you're beautiful. And we'll be all alone, so no one gets to look at you but me. And yes, I'm very ready."

Caterina cupped my neck and pulled me in for a kiss. It wasn't as frenzied as it had been Thursday night when all that bottled-up passion spilled out and blinded us both. My tongue glided along the seam of her lips until they parted for me. This kiss was slow, the yearning and need boiling over but not rushing us like before. I swallowed her sweet whimpers as our tongues explored rather than attacked, becoming reacquainted with the taste and savoring it this time. I'd savor her for as long as she'd let me.

"We need to get going," I panted after pulling away. A sexy blush crept up her cheeks as her dark eyes searched mine.

"Sorry, I get lost in you." She let out a breathless chuckle.

"I've been lost in you since Thursday." I let my thumb fall over her lips. "Let's get lost together."

# 17

## CATERINA

WHAT WAS it about Joe that made me lose every inhibition I had? From the time I met him, I just couldn't help myself. I *had* to kiss him, or something inside me would implode. Had I ever been this ravenous for anyone else?

Nope. Never.

Whatever I had with Joe was a very unexpected first, and I had no idea how to hold myself back. My attempt to stay away from him had lasted all of forty-eight hours until I couldn't take it anymore, and I was only in walking distance. What would happen when I left him for real? Clenching my eyes shut, I tried to push the thought out of my head.

"Hey," Joe whispered and reached over the console to squeeze my knee. "You look about a thousand miles away." My gaze flicked toward his raised brow, and I cursed the heat drifting down my leg from his touch. I almost pushed my knee into his palm to invite his hand to go higher.

"I'm good. Excited. Annoyed, I still don't know where we're going, other than the fact we needed to bring our own food." I shot him a glare. Between the amazing smells of whatever Joe packed wafting from the back of the cab, his dark T-shirt and worn jeans, exactly what he wore the night we met, my head spun. The last time he cooked for me and dressed like that, my panties had fallen off so quickly, I almost tripped over them.

He grabbed my hand and brought it to his lips. My skin tingled from the wet warmth of his lips and the tickle of his stubble. Even that first night we'd met, his touches meant something, *said* something.

"That's better," he said, still keeping hold of my hand as he pulled the truck into park. "We have tonight. I know you're a planner and all, but, just this once, maybe live in the moment a bit, and enjoy it." He grinned and laced our fingers together.

"I've been living in the moment since Thursday. I'm just not used to it." I choked out a laugh. "But, yes. I'll take tonight and whatever else we can get." His smile grew wider, and, hell, I wanted to kiss him again. I turned to climb out of the passenger seat before I leapt over the console for another Joe fix. There would be time for that later, I hoped. I supposed living in the moment meant not rushing it, and although it would be tough, I'd try my best. For more time with him, I'd try anything.

"Where are we?" Joe had taken us to a small, deserted beach. "Can we even be here?"

"It's public property. Not many come here since it's so tiny, but I stop by sometimes to think. It's quiet and has the best view of the lighthouse. Do you mind carrying this? I have two big, heavy bags to unpack for us." A grin lifted his cheeks before he handed me two folded blankets.

"Sure. Big blankets for such little sand, no?" I asked as I followed Joe onto the beach. Once I let the tension go, excitement stirred in its place.

"We need a place to set the feast I brought us." He flashed a grin over his shoulder.

"A feast?" My flat sandals filled with sand as I set down the blankets. "It's really sweet of you to go to all that trouble." The night was warm but breezy and made it easy to spread out the soft fabric over the sand.

"I own a restaurant, in case you forgot." He set the baskets on the corners of each blanket to weigh them down. "Besides..." His adorable, shy smile was the sexiest thing I'd ever seen. "I like cooking for you."

"And I like to eat, so we're a match made in heaven." I kicked off my sandals and reached for the top of one of the baskets. Joe pushed my hand away and shook his head.

"Nope. I serve *you*. I like doing that, too." He pointed to the blanket and motioned for me to sit down.

"Okay, if you want to cook for me *and* feed me, I won't argue." I plopped down on the blanket and crossed my legs under me. "Did you leave any for your customers tonight?"

"Some." Joe handed me a fork and knife. "I grabbed a few of the entree specials. I tried to pick closest to what you got the most excited about at the festival. I have shrimp, stuffed clams, and..." His eyes brightened before he handed me a foil covered container.

I peeled the top off and found mozzarella sticks and a tiny cup of marinara sauce. He'd thought of everything, even paying attention to what I liked as we strolled around the festival, despite me pushing him away both right before and right after. I already had trouble believing this guy was real. Any words I wanted to say in gratitude were stuck behind the lump in my throat.

"Joe, I—" I gulped in an attempt to will away the tears flooding my eyes. No man had ever made me cry tears of happiness before. I was touched, overwhelmed, and shocked that he'd gone to all this trouble for me with only a day's notice. "I know it's ridiculous to get this flustered over fish and mozzarella sticks, but no one has ever paid attention like this..." I set my plate on my lap as my nose burned. "I hoped just this one night, I wouldn't make an idiot of myself in front of you. No such luck, I guess." I cupped my forehead as if that would somehow push out a coherent sentence, but I was too choked up to be articulate.

As much as I attempted to write off what Joe and I had as lust and chemistry, what he'd done for me tonight transcended that. I still had a lot to learn about Joe, but he'd showed me the most important parts, and I was already hooked.

He looped an arm around my waist, yanking me into his side. "You're doing fine. And for the record, you've never made an idiot of yourself in front of me. You're brave and beautiful. And, since the second I met you, I couldn't get enough. I'm glad we're not fighting it anymore." He leaned forward and brushed my lips. They parted on a soft sigh when he grazed my bottom lip with his tongue. This man could *kiss*. It had taken me over twenty years to have a cinematic-worthy, toe-curling kiss.

It was as if my teenage years had been reset, and I was in one of those coming-of-age tales of self-discovery. Only I was closer to middle age, and the first kiss came at the beginning of the story, quickly followed by very dirty sex with the promise of more.

I sifted my fingers into his hair and laid back, pulling him down with me. Joe broke the kiss and shook his head.

"Dinner first, and dessert, *then* we see about extra dessert." He sat up and kissed the tip of my nose.

"You even brought dessert?" My mouth fell open. Joe was turning out to be my every fantasy come true. If there was chocolate cake in one of those baskets, my clothes would fly off of their own accord.

"If you're a good girl." His scorching smile and the husky way "good girl" rolled off his tongue made my silly heart trip over itself. "Now, eat."

"Can I ask you something?" I leaned back on my elbows, already stuffed after only two plates.

"Sure." He rested his elbows on his knees. "Ask away."

"We spoke about my less-than-stellar relationship history, but you said you didn't see women that much. Were you ever serious with anyone?"

He shrugged. "I wouldn't call anything serious. Like I told you, I tried to not start anything with someone out of town, and the women I dated around here got fed up pretty fast. The long hours I work and constant changing of plans had anyone I attempted to date pretty short on patience. And they were right. I never made time for anything other than the restaurant. I was always either brainstorming a new menu or obsessing over the financials. I honestly never wanted to make time for anything or anyone else. Until now."

My cheeks heated, matching the warmth flooding my chest. "It doesn't feel like we just met at all, does it?"

He laughed before slowly shaking his head. "No. No, it does not."

"I even missed you a little."

His jaw went slack before he pressed a dramatic hand to his chest. "You did?"

I held up my hand and pinched the air between my index finger and thumb. "A little."

"Only a little, huh?" He moved closer, mirth dancing in his blue eyes.

"Maybe slightly more than a little."

"You're only saying that because I fed you again." He

dropped his hand on my knee, causing a swarm of goose bumps up my thigh.

"Maybe." I shrugged, almost afraid to meet his gaze. Joe's smile was a lethal weapon, charming and paralyzing me at once.

"This was really incredible. Thank you for tonight."

"Hey, it's not over yet."

"Was I a good girl? Do I get dessert?"

"Yes, I think you were." Joe reached for a white paper bag. "And they stayed warm." He unfolded the top of the bag and handed it to me.

*"You found zeppoles?"* My eyes bulged before I dove into the bag and grabbed one. The powdered sugar melted into a glaze on my fingertips.

The first bite made my eyes roll back. "My God, Joe," I moaned, already going in for a second. "So damn good."

"Again, with the sex noises." He arched a brow. "You're making it hard to stay a gentleman tonight."

"Who said you had to do that?" I licked the grease and sugar off of my fingers slowly once I spied the heat in his gaze.

"Put the bag down," he growled, moving toward me on the blanket with a wicked gleam in his eyes.

A snicker escaped me before I shook my head. "Okay. I'll stop with the sex—"

"I said, put. The. Bag. Down." It was dark other than the lantern Joe had planted in the sand, but I couldn't miss the feral look in his eyes as they zeroed in on my lips. Heat ricocheted all over my body and pooled between my legs.

He dragged his finger along my top lip. "You have some sugar right here."

I ran my tongue over the trail of his touch. "Then take it off for me."

His hooded gaze locked with mine before our mouths

crashed together in a hungry, desperate kiss. I pulled him on top of me, tugging at the back of his shirt as our teeth scraped and tongues battled.

He muttered a curse before he dipped his head and trailed hot, open-mouthed kisses across my collarbone, pulling down the neckline of my shirt and sucking my nipple through my bra. I grabbed his head to pull him closer, writhing beneath him as I chased the friction my aching body craved so badly.

"I think about you," I admitted as Joe made his way down my neck with his lips. I felt him smile against my sensitive skin.

"Yeah?" He fisted the hem of my skirt and pushed it higher until it was a twisted denim belt low on my hips. My body quivered with a crazy want I'd never felt before, not even that first time. My limbs were liquid against the sand and about to give out any second.

"Good, because I think about you, too. No matter how I tried, I couldn't stop." His fingers dipped into the neckline of my blouse before tugging it down along with my bra. My breasts spilled out of the cups and into his greedy hands. I mewled as his thumb traced around my rigid nipples. "What do you think about?"

His hand delved into my panties, and he groaned when his fingers found me soaked and swollen.

"You, between my legs, like the night I met you." Coherent sentences weren't possible when his mouth and hands were all over my body.

He lifted his head, the singeing embers in his eyes stealing more of my breath. "I did a lot between your legs that night. Tell me what you think about. Coming on my tongue or on my cock?"

God, his mouth could get filthy, and I loved it.

"When," I gulped, so turned on my brain was about to short circuit. "When you made me come in your mouth. All I think about is you doing it again." I barely recognized the hoarse whisper falling from my lips.

He trailed tiny kisses up and down my core through my panties. Writhing against his mouth, I gasped for air, unable to utter anything but a muffled grunt.

"You make me crazy. Still so wet for me. Such a *good girl*," he murmured as he tortured me with more little pecks, this time pushing my panties to the side and dragging his lips up and down, so slow and light it was almost painful. If he didn't devour me in the next five seconds, I'd combust.

I still craved the friction he was deliberately holding back. I needed him to suck my clit into his mouth hard and bite it.

"Joe ..." My face was on fire as I rolled up on my elbows. "Don't be a tease."

"Tease? Maybe you need to be more specific." The carnal smile dancing across his lips, already soaked with me, was my undoing.

I grabbed the back of his head and thrust my hips against his face.

"Suck, Joe. Hard."

His laugh vibrated against my thigh when he slid his hand under me and cupped my ass. My hips bucked off the ground on reflex.

"All mine?" He squeezed before giving it a loud slap, sending a piercing sting down my thigh but triggering a blinding throb in other places.

That was new.

"Yes." My quick and desperate answer surprised me. Maybe it was a loaded question, but, in that moment, I was his —and he could do whatever he wanted.

He dragged wet kisses across my hip before raising his head with a panty-incinerating, devious smile.

"You better hold on, then."

He hooked his fingers into the waistband of my panties and dragged them down my legs. I didn't see where they landed but didn't care when his mouth was on me, licking up and down and around my clit before sucking it into his mouth.

"Harder," I begged, my vision already going hazy.

He had enough of his own teasing, sucking hard and sinking his teeth into the most sensitive parts of me. I rocked my hips against his mouth and bit my lip, unable to stop my ear-piercing scream when the tremors hit their peak.

He didn't waver after my body stopped quivering, never taking his mouth off me and kissing me between my legs like he'd kissed me on the mouth before we stepped into his truck, exploring and tasting as if he couldn't get enough. Everything tingled below my waist as I tried to remember how to move my legs.

"What do you want, Caterina?" He lifted his head, his face flushed and his lips and chin still drenched.

"You," I breathed out once my lungs found air again.

"Come home with me," he whispered as he settled on top of me. "I want you in my bed tonight and tomorrow morning and however long I can have you. Fuck how fast it is, I just want to be with you."

"I want that, too." I framed his face and brushed his lips.

"Let's get out of here."

## 18

## JOE

AFTER I SNOOZED the fifth alarm, I finally lifted my head off of the pillow and glimpsed a bit of sunlight through the blinds. When was the last time I'd woken up after sunrise? My sleepy brain couldn't remember.

"I should go." Caterina yawned and burrowed into my side. "You have to go to the restaurant."

I tightened my arms around her still naked body and rolled her on top of me.

"Didn't I say I wanted you in my bed this morning?" I whispered and threaded my fingers through her dark tangles. "I'm not rushing anywhere, and neither are you." I dragged my hands down her bare back, digging my fingers into her ass as I lifted my hips off the bed, showing her how much I wanted her to stay.

Dominic told me to consider taking a late morning. When Caterina reached between us to palm my hard length, I decided to, for once, take him up on it without a fight. She made lazy strokes up and down before meeting my gaze with a sleepy smile. I'd taken her in a thousand different ways after we'd returned from the beach. The short drive back to my apartment had made us so crazy with need, I was inside her the second I shut the door, her leg looped around my hip as I plowed into her against the wall. We were slow and sweet one minute and desperate the next, but other than tiny intervals of recovery, we hadn't stopped. I'd never been so starved for a woman in my life, and having her all night did nothing to satisfy the hunger. If anything, I craved her more every time.

I was fucked for sure, but too high on the beautiful woman stroking my cock to care.

"Can I taste you?" Her grip on me tightened as her eyes glazed over.

"That's a question you never have to ask." I sifted my hand in her hair and grabbed a fistful. "May I make a request?"

"I'm pretty agreeable after last night." She giggled, kissing the corner of my mouth and swiping her tongue along my jaw. "Go on."

"Put your glasses on and look up at me while you do it."

Her hand stilled as she sat up. "Do you have a librarian fetish? I'll go along with it, but I'm a little curious."

I pulled her in for a kiss, laughing against her lips. "You're gorgeous either way, but something about you in glasses with your mouth full of me...well, I'm warning you now, I'm going to come *hard*."

Her eyes narrowed into slits as she shook her head. "How are you even real, and where were you when I was sixteen and crying because I needed glasses all the time and wasn't allowed to get contacts? They're in my purse, which I think I dropped next to the door. Give me a minute." She kissed my lips, small little lingering pecks that drove me out of my mind. "You're filthy, and I like it way too much."

She rose from the bed, naked and making no attempt to cover up. My eyes feasted on her when she ambled into the living room, just like my mouth had for most of last night. My heavy eyes closed as I tried to figure out how much, or how little, sleep we'd actually gotten. A tired smile lifted my cheeks when soft lips painted kisses down my chest. I opened my eyes to a gloriously still-naked Caterina in nothing but glasses crawling over me, her chestnut locks tickling my stomach as she traveled lower, dragging her tongue across my hip before she took me in her mouth.

Her cheeks hollowed as she worked her mouth up and down my cock, all while she peered up at me from behind her glasses. Sitting up and leaning on my elbows to get a better view, I almost swallowed my tongue, not at all prepared for the sexy-as-all-fuck sight in front of me. She moaned as she took me even deeper, the vibrations traveling down my legs like an electrical current, sparks and all.

"Caterina," I croaked out almost like a plea as I wrapped my hand around a fistful of her hair. Everything between us was too intense and too good.

"Up." An urgent need rushed through me as I pulled Caterina toward me by her underarms. She pressed her hands on my chest, breathless and dazed, reflecting the craziness I felt hammering against my rib cage.

I flipped us over so that I was on top and reached into my nightstand drawer. Groaning in relief when I palmed what I was looking for, I knelt between her legs and tore open the foil packet, cursing myself for not being fast enough.

"I want to ride," she purred as she raked her nails down my back.

"You will, baby." I covered her mouth with mine, swallowing her whimper when I was fully seated inside her. She gasped into my mouth, lifting her hips to meet mine with each thrust. This wouldn't be slow. I pounded into her over and over again, and I still couldn't get deep enough.

"I need you like this now." I broke the kiss and rested my forehead against hers, still moving inside her, harder and faster as if I were chasing some kind of clock. Maybe I was, but wouldn't allow myself to think about it.

"Joe, I ..." Caterina's head fell back as her eyes clenched shut. I licked along her jaw before covering her mouth with mine again, our kiss messy, deep and desperate, just like where we were heading.

Her legs quivered just before she pulsed around me, and I came hard with a grunt, my head dropping to her chest as I spilled into her.

"Holy shit." Caterina's hooded eyes grew when they met mine, her voice small as she chased her breath.

I kissed the tip of her nose as I straightened her glasses.

"Holy shit is right." I brushed the hair off of her sweaty brow and pressed a kiss to her forehead. It'd been like this all night long, and neither of us could get enough. I worried she was sore since I hadn't exactly been gentle, but she was right there with me every time.

"I like you here." I slid my arms under her and pulled her to me. Deep enough and close enough didn't apply to this woman.

She grinned and looped her arms around my neck. "I like me here, too."

"My kitchen is small, but there's a table, and I make an awesome French toast. I have a couple of hours before I have to be at the restaurant."

"If you keep cooking for me, I'll never want to leave." A sad smile stretched her lips.

"Ah, you see my plan. If you want, you can take a T-shirt from my top drawer." I slid out of her and stood, grabbing a T-shirt and shorts from my dresser.

"Like what you see?" I asked, purposely taking my time leaving the bedroom after feeling her eyes on me.

"Yeah, I do. Is that a problem?" She shot me a glare but couldn't help the twitch at the corners of her mouth.

"Nope, not at all." I winked over my shoulder from the doorway. "Look and take all you want, sweetheart."

After I got rid of the condom and headed into the kitchen, I grabbed my phone to shoot Dominic a text.

**Joe:** *I'll be in around 10 if you can handle it.*

**Dominic:** *10?? Wow! Good for you. And of course, I can handle it.*

**Joe:** *Again, not a virgin or a monk. I've spent the night with a woman before.*

**Dominic:** *But never the morning.*

**Joe:** *Maybe I'm not the only one who needs to get out more. You seem to be keeping track of what I do and who I'm with a little too closely.*

**Dominic:** *Nice dodge. See you at 10.*

I pulled the eggs and milk out of the fridge and reached for a couple of bowls, my gut not as light as when I'd woken up. Dom was right. I never lingered after spending the night with someone, even if we were dating. Caterina was changing me at a fast pace, and, before I knew it, she'd be gone. It was too early to suggest something long-distance or to even fathom how she'd react. I'd told her to live in the moment last night, and I had to force myself to do the same. I focused on the sizzle in the pan instead of the new weight on my chest.

"You wouldn't have a coffeemaker, too, would you?" I turned to find Caterina sitting at the table, my Rangers shirt hanging off her slim frame, her nipples poking out just enough to reveal the absence of a bra. My heart did a sad leap at the sight of her in my clothes.

"I do," I replied as I flipped the bread in the skillet. "Iced or hot? I have cold brew in the fridge, and there's half-and-half in there."

"Cold brew is great; where are your glasses?"

I reached into the cabinet above the stove to grab a glass.

Caterina wrapped her arms around me from behind and pressed a kiss between my shoulder blades. "Thank you, but how about you cook and I pour the coffee." She took the glass out of my hand and reached over my shoulder for another one before opening my refrigerator.

"I can't help it, I guess. Occupational hazard to want to serve." I plated our breakfast and set it on the table.

"That looks amazing," she gushed before pouring two glasses of cold brew. "How did you get so good at cooking? Did you go to school for it?"

She sat back down and dug in. I found her appetite—for everything—sexy as hell.

"I did. I studied to be a chef and then went back to school for hospitality. I always loved cooking, but I wanted to be my own boss and run things my way. Took me a little while, but I got there."

She set down her glass and squinted at me. "A little while? You're only thirty and already running a successful business. I saw the reviews on Yelp. The Beach Pub is a big deal around here."

"So, you checked up on me?" I smirked around my fork.

An adorable blush spread on her cheeks. "Megan and Claire said they found The Beach Pub online, and, yes, I checked it out. You should be proud."

"I am. It's harder than I thought, but I'm managing so far. What about you? I know you said you worked in advertising, but you never said where."

"My office is located near Grand Central Station."

"Wow, so you're in the thick of it all."

She shrugged. "I guess. I went to college in Manhattan, so crowded subways and streets are all I know. I started as an account executive but was promoted to account manager this year. It's stressful, but I enjoy it. I just need to learn to leave work at work and go home at a reasonable hour. My boss even gets on my case over my hours."

"Why put in so many then? My mother works in advertising, too. She sometimes had the occasional late night or trip, but most of the time, she was home for dinner with us. Burning yourself out isn't healthy."

"I've actually been thinking about that. I had a day to myself at the rental before the girls came in." She rested her fork on the side of the plate. "Your mother had reasons to leave work at a decent time and people she wanted to see. For the past year or so, I guess I didn't. That, I promise you, is changing when I get home. There's no reason to leave work later than six most nights, and I miss seeing my friends. I'm actually grateful for the fucked-up wakeup call I received."

Caterina had the livelihood I ran like hell from. I was happy at the shore and couldn't see heading back to the city for anything else but a visit. And, even if I wanted to go back, everything I had was here. The commitments and obligations of owning a business weren't something I could just walk away from, but I hated not being able to offer her that normal she deserved: a man waiting for her every night. Even if we tried this long-distance, she wouldn't have that. At the end of the week, I had to decide how selfish I was where she was concerned.

She rose and planted herself in my lap. "Can I tell you something that's going to sound crazy?"

I wrapped my arms around her waist and pulled her to me. "I'd say we passed crazy a few days ago. You can tell me anything."

"I loved last night." Her nails scraped along the bristles of stubble on my chin. "It was incredible. All of it."

"That's not crazy." I brushed her hair off her shoulder. "I feel the exact same way. I loved every second."

"But this..." She looped a stray thread on the edge of my sleeve between her fingers. "I love talking to you as much as I love *not* talking to you." A sweet giggle fell from her lips. "I keep thinking how great it would be to have this every day— with you. I want to know everything about you, and it feels like time is already running out. We could be so amazing together, but—"

"You don't know how it's going to work?" I lifted an eyebrow.

"Exactly," she whispered before cuddling into the crook of my neck.

"Tell you what, how about we wait to figure out... after... until we're almost at that point. I don't want to talk about letting you go until I have to."

She grimaced before nodding, looking as crushed as I was feeling at the notion of letting her go.

I'd already realized that a week would never be enough.

## 19

## JOE

"It's a beautiful thing, isn't it?" Dominic jerked his head toward the line of customers waiting to get in. Someone with a ton of followers had posted The Beach Pub on a couple of social media platforms last night, and it brought in droves of customers today. Thankfully, we'd doubled the staff during the past couple of weeks like we usually did by midsummer. The restaurant was happily buzzing without both of us breaking too much of a sweat.

"Free advertising is a very beautiful thing," I agreed as I glimpsed the dining area from the inside of the kitchen. If only I could figure out how to make Instagram and Twitter work for us instead of hoping for the occasional fluke here and there. That first night I'd met Caterina, I'd been honest about wanting to figure out how to promote this place better, and she'd said she could help me, even if my motives for taking her up on it were a bit clouded.

Our new hostess, Tina, fluttered from her post in the front to the back, most likely scanning the room for one of us. Her father was a faithful customer of ours and asked us if we'd consider giving her a job this summer. For hiring waiters and waitresses, Dominic and I were more selective. When we were busy, especially at night, we needed workers with experience. Tina was a pretty, but timid, little thing, always regarding Dom and me with wary eyes but seemed to be doing all right her first week.

Some employees came back from the previous summers, and that filled me with an enormous pride. To make the restaurant a town staple and local tradition felt like the beginnings of success. It was also something I wouldn't get in a crowded city. I belonged here and had never doubted it. Maybe I'd cursed it a little since last Thursday but never doubted.

"Joe, there's someone in the front here to see you. She said her name was Caterina? She went to follow me, but I told her she needed to stay there."

"Thanks, Tina," Dominic told her before smirking at me over his shoulder. I found this tiny thing attempting to be our security a little comical, too. "We appreciate that."

I ambled out to the dining area, spotting Caterina near the front desk. She was impossible to miss with a white sundress and the shadow of a pink bikini underneath. Her dark hair was piled on top of her head with loose wisps tickling her neck and cheeks. My cock gravitated toward her on sight, pushing against my zipper as if it were angling to get as close to her as possible.

"Is this okay?" She stepped back and held up her hands with a playful scowl on her face. "I know I'm not supposed to go back there."

"You don't need to follow the rules." I grabbed the nape of her neck and pulled her in for a kiss. I had to make it quicker than I would have liked since we were in public. But I flicked the seam of her lips with my tongue when I pulled away, not able to resist getting a taste. "You can get as close to me as you want." I traced the shoulder strap of her bikini, my finger stopping at the top of pink triangles teasing the shit out of me. "Anytime. Anywhere."

She grinned, a blush spreading across her sun-kissed cheeks.

"Would Dominic be really mad if you left early after coming in late today?" Her fingertips flirted with the edge of my collar. We were like two lovesick teenagers, drunk and stupid from the passion between us.

"Maybe." I shrugged as my hands traveled down her back. "I'm technically his boss, so he can't tell me no." I'd memorized her entire body last night, but thinking of her full, beautiful tits spilling out of the top with hardly anything covering the bottom made me hard to the point of pain. "What did you have in mind?"

"Well," she started, tilting her head to the side. "I'd like to make you dinner at the rental. Claire and Megan are going out for the night and meeting up with friends a couple of towns away and may stay over. But I'm not feeling it, you know?" Her lips puckered in an adorable purse. "I won't be as good as you since you're the professional and all. But I make an awesome shrimp parmesan, and the kitchen at the rental is Food Network quality." Her bright smile faded. "No pressure, of course."

I put my finger over her lips. "If I didn't own this place, I would have called out for the day and still be in bed with you right now." The pad of my thumb skimmed across her bottom lip. "Yes, I'd love to have dinner with you tonight. I can be there around eight if that's okay."

"Perfect. So," she waggled her eyebrows, "what's back there that I can't see?"

"Tina's new and a little overzealous. If we weren't so busy,

I'd take you back there and show you my office." My brows shot up as I pulled her close.

"What's so great about your office?"

"Oh, *lots* of things," I told her while my hand roamed down her hip. "Starting with the lock on my door."

"Rain check," she whispered and pecked my lips. "See you at eight."

"See you at eight." My eyes stayed glued to her as she sauntered out the door. I was fixated on the sway of her ass in that damn bikini bottom.

"Am I closing again tonight?" Dom asked from behind me.

I nodded before I turned around. "And the rest of the week." My gaze still clung to Caterina.

I'd make it up to him when she was back in Brooklyn, and I had nothing to do but wallow.

As if she sensed my eyes on her, she turned around, flashing me a sexy grin when her gaze met mine.

I had her now, and like a glutton, I would devour every second up with her I could get— until they ran out.

Thanks to a full day of steady crowds, eight became nine and then close to ten. I texted apologies all night long until I pulled up in front of the rental and sprinted up the outside stairs, praying I hadn't screwed up the little time we had together by pissing her off.

"I'm so sorry," I blurted before even saying hello. Caterina looked me over with a crinkled brow, leaning against the doorjamb without a word in reply. She was so damn beautiful in a simple black dress that clung to all my favorite places. "It was packed, and two waiters called out sick, and every time I headed for the door something else happened— "

She cut me off with a kiss and pulled me inside, shutting the door behind us. I moaned into her mouth before I backed her against the wall, apologizing the best I could with every stroke of my tongue against hers.

"All I wanted was to be with you tonight. Please believe me," I begged between kisses.

"I know, Joe." She pushed against my chest. "I saw how busy it was. You texted me a thousand apologies. More aren't necessary unless you want to do that thing with your tongue again." She wagged her eyebrows and pressed a kiss to my chin. "You're the owner, and sometimes you can't just leave. You and I have that same pain-in-the-ass sense of over-responsibility in common. All is forgiven, and this high-tech oven has a fancy warming tray, so I can still offer you a hot, rental-home cooked meal." She slid her palm against mine and entwined our fingers. "Still hungry, I hope?"

"Starving," I growled before I leaned in for another kiss. How could a man live with someone as amazing as she was and bring other women home behind her back? If she lived with me ...

I forced my brain to not complete that thought. We'd only just met. Five days wasn't enough time to really fall for someone, no matter how real it all seemed—real, yet hopeless.

"Time for that later, come." She jerked her head toward the dining room. My chest pinched when I spied the half-wicked candles. "I'll get you a plate. What would you like to drink? Beer or wine?"

"Whatever you're having is good." I settled at the table and watched her flutter around the kitchen. Her hair spilled down her shoulders in dark waves, and her olive skin had caught a little sun. The last time I was late for a date after being stuck at the restaurant, the woman I was seeing wouldn't even let me on her stoop. Caterina didn't seem to care. She just wanted me here, no matter what time I happened to arrive.

"What?" she asked when she caught me staring. My mouth watered at the plate she set down in front of me: shrimp parmesan, garlic green beans, and a large piece of Italian bread.

"You're something else, Caterina Rose." I wrapped my hand around her waist and dropped a tiny kiss on her arm, cracking up as her face crinkled in disgust.

"I told you before about using my full first *and* middle name. Eat."

I moaned around a piece of shrimp. "Wow, this is delicious. Want a job in my kitchen if the whole advertising thing doesn't work out?" I smiled around my fork.

"Well, I've already had sex with the boss—a lot—so I'm guessing I could skip the interview." A wide grin lifted her cheeks before she slid into a chair next to me at the table.

"Not so fast. You have to interview like everyone else. That's what the lock on my office door is for." I winked.

She laughed around the rim of her wineglass. "My mother gets on my case for not making my own sauce whenever I make this. She showed me a couple of times, but the real deal is an all-day endeavor, as I'm sure you know. Plus, we only have so many pots here. So, thank you for enjoying my dinner even though I'm a disgrace to my heritage and used tomato sauce from a jar."

"Are you close with your mother? You said it's only the two of you, right?"

She nodded around a mouthful of bread. "My father died when I was little. My memories of him are a little fuzzy since I was only six. My mother went back to work full-time, and we moved in with my grandparents. Our apartment was always bustling with some kind of extended family. Sunday dinners and holidays were full of people and non-stop food, but it still always seemed like just my mother and me." Caterina lifted a sad shoulder. "She was strict, but I never wanted for anything. I was a good kid, earned good grades, and never got into trouble. I felt as if I owed her that. But even she's on my case for working too hard." A humorless laugh fell from her lips.

"You're an amazing woman who deserves to enjoy her life. It doesn't sound like you've done much of that. Well, not before last Thursday." She laughed and nodded slowly.

"No. No, I haven't. I have a good job, money in the bank, a nice apartment—once I get rid of the squatter." She pushed her food back and forth on her plate. "But I want more. I always did, but I guess I pushed it aside because I felt I shouldn't. That it was silly. Now I'm thirty-three, and look at me." She blew out a long breath and shook her head.

I put my fork down and leveled my eyes on her.

"I am. Trust me, I am." I reached for her under the table and squeezed the inside of her thigh. "And what I see is beautiful." My voice croaked at the end, all this weird emotion filtering through me. I'd thought I never cared about dating because it simply wasn't for me. I didn't have time for another hassle, and I'd always believed finding "the one" was a bullshit impossibility for me. I never thought I'd actually find her, but not be able to keep her.

She sank her teeth into her bottom lip and narrowed her glossy eyes at me. "Do they teach that to hospitality majors? How to sweet talk new customers?"

"No, that comes natural. All me, baby."

Her smile faded when her eyes found mine. "Can you stay, Joe?" She draped her hand over mine, where it was still laying on her thigh. "I have dessert, and I found out this morning that the bathroom upstairs has a jacuzzi." Her eyebrows shot up despite her watery gaze. "It would be a shame if no one used it, right?

"Big shame." I squeezed her thigh but didn't get the smile I'd hoped for.

I rose from my chair and kissed her cheek before I dragged my lips down her neck.

"You have me as much as you want me, for as long as you want me."

## 20

## CATERINA

"I AM happy you're finally on a vacation. I've been so worried about you." My mother sighed into the phone. "You're going to burn yourself out."

"I'm okay, Mom. It's nice here—nice being with the girls."

"What else is *nice*?" She laughed. "Usually nice means borderline okay."

I kept saying nice to avoid the real highlight of my vacation: the gorgeous restaurant owner who I was about to spend the night with for the third time in five days after I met him five days ago. Mom wanted me to have fun, but not that much fun.

Joe pushed me out of the kitchen and insisted on cleaning up, and I took the opportunity to check in with my mother. Some of my friends spoke to their parents once a week, but that would never fly with her, and I wouldn't want it to. I checked up on her as much as she checked up on me.

"It's good, Mom. I promise. How is it there?"

"I ran into Trent on the street this afternoon." I could picture her mouth flattening into a hard line. One thing my mother did not have was a poker face. "He asked me when you were coming home. I thought you broke up?"

"We did. I told him to get out, but I had his name added to the lease, so he's not moving. I'd hate to leave the apartment and give him what he wants, but I don't know how to get him out."

"Are you ever going to tell me what happened?"

If I told my mother exactly what happened, an uncle or cousin would be at my place in less than twenty-four hours to drag him out by his feet. As awesome as that would be, I needed to handle this myself.

"Just know he did something awful enough to end us for good."

"I told you not to put his name on the lease if you weren't married."

"You did," I agreed while rubbing at my temple. "I didn't listen, and I'm learning my lesson."

"I always thought you deserved better, and I hope you're smarter when the next one comes along." She clicked her tongue against her teeth.

I didn't have the heart to tell my mother I was even stupider this time. There was no way I could explain what was going on with Joe and me, especially since I didn't totally understand it myself. All I knew was in between all the amazing conversation and incredible sex, I'd caught real feelings for Joe. The whole thing was ridiculous even in my own head, much less explaining it to someone else. Megan and Claire thought we were just having fun, but it was more. From the beginning, it had been *so* much more. Explaining to my mother how I may be falling for a man I'd known for a week was in line with telling her I met Santa Claus at the shore. I'd receive the same "are you high?" reaction. But I guessed I was high because all I did was dread the inevitable low.

"I do, too. I'll call you tomorrow, Mom."

I ended the call and let my head fall back, searching the ceiling as if it had an answer. This could work long-distance, right? Maybe? Was I prolonging the inevitable or living in the moment? Both I was sure, but I couldn't stop.

My eyes roamed our pristine kitchen. I guessed working in restaurants for so long made Joe quick and thorough with cleanup.

"Joe?" I called out. "Did you clean the whole kitchen? Where are you?"

The flick of a switch followed by a loud whir wafted from the bathroom. I knocked on the door. "Hey, you decent?"

"No, but come in."

I pushed the door open and found Joe laying in the jacuzzi, with jets blowing water around him as he stretched his arms along the back of the tub.

"Started without me?" I crossed my arms and aimed the best glare I could muster at him, all while a hot shiver broke out along my skin. Joe was naked. And wet. A naked and wet Joe, with water dripping along every muscle, was sprawled out in the tub, casting me a heated glance before he beckoned me with the crook of his finger.

"Lose the dress, and get in here."

With shaky hands, I slipped my dress over my head and dropped it on the bathroom tile. I stripped off my bra and underwear and climbed in with Joe.

"I thought it was a little bigger than this. I guess two people don't exactly fit." I crouched down in the tub, and Joe pulled me between his legs.

"Plenty of room." He rubbed my shoulders and slid his

hands down my damp arms, over my torso, and along my hips. "I still need to teach you to relax." Joe pulled me against him, his erection digging into my back. "I want you so fucking bad right now. I want my mouth and my hands on every part of you." His voice was hoarse, almost pained. "Where should I start, Caterina Rose?" His hands left my hair and traveled down my stomach. The shiver was replaced with a blinding ache.

"Joe, please," I begged. "Please touch me."

"Where, baby? Where should I touch you?" He thrummed my clit underwater, drifting his thumb back and forth and around. My hips rolled, pushing into his hand for more friction.

I craned my head toward his wolfish grin, looping my arm around his neck and pulling him in for a kiss. I flipped around and straddled his lap, water sloshing everywhere, and neither of us giving a single fuck.

My head fell back as his lips closed on a nipple, sucking hard and pulling the rigid peak between his teeth. I raked my hands through his wet hair and ground against him as his cock thickened against me.

"We can't." Joe grabbed my ass with both hands and pulled me up. "Too risky in here. Lie back, Caterina."

I climbed off of him and lay on the other side of the tub. Joe lifted my legs out of the water with a loud splash and buried his head between my legs.

His heated gaze lifted to mine. "So good. You taste so goddamn good. I'll *never* get enough." Anguish dripped off of every word as if he really *wouldn't* ever get enough. He slipped two fingers inside of me, curling them before pulling out, and I lost control of the lower half of my body. I came so hard I lost my breath and even my vision for a moment as hot white stars flashed behind my eyes. His lips and tongue stayed on me, still tasting and exploring even when my body jerked against him from aftershock.

"Joe," I breathed once I found my voice again. I dipped my head to meet his hooded eyes.

"Lie back, Joseph." I sat up and pushed against Joe's chest. His cock peeked out of the water, still hard and huge. I palmed the weight of his length, gliding my hand up and down before bending to take him in my mouth. I let my tongue trace the water droplets streaming down his shaft and swirl around the top. His chest heaved as he muttered a tortured curse.

"Caterina, baby, I'm close." His mouth fell open when I took him as deep as I could, still working him with my hand until he went rigid under me and spilled down my throat.

I'd given a few blow jobs, even enjoyed it at times. But I'd read the signals and would tear my mouth away right before the guy came. It always seemed too intimate and just too *much* to do that. With Joe, I wanted everything. He made me crave and want and need. It was as if I were taking everything I could from Joe and saving it for later when he wasn't within my reach anymore.

My breaths were quick again as I rested my head on Joe's stomach. He sifted his hands through my wet hair as his own breathing slowed.

I lifted my gaze to his, a slow smile lifting my cheeks. His eyes were hooded and wet, reflecting the same sad need that coursed through my veins.

His fingertips drew soft circles along the nape of my neck, and I heaved a long, contented sigh.

Reality would rear its ugly head all too soon.

Exhaustion barreled over me like a freight train the second I opened my eyes, but after the night we'd had, it was worth it. I hated to leave Caterina so early, but I couldn't bail on Dominic today. Summer events and the revenue they brought in were our bread and butter, but right now, I hated anything that took me away from the beautiful woman lying on top of me. But, I had to cash in on these busy weeks at the restaurant to keep us going for the rest of the year. I needed to fish my head from out of the clouds and focus—at least for the day.

Caterina groaned and tightened her hold around my waist while burying her head into my chest.

"I hate that morning comes so fast." She cuddled into my neck, her tiny kisses along my jaw chipping away at my pain-in-the-ass resolve.

"Me too, baby." My lips found her forehead before I gently pulled away, trying to remember where I'd dropped my clothes. "I can't leave Dom today. We have a lot of rearranging to do to make room for the live band, so we need everybody." Her hazy eyes met mine as she nodded into the pillow.

"A live band sounds fun. Maybe we'll stop by." She yawned into a sleepy smile.

"You should. These guys are pretty good." I brushed her tangled locks off her forehead and ran my fingers through her hair. "And I'd love it if you stopped by. I..." I trailed off, cursing myself yet again. "I'll be working late if the night goes like we hope it will."

"That's great, Joe." She rolled up to sitting and rested her elbows on her knees, the sheet covering her but loose enough for me to glimpse her gorgeous naked body. If the sheet fell another half inch, her breasts would be in full view, screaming for my tongue, but I'd have to resist this time. This woman was too perfect, and it was too easy to get lost in her. "Don't worry about it. Do what you have to do." She tilted her head. "We'll stop by, but I won't get in your way."

"What if I want you in my way? Come tonight, and, when you get there, come find me." I sounded needy and pathetic to my own ears, but I wanted her there. Our time together was too short to worry about pretense. I'd figure out how to be with her tonight and still keep an eye on everything.

"Okay." Her sleepy eyes twinkled. "A live band means there's a dance floor, right?"

"You dance?" I lifted a brow.

"On the nights my friends were able to force me out in college, yes, I loved to dance, especially if there was a live band. It's been a while, but I'm on vacation, right?" She coughed out a laugh. "Do you dance?"

I shrugged. "If I get a couple of drinks in me, maybe. Dominic is the one you usually have to pry off a dance floor."

"But I don't want to dance with Dominic." Her bottom lip jutted in a pout.

"Damn right, you don't," I growled and pulled her to me.

"I'll come find you. I wish I could make you breakfast, but

my scrambled eggs are sad compared to your French toast, anyway." She pushed off the bed and headed to her dresser to pull out a T-shirt as my eyes canvassed every gorgeous inch of her. *Fuck, she was killing me.*

"I'll walk you out, but you may want to find your clothes in the bathroom first." She jutted her chin toward the hallway, and we shared a laugh.

"Ah, so that's where they are; I couldn't remember. It was all a blur." I brushed her lips and headed into the bathroom. Once I scooped up my clothes and pulled them on, I felt the heat of her stare burning into my back.

"Staring again?" I flashed a grin over my shoulder, loving the scowl I got in return. "I feel like a piece of meat."

She crossed her arms and leaned against the wall. "I'm too exhausted for a dirty comeback for that." She snaked her arms around my waist and peered up at me. How could she be this goddamn beautiful first thing in the morning? She pressed a light kiss to my jaw. "Don't work too hard, okay?"

"I'll try." I took her face in my hands and kissed her, long and deep enough to make her slump against me. I laughed against her lips before I pulled away. "Throw me out before I blow off the whole day and drag you back into bed."

"I wish." The sweet smile on her face as she beamed at me made my heart sink. "Go. I'll see you later." How amazing would it be to have her waiting for me, or to wait for her at the end of a day? I was having those getting-ahead-of-myself thoughts again, but we fit too perfectly together not to think of what ifs. Our problem was the pieces wouldn't click so well when she was back home, no matter how much I wanted to pretend they would.

"I didn't expect to see you this early," Dominic said over his shoulder when I strolled into the restaurant. He was already moving tables around to make room for the band to set up. "I'm guessing she wasn't that pissed you were late?"

"Nope, not at all—and I was *two hours* late." I picked up a couple of chairs and carried them over to where he'd already started stacking them in the corner. "She had dinner waiting for me when I got there."

"Wow." Dom shook his head. "That's...rare. I once was an hour late to a woman's apartment, and she wouldn't even open the door for me."

"Caterina is rare." The pang of something I couldn't describe swirled in my gut. We had a night full of awesome conversation and amazing sex. I loved every second of the time we spent together, but we were getting too used to it. *I* was getting too used to it. After she left, there would be a void that hadn't existed before we met. How could someone have this much of an effect on me after only a week? The smart thing to do would have been to back off. But it didn't matter how long I'd known Caterina or how much we were setting ourselves up to get hurt. I was already in too deep.

"Let me ask you something." Dominic lifted the last of the chairs. "What do you see happening next week? I know you think I'm a little too into your business—"

"A little?"

"Seriously. Or should I say what do you *want* to happen next week?"

"This is a conversation a little too deep to have before my second cup of coffee, man." I plopped down the last chair harder than I meant to. "What do you want me to say? She lives in Brooklyn, I live here."

"It's not like she's in another country." He shrugged and rolled his eyes. "You can figure it out if you want to."

I blew out a long breath. "She deserves better than what I have to offer her, which isn't a hell of a lot. How many weekends can I just drop everything and head to Brooklyn? Even when the summer ends?"

"Maybe you could work something out. She could come out here sometimes."

"It's only been a week. Less than a week, in fact. I can't ask her to change her life for me." I made my way into the kitchen for some breakfast, knowing Dominic wouldn't let this go and would be right on my damn heels.

"I think you've spent more time with her this week than you spent with Jill in the whole time you guys were dating. In fact, any woman you were with seemed like an afterthought to you, until this one."

I grabbed a bagel off the counter before I turned back to Dominic. "What do you want me to do?"

"I'll say one more thing, then I'll drop it."

I highly doubted that but nodded anyway.

"Stop blowing it off as temporary when you don't want it to be. Ask her what she wants to do instead of assuming. Do you know what *you* want?"

"Her." My answer came quick and with zero hesitation.

"When you bought this place, and everyone told you how nuts you were, you said life was too short to not do what you want. Take your own advice, dude. So what if it's quick? Don't throw away something real just because you think it's not supposed to be."

I drew back, squinting at my best friend. "Since when did you get so philosophical?" I had to laugh.

"I'm the brains *and* the beauty around here. It's exhausting." He shook his head before pushing the door open. "Plus, I'm dreading next week, too. I'm the one who's going to have to deal with the brunt of your heartbroken, cranky ass."

Dominic's words rattled around in my brain as I poured a cup of coffee. The annoying bastard was always right.

Contemplating a future with her after the short time I'd known her seemed ridiculous, but it was all I could think about. I'd already mapped out the drive from Ocean Cove to Bay Ridge, Brooklyn a hundred times—three and a half hours. Maybe not across the country, but far enough to have completely separate lives.

Maybe we could work out a way to see each other—sometimes. The old me would love an arrangement like this: casual and part time, nothing dragging me from all the things in my life that needed to stay a priority.

But I already knew that when it came to Caterina, casual would never be enough.

## 22

## CATERINA

"Wow," Claire gasped as we walked closer to Joe's restaurant. "Good thing your boyfriend is the owner, or we'd never get in."

"He's not my..." They both turned to me with raised brows. "Ugh, just push the door open."

Claire was right; this place was so packed, we could barely close the door behind us. I hadn't seen this many people collectively in this town all week. Granted, my days were spent on the beach, and my nights were spent with Joe, but it still seemed like a much bigger crowd than I would have expected judging by the amount of people I'd seen out and about.

Joe didn't give himself enough credit. He was smart enough to know how to keep a business in a summer tourist town going all year long by cashing in when it counted.

But...he wasn't my boyfriend. Claire's little quip upset me more than it should have. We were heading home on Saturday morning, and then what? Would Joe only be a memory, a hot and heavy fling I could reminisce about when I crossed the bridge back into Brooklyn and went back to my old life?

He was more than that. Or, I wanted him to be more. I'd caught him referring to our time together as limited, and he'd mentioned not wanting to talk about letting me go until he had to. Not *if* he had to. It was an eventuality, not a possibility that whatever this crazy thing between us was would end. Thinking about it hurt more than I expected it to. I sucked in a shaky breath, needing a drink to numb the shitty feeling now lodged in the pit of my stomach.

"I'll get us some drinks; you guys find a table." I ambled away from my friends and headed to the bar, scanning the room for Joe but not finding him anywhere.

I searched the crowd to find where the girls were sitting, but my friends were already lost in the sea of patrons. It was dark and loud, the bass from the speakers echoing in my ears. The band sounded great, playing an old eighties cover with different guitar riffs.

"What can I get you?" I barely heard the bartender over the noise and my turbulent thoughts.

"Three cosmos, please." I tried to ignore the doubt creeping into my veins and resolving to enjoy my vacation for what it was. I'd have fun tonight if it killed me—no matter if I could be with Joe or not.

I pulled out my phone to shoot him a text.

**Caterina:** *We just got here. I'm at the bar getting drinks. Congrats, this place is packed!*

After shoving it back in my bag, I paid for the drinks and prayed I'd be able to make it to wherever the girls were sitting without spilling. I spotted Megan's wave and headed in her direction.

"I'm on my game tonight, didn't miss a drop!" I gingerly

placed the glasses on the tiny table the girls found in the corner.

"Cosmos? Have we finally become the *Sex and the City* girls? Over thirty and still going out for cocktails?" Claire joked before lifting a glass and taking a sip.

"Hey, when I watched reruns in college, they were my idols." I took a big gulp of my sweet drink, welcoming the relaxing burn down my throat. "They never had their shit together but looked like they had fun anyway. That's going to be my new life when I get back to Brooklyn. I may be a mess, but I'll figure out how to enjoy my life."

"Oh, I'd say you're enjoying your life just fine, right now." Megan raised her glass in my direction.

"I meant in the long term. This..." I trailed off, my eyes darting around the room in search of Joe. "This is temporary."

"How do you know that? I saw that kiss on the porch the other day, and nothing about it looked temporary." Claire drew back in her chair and crossed her arms.

"Great chemistry doesn't mean anything permanent." I shrugged and drained my glass. I wasn't calm, only flushed and hot. Remembering the sangria/ice cream incident, I resolved to pace myself. Dousing my feelings with alcohol wouldn't provide any true relief.

After chatting at the table for almost an hour and three rounds of drinks, although the last one was water for me, I surveyed the growing crowd around us and still found no sign of Joe.

"Why don't you ask someone to find him for you?" Claire asked as she played with the stem of her cocktail glass.

"He's probably busy; he knows we're here." I picked up my phone, glancing at the still blank screen. I could have asked the bartender to find him for me when we'd arrived, but the Eeyore cloud that settled over my head since Claire had uttered the word "boyfriend" had me playing distant and childish tonight.

"Do you like him? Not just his dick, but *him*?" Megan lifted an eyebrow and tapped her finger against the table.

"Well, we don't know how much they've been actually talking all this time." Claire nudged Megan.

"We've talked a lot more than you think." I narrowed my eyes. "Awesome conversations about everything. He's smart and funny and...yes, I do like him. There's a lot to like." I averted my gaze. "He's amazing, and not just because he's gorgeous and sexy, but he's a good guy. He has this caretaker thing about him that's so damn sweet. He's a great businessman at only thirty." I played with the tiny napkin under my empty glass.

"Do you want to tell us how this is only temporary again?" Claire glanced at Megan and jerked her head in my direction.

After glowering at them both, I continued. "It's temporary because I can't see how it could be anything else but. I'd love to keep seeing him, but I'm not sure how it would work, or if he'd even be up for figuring it out. So yes, even though it's pretty fucking spectacular, I don't only like Joe's dick."

"Well, that's a relief."

My body went rigid at the recognition of the deep voice behind me.

"You guys couldn't give me a signal or something?" I glared at my traitorous friends, collapsing in giggles.

I swiveled my head toward where Joe stood. "How much of that did you hear?"

"Enough to make my head swell a little bit." A smirk tickled the side of his mouth as he reached into his pocket. "I left my phone in the office and just noticed your text." He nodded hellos at Megan and Claire before holding out his hand to me. "Mind if I steal her for a bit?"

"Oh, not at all." Claire waved a hand and shooed us away.

"Thank you," he replied before pulling me past the bar and down a long hallway in the back. Before I could say anything, he pinned me against the wall and covered my mouth with his. I stiffened at first but, as usual, melted into his arms.

"The truth," he whispered, his lips still close enough to brush against mine. "You've been here for an hour and didn't try to find me. Why?"

I turned away from his scrutinizing stare. "I like you too much, Joe. And after this week..." I shrugged, not wanting to acknowledge what we both knew. "I guess I'm preparing myself a little."

He took my face into his hands, his hold tight as his gazed locked with mine. "What if I don't want you to prepare yourself? What if you stay with me for a couple of days after your friends leave? Didn't you say your boss told you to take more time off since you have so much saved?"

My jaw went slack as my words escaped me. "I can't just do that—"

"You *can* just do that." His shoulders jerked with a husky chuckle. "I'd still have to work, but I'd make sure my nights were free. You can be a beach bum for a couple of more days or hang out here." He wrapped me in his arms and yanked me closer. "Come on, Caterina. And I have a surprise for you." His lips curved up. "I'm off tomorrow."

"You're off tomorrow? Are you sure that you can do that with it this busy?" My brows pulled together.

"I own the fucking place, so yes, I can." He kissed my temple. "I'm taking you sightseeing. Well, what little we have to see around here." He leaned his forehead against mine. "Then, we figure things out. Okay?"

My heart soared as I looped my arms around Joe's neck

and attacked his mouth, still having no clue how we would actually work, but putting off goodbye was enough for me, right now.

Joe pulled me back inside the main part of the bar, seeming lighter himself as he led me to the crowded dance floor. He twirled me a couple of times, both of us laughing and falling into each other without a care in the world. I wished it could always be like this, and worried settling for less wouldn't eliminate a goodbye, but make it that much worse.

## 23

## CATERINA

JOE TIGHTENED his hold around my waist with a sleepy grumble before burrowing his head into the crook of my neck. Today made exactly a week since we'd met, and we were essentially in the same position then as we were in now: naked, legs entangled, although minus my morning after freak-out.

Quality of time—not amount of time—was what counted, and Joe had given me more quality in one week than I'd had for most of my life.

"Stop thinking so much so early in the morning."

I smiled into the pillow at Joe's gravelly voice and his warm lips dragging across the nape of my neck.

"It's not early at all." I reached behind me to wrap my arm around Joe's neck before squinting at the alarm clock on the nightstand. "It's nine o'clock. You think you're so smart."

"I am smart, but you're not hard to read. Relax, beautiful." He climbed over me, my legs parting on their own accord so he could settle between them. "You're all mine today. How's that sound?" He leaned his forehead against mine.

"That sounds great." My nails scraped up and down his

back. "Are you sure you want me here until Monday? You've only spent nights with me, you don't know the kind of house guest I am."

"I don't think I have anything to worry about." He kissed me, tugging on my bottom lip with his teeth as he pulled away. "I couldn't care less if you like to leave your clothes laying around."

"I don't leave clothes laying around." I shot him a squinty glare. "I may not be OCD neat, but I'm not messy."

He tapped his chin as he looked down at me. "There are two sets of clothes scattered all over my living room floor, and, if memory serves me right, *you're* the one who stripped us both and let everything fall where it may. Not sure if you just really wanted to get me naked or you're messy. Either way is fine with me."

I jabbed his shoulder, but he wouldn't budge. He was right on both counts. I did tend to be on the messy side. My bedroom back in Brooklyn always had a small pile of clothes on the chair next to my bed that I was too lazy to put into the dresser five feet away. Whenever I had more than ten minutes alone with Joe, my goal was always to get his clothes off as soon as possible. After our date at the beach I ripped the button straight off his jeans the second he got his front door opened, leaving a gaping hole he loved to tease me about.

Rational thinking hadn't applied once since I'd arrived at Ocean Cove, and I'd finally decided to just go along with it. I was indulging and not denying, and I'd never felt more alive in all my thirty-three years.

"I just want you with me. Nothing else matters." He pressed into me, already hard as a rock and drawing a whimper out of me at the subtle but sublime friction. "Stay with me, Caterina," he pleaded against my lips.

We broke apart at a loud knock at the door. Joe groaned as

his head fell to my chest. He reached for his phone with his brows knitted together and glanced at the screen.

"The one time I decide to take a damn day off. I would've thought if something was wrong, I'd get a text, but nothing." He rolled off me and dug into his dresser drawer for a pair of shorts. I grabbed my glasses from the nightstand and slipped them on before I was treated to the flexing of his muscular back and perfect ass as he stepped into gray sweat-shorts.

"I feel your eyes on me." He turned, reaching over to slap my ass with a loud smack. "Don't move; I'll be right back."

Straining to make out the voices of who Joe was speaking to, I covered my mouth to muffle a loud yawn. This week was both exhilarating and exhausting.

Joe came back into the bedroom holding all our clothes from last night. He set them on the bed and turned to me with a crinkled brow.

"So," he came to where I was laying on the bed and leaned on the edge, "my parents decided to make a surprise visit. They came to the restaurant first, and, when Dom told them I took today off, they came here to see what was wrong. Guess I surprised them instead." His shoulders shook with a laugh before my sleepy head caught up to what he was telling me.

"Your parents are here, and saw all our clothes on the floor, so they know you have someone here?" My panicked hand smoothed my matted hair as if that made all the difference in this awful situation. I wished I could run into the bathroom to fix myself, at least a little, but it was down the short hall next to the living room.

I sifted through the pile for my bra and underwear. "I'll go back to the rental." My panic had me attempting to fasten my bra and pull up my panties at the same time. "Your parents came all this way, you should—"

"No." My head jerked up to the sound of Joe's raised

voice. "I took today off to spend it with you, and that's what I'm doing. We can see them later." He grabbed my shaky wrists and pulled me toward where he was still sitting on the bed. "We're all adults. There's no reason to be ashamed."

"For *you*, there isn't." I dropped my head into my hands and pinched the bridge of my nose. Joe peeled my fingers off my face and shook his head.

"Aside from not calling first today, my parents are pretty chill. In fact, my family is always worried that I'm alone too much, so meeting the beautiful woman I've been spending all my time with will be a huge thrill." He lifted my hand to his lips and pressed a kiss to the top of my wrist. "I want you to meet my parents and be with me today. *All* day." The plea in his crystal blue eyes made me stumble.

He rubbed my back and kissed my forehead. "And stop worrying about how you look. You always wake up gorgeous. Another reason why you'll be a great houseguest." Joe's easy grin made him impossible to refuse.

"Yes."

"Yes, what?"

"Yes, I'll stay with you." I grinned, warmth flooding my chest when Joe's entire face lit up.

"I'll get rid of these two, and I'll show you how happy I am that you finally agreed." The heat in his gaze made me squirm to the point that I almost forgot the humiliation waiting for me on his couch. "I'll meet you outside." He planted a quick kiss to my lips before rising from the bed and shutting the door behind him.

I pulled on my dress from last night and reversed the camera on my phone to survey the damage. My mascara was smudged under my eyes, and my hair was still sticking up every which way. I wiped under my eyes with my finger, hoping to appear more smoky-eyed than raccoon before I headed for the living room.

"We are so sorry." A beautiful woman with long dark hair rose from the couch and rushed over to me. "We're usually not the kind of parents who barge in unannounced. I'm Samantha." She held out her hand with a warm smile.

"Nice to meet you." I took her hand and exhaled some of the tension. "I'm Caterina."

"What a beautiful name!" She squeezed my hand.

"Everyone calls me Cat, except for your son." I turned my head to where Joe was beaming on the couch next to who I guessed was his father. I did a double take as I looked between them. Joe's father was his older identical twin.

"Spooky isn't it," Samantha said in a loud whisper when she noticed me staring.

"Yes, it is a little," I agreed, my gaze still fixed in their direction.

Joe's father grinned as he came over to where we stood.

"I'm Lucas. Nice to meet you, Caterina." He took my hand in both of his. I could tell right away that he and Joe had the same personality, too. It made me wonder why whenever Joe brought up his father, it sounded like they had a strained relationship. "I'm sure on my son's only day off, he has better plans for both of you than being stuck with his parents all day." He lifted a brow before craning his head to Joe. "But maybe you both wouldn't be against a little dinner?"

"They love this steakhouse one town over and use seeing me as an excuse to go." Joe's lips twisted into a smirk at his father.

"Now, Joey, that's not true. Seeing our baby boy is always our first priority when we come here." He ruffled Joe's hair, and I laughed at Joe's groan. "Yes, that's the place. Good food, and right on the beach. I hope you'll join us."

"I think we can do that." Joe's eyes locked with mine, and I responded with a tiny nod. I didn't think I could say no, and his parents seemed easygoing and friendly. New boyfriend's mothers usually made me uncomfortable, but I didn't feel like either of them were sizing me up. Joe was right, they were simply happy to see me and their son.

"We'll let you get back to your day." Lucas draped his arm around his wife's shoulders. "Eight o'clock sound okay?"

I lifted a shoulder at Joe, as he was the one with all the plans for today.

"Sounds fine, Dad." Joe breathed out with the tiniest bit of exasperation. Samantha kissed his cheek before they said goodbye to us both and made their way out of his apartment.

"I'm sorry we got suckered into that. The drive from Queens is long, and I couldn't tell them no." He shrugged and sat back down on the couch.

"It's fine. Steakhouse sounds nice." I settled next to him. "Are you sure you want me to go?"

Joe drew back on the couch and squinted at me. "Why wouldn't I want you to go?"

"Dinner with parents is something you do when you're a little further along than we are." I lifted an eyebrow.

"I want you there. I'm glad you met my parents. I think boxing us into a timeline doesn't make sense, and we need to stop doing it." Joe slid his hand under my legs and lifted me onto his lap. "It doesn't matter if we just met or if I'd known you for years. I feel what I feel, and that's fucking crazy about you."

I shook my head and cuddled into his chest. I was fucking crazy about him, too, and wished I could get rid of the stupid commonsense that kept telling me this shouldn't be happening so fast. For us, at that moment, the timing was perfect.

"Can I ask you something?" I pushed off of Joe's chest. "They both seem really nice, but you always talk about friction between you and your dad. Did I miss something just now?"

"No, they're both really nice and weren't hiding anything." He laughed. "My father and I are the same in a lot of ways. But, like I told you, he's this big financial executive, brilliant and successful. I'm happy with the path I chose, but I never felt he was. So..." He shifted on the couch and pulled me closer. "I lash out when I shouldn't which makes everything that much worse."

"You *are* smart and successful, Joe. What do you mean by lash out?"

"Well," he tightened his hold around my waist, "we'll go out tonight, and he'll insist on paying. I'll take that as an insult that I'm not successful enough to pay, and I'll fight him on it for a few minutes. And then he'll ask questions about the restaurant out of genuine interest, and I'll again get annoyed that he's nit-picking at all the business decisions I make. I'll most likely come home feeling like shit for either not being as good as him or for being an asshole because I don't know how to deal with my insecurities."

"Self-awareness isn't any good if you don't try to get ahead of it, *Joey*."

"I knew you'd pick up on that," he groaned as his head fell back. "I'll probably need comfort when I get home." Joe's hand skidded up my thigh until his finger grazed the edge of my panties.

"What kind of comfort?" I jumped when his hand traveled lower and settled between my legs.

"Maybe ride me for a little while, sit on my face. Feeling you come on my tongue should make me forget my troubles for a bit."

I shook my head and lifted my leg to straddle his lap.

"You're filthy," I whispered before dipping my head to kiss him. He laughed against my lips before he pulled back.

"And you're mine for the entire day. Ready?"

After a week of fearing the worst and focusing on how we'd end, I wanted to embrace the ride, no matter where it led.

I replied with a kiss. "Absolutely."

"Tired?" I glanced at Caterina over my shoulder as she trailed behind me.

"No, but maybe like slow down for just a minute." She glared at me while fighting a smile.

Ocean Cove was small, but I made sure she saw all of it. I took her to the tiny coffee shop that, like my place, saw a big boost in business each summer but had enough of a local following to stay open all year long. Moving out here and running a business wasn't easy, but I loved it. The local merchants joined together to keep revenue up with seasonal events, and fall was becoming more popular around here. I always saw possibility here and still do, but I suspected showing Caterina all of my adopted hometown had to do with a subconscious need to convince her to stay.

We wound up on my favorite pier, the one no one seemed to know about but me. From the end, you could see the board-walk and rides from the more popular shore towns, and, even with the crazy lights in the distance, I'd always found peace here. I came here to think, even in shitty weather that rocked the old wood and made it creak, and I'd always leave with a little more clarity than when I'd first arrived. Now, I realized, I'd come here next time and remember who I'd been with today and would be sad instead of soothed.

"You said no one comes here but you?" Caterina walked up to the edge and leaned over the railing. "Seems like such a shame, you know?"

I came up close behind her and looped one arm around her waist. "Can you see Wildwood in the distance? You can tell by the big Ferris wheel from the water park. At night, when it's lit up, it's pretty cool." I leaned into her, my eyes clenching shut as I tried to memorize how her body felt against mine, the scent of her hair, and the little noises she made that she wasn't even aware of.

As if she could read my mind, she drew back, tilting her head so I could rest my chin on her shoulder.

"You're a bit of a loner, aren't you?" She turned and wrapped her arms around my neck. "This place is about as different from Queens as you can possibly get, and you moved here alone. Dominic came later, right?"

"Yes. Not too much later, but," I shrugged, "I was okay coming out here alone but thankful he was here to help me, then and now. Sometimes it's hard to admit I have limitations." I yanked her closer, drawing out a laugh. "I think you can relate."

"I'm working on it." Her fingers played with the collar of my T-shirt before her dark eyes came back to mine. "You really never had a girlfriend? As ridiculously good-looking as I'm sure you always were, not even like in high school?"

I laughed and lifted a shoulder. "I had dates. Some repeats. But nothing I would call anything special. I know I sound like an asshole. But I never led anyone on, at least, not intentionally. When I go back to my old neighborhood, I don't walk the streets in fear of some kind of retaliation."

She smiled and shook her head. "Lifelong bachelor even back then?"

"What about you? I'm sure you had a ton of guys wanting to take you out in high school."

"Nope. I was sort of a late bloomer. Product of an overprotective mother. I was always more in the background: the girl with glasses who always got good grades and did what she was supposed to."

"You're hot as *fuck* in glasses." I yanked her closer.

She cupped my cheek. "Your kink is cute. But back then, not so much. Anyway, we're changing the subject. We were talking about you. My past is non-existent."

My head fell back on a sigh before my gaze came back to Caterina's.

"I liked the girls I dated. But none of them..." My eyes darted away from hers and focused on the water behind her. A confession dangled between us, but I couldn't look at her when I let it out.

"None of them, what?" She squeezed my shoulder, so I'd bring my gaze back to hers.

"I saw women for fun. But then I saw you, and something in me wouldn't let you leave. I cleaned out my kitchen trying to get you to stay, in fact." My thumb slid back and forth over her jaw. "I've never been drawn to someone like that. I actually never thought it was possible." I remembered what Owen said about being "hit." I didn't believe him at the time, but now there was no other explanation. "You were everything I didn't know I was looking for. And I don't think I can let you go."

Her eyes watered as she sank her teeth into her bottom lip. "I don't think I can let you go, either. This sucks." Her sad laugh didn't mask the crack in her voice on the last word.

I pulled her into my chest. "Yeah, it sucks. But we'll find a way."

"What way is that?"

"I don't know. Why I said we'd find it." The sides of my mouth curled up until I spied the brokenhearted defeat in her eyes.

"We have an uncomfortable steak dinner to go to." I stepped back and grabbed her hand. "You said you wanted to stop by the rental and change, come on." I brushed her lips with mine. "Faster we go, faster we could come back and get naked until tomorrow morning."

"WHAT WAS your favorite part of today?" I asked Caterina as we pulled into the steakhouse parking lot. She wore a red dress that hugged every part of her, matching red lips and glasses. I hated myself for agreeing to see my parents tonight.

"Well, the pier was beautiful. This town is so much bigger than it seems. I love how you know all the ins and outs and backroads, like that beach you took me to for our first date."

"You count that as our first date?" I cast a quick glance at her. "Not the night you came into the restaurant?"

In my periphery, I saw her shrug. "That was more...fated. The beach was planned."

"So, you're saying we're fated." I picked up her hand and threaded our fingers together.

She rested her chin on my shoulder. "What else would you call it?"

"Good point. What else did you like?"

"Honestly, being with you. You were my favorite today."

I pulled into a spot and covered her mouth with mine the second I put my truck in park.

"You know," I panted against her lips, her lipstick smeared across her swollen mouth. "You don't have to say nice things to get into my pants later. I'm a sure thing. A *very* sure thing."

"Oh, I know that." The side of her mouth curved up before she kissed my cheek.

"You were my favorite, too." My thumb skidded along the delicate curve of her jaw. "You've been my favorite since last Thursday."

She could be my favorite for a lot longer, like maybe forever.

If I could just figure out how.

MY PARENTS WERE so overjoyed I'd brought a woman to dinner with me, they fell all over Caterina from the second she sat down. They asked her question after question, but not in an intense inquisition sort of way. They were so happy she existed; they wanted to know all about her and barely uttered a word to me since we'd arrived.

"Where do you work? I know you said you were in advertising. Our son doesn't tell us much," my mother said to Caterina while arching an eyebrow at me. While that was true, this thing we had was such a whirlwind I didn't tell anyone except Owen when he dragged it out of me. I hoped he hadn't mentioned it to my sister, but now I wondered if my parents' oddly timed visit wasn't only for a good piece of steak. If Bella had told them about Caterina—like she told them everything else—I wouldn't be surprised if their spur-of-the-moment visit was for a little intel.

"I work for an agency in Midtown. I was just promoted to account manager."

"I used to be a marketing manager at Copeland. I worked with agencies all the time. I'm still there, but I work from home part-time, and I take full advantage of all six weeks of vacation I've earned."

"Something this one needs to learn how to do." I nudged Caterina with my shoulder.

"I know." She nodded. "My boss is always after me to take more time off. With the rollover from the last two years, I have almost three months of vacation days. I'm an HR nightmare."

"I'd never let that happen if you worked for me," Dad told Caterina while he poured my mother another glass of wine. I agreed to let him pay without a struggle, and, after he'd ordered a $300 vintage bottle of Merlot, I wouldn't have been inclined to fight him that hard this time. "Time for yourself is important. I've seen the best employees get burned out because they think the world will end if they take a day off."

"Well," Caterina set down her fork, "I haven't told Joe this yet, but I've actually extended my vacation until Wednesday. I may have to work a little Monday, but..." she turned to me, her eyes bright and a hint of a smile curving her lips. It was all I could do not to leap out of my seat and crash my mouth into hers. I had her until Wednesday. It was only three extra days, but I'd gladly take every second I could get, that *we* could get.

A slow smile curved my lips, and I spied her shoulders relax. More time with her was all I wanted, and I was fucking thrilled to get even a little more of it.

"You can work in my office as much as you need to."

"I know, but I don't want to get in your way." She nodded a thank you to my father when he refilled her glass. "If you get really busy—"

"You are *never* in my way, and I think you should know that." I grabbed her hand and squeezed, oblivious to the fact we weren't alone. We were grasping at every second we could get. This pull between us took over everything, including logic. But right now, I got to keep her for longer, and that was all that mattered.

Sensing my parents' stare from across the table, when Caterina peeked at her phone screen, I turned to their identical dopey smiles as they looked between us. Their eyes literally twinkled as they regarded me with both elation and relief. My mother and I had the same conversation over and over again about how unhealthy it was to be so focused on my business. She constantly worried I'd gotten too used to being alone. Every phone call ended with my reassurance to her that I was fine, and I didn't have room in my life for anything other than running the restaurant. To my shock, one week had changed all of that. I was still dedicated to making The Beach Pub a success and keeping it that way, but I wished Caterina could be a real part of all of that, not just someone I'd get to see once a month if I was lucky.

"I'm so sorry. This is my boss, probably wondering if I've been kidnapped since I asked for more time off. Please excuse me." She rose from the table and rushed to the patio outside.

When I was sure she was out of earshot, I drew back in my chair and crossed my arms.

"Go on. I know the both of you are on the verge of exploding, so ask me what you want to ask me."

"She's beautiful and a sweetheart. I'm thrilled for you, Joey." My mother reached over the table with a watery gaze to squeeze my arm.

I smiled back, despite myself. "Well, she's going back to Brooklyn, eventually. I don't know what's going to happen after that." My voice was small as my eyes landed on Caterina, leaning against the patio door outside. Sometimes, the air whooshed right out of my lungs when I looked at her. I wasn't sure if it was the urge to grab her by the ankles so she wouldn't leave, or that I couldn't process how amazing she was, or how great we were together, and *would be* together if she didn't have to go back home.

"I see the way you're looking at her now and how you've looked at her all evening." Dad's gaze darted between Caterina and me. "You're a smart guy. I think you'll find a way. Have faith, Joey."

If only I was smart enough to close the distance between Brooklyn and Ocean Cove.

"I'm glad to see you doing so well. The restaurant was packed when we stopped by. Is this your busiest summer?" Dad asked, and I braced myself on instinct. The honest question came with a sincere compliment, but, for some reason, I went on auto-defense as usual. Trying to remember what Caterina said about self-awareness, I nodded and willed myself to relax.

"Actually, yes. I think it is. Customers like sitting on the patio in the back near the beach since we opened it this year. We had a successful event last night and a few more planned this summer and early fall. Caterina has been showing me how to better use social media to my advantage, and it seems to be helping."

"That's great." Dad beamed before he took a sip of wine. "Maybe I could be an investor, too, one of these days."

My stomach dropped as my body stiffened. "What do you mean by investor?"

He shrugged. "Like Owen is. If you want to keep things going in the fall, more revenue can only help, right?"

Mom draped her hand over her eyes and shook her head, and it wasn't hard to figure out why. I was sure Bella finally mentioned Owen's loan to my parents, and my father couldn't help digging into why I'd asked.

"Owen isn't an investor. Or he wasn't supposed to be." My eyes narrowed as I fell into the same awful pattern with my father. The question had no intended malice, but like always once my guard went up, I couldn't go back. "He gave me a loan early on that he refuses to let me pay back, so he likes to call himself an investor instead. And he was supposed to be a *private* investor, but, as usual, my sister can't keep anything quiet when it comes to you." I drained the wine in my glass with one gulp.

"And it was easier to go to Owen than to me. Like everything else. Right?" Dad's icy glare matched my own. We really did appear to be identical twins, but looks and sense of humor were the extent of it. I wasn't the great Lucas Hunter and never would be. Even though I was happy with who I was, the bratty kid in me always wanted to be more for his sake.

"Sorry about that." Caterina breezed back to the table and settled next to me. "Good news, I get to stay until Wednesday with no issues at all!" Her grin faded once her gaze stumbled onto mine. Squeezing her hand, I jerked my head slightly to the other end of the table so she'd know my change in demeanor didn't have anything to do with her staying and everything to do with my insecurities getting the best of me once again.

Caterina and I had more in common than I realized. We worked our fingers to the bone in a chase for a perceived unattainable validation that only exhausted us. I'd fought hard for the life and livelihood I had, but lately, all I could focus on was what it cost me in the long run. I had what I thought I wanted, but didn't realize how miserable I'd be in the end.

THE REST of dinner was spent in an uncomfortable silence. Caterina and my mother had hit it off in a big way, but my father and I didn't utter a word to each other than a tense goodbye in the parking lot. I didn't even ask how long they were in town for before we parted ways. I was angry—mostly at myself—and ashamed for how I acted.

My stomach turned at Caterina seeing me at my worst. At least, she hadn't been there when Dad and I had actual words, but I wasn't acting like the guy she'd known for the past week.

I pulled into my spot in the driveway and climbed up the inside steps to my apartment with Caterina following behind me. If not for my childish outburst that ruined what had been a nice night, the both of us would have come back here thrilled and probably naked already. I'd fucked that up, too.

"Hey," Caterina whispered as she dropped a hand on my forearm. "Feel like sitting outside for a little while?" She nodded to my tiny patio that I never used since I was rarely home.

"If you want. Let me grab a couple of towels; those chairs have seen better days." I trudged over to my hall closet. The lousy feeling in my gut always took a while for me to shake, but I pushed through it for her sake.

After I draped towels on both chairs and fell into a seat, Caterina planted herself on my lap, gasping at a loud creak.

"I didn't break the chair, did I?" She grimaced and drew an unexpected chuckle out of me.

"No, baby. It's old but sturdy. Your cute little ass didn't break it, I promise." I wrapped my arms around her and drew her closer, burying my face into her neck. "I'm sorry, Caterina," I whispered before pressing a kiss behind her ear.

"No need to be sorry." Her hand drifted down my cheek. "*I'm* sorry you're upset."

"I need to grow the fuck up finally." I shut my eyes and leaned back on the chair. "I fought hard to live the life I wanted, and I need to own it and not worry about who I disappoint."

"But you don't disappoint. Your parents love you, that's easy to see. What happened when I left the table?"

"Someone—most likely, my sister—let it slip to my parents about Owen's loan. My dad asked how he could become an investor, too, and that set me off. Thing is, I know he was only asking to help, not make me feel like I was failing, but I wanted to do this myself. Be a success *without* his help."

"Well, what would be so bad about him helping you?" She turned to face me. "Would he hold it over your head?"

"No, but I guess if I asked him, he'd maybe think he had a say in how I do things and point out what I was doing wrong without meaning to if that makes sense. Like, in my head, I know he wouldn't do it on purpose, but it would feel that way and make me crazy. I sound like a petulant little punk. Are you sure you want to stay with me now?"

She jabbed my shoulder. "Stop it. You don't, because I get it. I'm close with my mother, and we have a great relationship, for the most part. She still kinda hovers, for lack of a better word."

I laughed at her eyeroll. "When I first moved into my apartment, I asked her for a loan that I swore to her I'd pay back in a couple of months."

"But, at least you had the guts to ask." Sifting a lock of her hair between my fingers, memories of my father and me raced through my head as I tried to pinpoint when things had shifted between us. As hard as I always tried, I could never figure out the exact day he'd gone from my hero to an unattainable ideal I never felt I'd measure up to. "Did she give it to you?"

"Yes, but she pointed out how important it was to save if I wanted to live on my own, and I should give her part of my paycheck every month. She offered to start a savings account for me and hold it."

I nodded. "Always good to have savings—but not what you needed to hear, right?"

"Exactly." She pushed her finger into my chest. "I took it as making sure I saved money so I wouldn't screw up and run out—again. I'm sure she meant well, mostly, but it made me feel small—like a kid who didn't know what she was doing. I paid her back within a month and haven't asked her for another dime since."

I kissed her cheek and anchored my forehead to hers. "We're two stubborn idiots, aren't we?"

"Maybe. It's hard to take guidance or what's meant as friendly advice from your parents when you feel like you already have something to prove. Especially when you put unnecessary pressure on yourself to be perfect. I'm definitely guilty of that, as you may have noticed." She shifted in my lap before cuddling into me. "Starting a new business isn't going to be a huge success right away. I think your head knows that."

She tapped on my temple. "But you keep expecting it to be anyway."

Why was it that every time I saw my parents, I went home feeling like both a fuck up and a jerk? Something had to give because my father didn't deserve the way I froze him out every time. I knew that, yet I kept doing it.

She pushed off my chest and took my face in her hands. It was hard to see with only the soft light from my kitchen filtering out to my dark patio, but I was still trapped by Caterina's dark eyes and long lashes. Her lipstick had faded since dinner, but it was impossible to miss that mouth: full and lush and so damn soft. I needed to get lost inside her tonight. I wanted her to make me forget all the ways I'd made life impossible for myself and how lonely I'd be without her once Wednesday came. Here, with this beautiful woman draped over me, all the obstacles and silly issues in my life dissipated into the ether. She was all I needed.

"You're amazing, Joe. Don't let your fear of falling short make you ignore all you've accomplished. Promise me that."

My heart swelled then sank because that sounded a lot like part of a goodbye. I wouldn't entertain any of that tonight. Tonight, we were together, and she was mine. It didn't matter if the timing didn't make sense. *We* made sense.

"You're pretty amazing yourself." I nipped at her earlobe, smiling at the giggle vibrating against my lips.

"I wish there was something I could do."

"You're doing it now. You're here. But there is one thing that could make me forget for a little while." I grabbed her hips and brought her closer. "Kiss me," I hissed before she brushed my lips, teasing me as she grazed her bottom lip along mine. A growl erupted from my throat before our lips fused together. I licked inside her mouth and swallowed her sweet whimpers when my tongue stroked hers. As she squirmed on top of me, the chair under us continued to creak as our kiss caught fire. I caressed the sweet curve of her ass and brought my hand lower until I fisted the material at the hem of her dress.

"Still need me to ride you?" she giggled against my lips.

"Definitely later, but for right now..." I slid my hand back up her thigh, taking the bottom of her dress along with it. "Right now, I need you to come all over my fingers." I hissed when I found the lace of her panties. "You can't scream that loud, but no one will see you but me." I pushed her panties to the side and ran a finger up and down her slit. She was silky and soaked.

"There's my girl. So wet." I made circles around her swollen clit, slow at first but picking up the pace the harder and wetter she became. "That's it, beautiful. Drip all over me. Tell me how good I make you feel." A guttural moan fell from her lips, her legs shaking as they always did when she was close. She clutched my bicep, digging her nails into my arm as her body went rigid on top of me.

"Tell me, baby." Need strangled my words as my fingers twisted deep inside her. I ran my thumb over her clit and smiled when she jerked in my arms. "Tell me how good it feels when I make you come."

"So good," she panted, lifting her hooded eyes to mine. "I've never felt like this. I don't want to leave." Her voice was barely audible as if she didn't want me to hear.

"I've never felt like this either, baby." I came back to her lips, our kiss sloppy and desperate. "And I don't want you to go," I admitted, my words slipping out like a plea. "But you're mine right now. All mine and—" Her pussy clenched around my fingers, and all the blood in my body redirected to my dick.

Her mouth fell open with a silent scream as her whole

body shuddered. She rocked against my hand until her orgasm subsided, collapsing on top of me with a tortured groan.

"How could it be this good?" She met my gaze, her words full of both wonder and dread.

"It doesn't matter," I whispered and pressed a kiss to her forehead. "Because it is."

## 27

## CATERINA

"I can't believe this week is over, and I have to go back to work," Claire whined as she plopped into one of the patio chairs.

"All good things must come to an end, I suppose." I flipped the burgers on the grill, focusing on the sizzle of the meat and smoky aroma of the charcoal, not the sour taste the words left in my mouth. I'd been MIA all week long, and, although my friends understood, I promised them a barbecue on their last night while promising *myself* to dwell on the wonderful things this getaway brought me instead of dreading the end.

"You didn't have to go to all this trouble, Cat," Megan said, handing me a glass of wine. I put the grilling tongs down and took a long, wonderful sip. Nothing was better than ice cold Pinot Grigio on a hot day, and, while I didn't want to get drunk, a little numbness from a glass or two would be welcome.

"Yes, I did." I closed the hood on the barbecue and settled into a chair next to Claire. "I was an awful friend this week and left you pretty much every single night. Making you guys dinner will relieve my guilty conscience."

Claire nudged my ankle with her foot. "There is no need to feel guilty. A hot vacation fling was exactly what you needed to cleanse that jackass from your system. I'm thrilled you had a good time."

"Right," I breathed out, my gaze dropping to the ground as I took another sip.

"I don't know if I'd call it just a vacation fling." Megan scooted her chair closer to me. "He asked you to stay with him after we left. And I see how sad you are even though you're trying to hide it. Have you talked about what happens after you leave?"

I gave her a slow shake of my head. "Not really, other than we'll figure it out. Claire may be right. It's all hot and heavy now, but, in the end, it'll probably just be a fling. What else could it be after only a week?"

"Do you really believe that?" Megan arched a brow.

"I don't know. I don't want to believe it." I rose from my seat and again tried to forget my troubles and focus on my burgers. "When we're together, it's as if I've known him forever. And it's good, guys. So, *so* good," I lamented as I covered the burgers with slices of cheese.

"Get away from the grill and talk to us." Claire patted my now vacant chair and crooked her finger.

I plopped back on the seat, ready to finally unload to my friends what had been eating away at me all week.

"I don't want it to end. It's crazy to feel this strongly about someone I've only known for a week, but it's never been like this with anyone else. We're like kindred spirits in a lot of ways. Fighting the same annoying demons. He's..." I rested my elbows on my knees and dropped my head into my hands. "Wonderful. But how can this continue?" I sat up and looked between them, their faces unreadable other than sympathy. "Like maybe at first we talk all the time, and we try to see each other, then when I can't make it, and he's busy here, it just fades. I don't know if it's better to not even try and set ourselves up like that. Bad enough prolonging my stay is going to make leaving that much worse."

"Oh, Kit-Cat," Claire looped her arm around my shoulder. "Don't give up so soon."

"I have never seen her this sick over a guy before." Megan studied me with a pinched brow. "Have you, Claire?"

"Nope. Not once. Even that dude you broke up with in college, after what was a long time, too, right?"

"Six months isn't a long time, Claire." I drained my glass and pushed off the seat.

"Oh, I remember him!" I spotted Megan nodding in my periphery. "The football player, right?"

"Baseball," I answered, not looking up as I piled the burgers onto a platter and set them down with the rest of the food on the glass patio table. "He was too busy for a girlfriend, and I was doing that double internship, anyway." I shrugged before waving them over to sit.

"See!" Claire yelled and stalked over to me before poking my shoulder with her finger. "You were always too busy to care when it came to men. Even..." She nodded to the street behind the yard.

"You can say his name. Trent." A laugh escaped me before I reached for the salad. "And I'm not sure that's the right direction toward Brooklyn, I think it's to the left."

"I mean that yes, you were pissed off at what he did, but breaking up was more aggravating than heartbreaking for you." She held her hands up. "In my opinion, anyway."

"What she's trying to say—I think—is that you really care about this guy. How long did it take us to convince you to take this week off? I think we worked on you for over a month. When Joe asked you to stay with him, how long did it take you to say yes?"

"Not right away," I whispered as I darted my eyes from hers.

"By the next morning?"

"Maybe. I don't remember." I wouldn't look her in the eye as I stabbed my fork into an innocent piece of macaroni salad.

My phone buzzed across the glass table next to my plate. I took a quick glance at the screen and couldn't help the smile pulling at my lips.

**Joe:** *One more night, and you're all mine.*

"I think I know who texted her," Claire sang from across the table.

"Look..." Megan dropped a hand to my forearm. "Maybe I'm a sap, but don't dismiss what you guys have as a fling only because you think it happened too fast. Brooklyn isn't that far from here."

"It's far enough." I sighed. "I want what we had this week. I want us to be together every day, not once in a while, if we're lucky. I'm afraid part-time isn't going to be enough for either of us." I set down my fork and draped my hand over my eyes. "This is ridiculous; it's been a week. I shouldn't be planning for my future after a week."

"You didn't plan a future with Trent after *two years*, or put this much thought into when you could see him again," Claire noted as she poured us all more wine.

"I put his name on the lease. That was planning."

"But why did you even do that?" Megan asked.

Why *had* I done that? It felt like the natural next step, but maybe it had been sidestepping a real commitment. Yes, his name was on my lease, but we'd had no other real plans with each other for the future. It was convenient, like every other man I'd been with until it wasn't.

Joe and I were about to get very *in*convenient, but, unlike all those who'd come before him, I knew I couldn't drop it all and walk away unscathed. And that scared me most of all.

## 28

## CATERINA

Since checkout time from the rental was noon, all three of us were up early, going through the entire house to make sure we didn't leave any souvenirs for the cleaning crew. I gathered what was left of the food, which ended up being a lot since we weren't home other than to sleep.

"I hope leaving at this ungodly hour means no traffic," Claire whined, and we loaded their suitcases into the back of Megan's car. My suitcase was packed last night and in my trunk, before they'd even woken up. I was a mix of nerves and excitement, and I hoped Joe didn't mind starting our weekend together this early.

"Claire, please." Megan stifled a yawn. "There's always traffic on weekends in the summer. Suck it up, buttercup. And you," Megan said as she grabbed my shoulders, "have fun, relax, and let things happen. Okay?"

"Sure, that's easy enough." I coughed out a laugh and hugged them both goodbye.

I leaned against my car, watching them drive off, still feeling a little guilty. I didn't spend as much time with them this week as I'd intended, but they understood and were truly happy for me. When I'd come to Ocean Cove alone, not knowing what the hell I was doing here other than trying to get some kind of bearing on my life, I'd never planned on Joe.

But I would have fun, relax, and let things happen—three things everyone else found easy but went against everything I usually was. An unexpected laugh tumbled from my lips when I closed my car door and started the engine.

At thirty-three, I felt young and alive for the first time in my life, and I didn't want it to end.

The restaurant was dark when I pulled up, but I spotted a light filtering through the front window of Joe's apartment. Fishing my bag out of the trunk and rolling it to the side entrance, I took in my surroundings. The street was so quiet, it was almost creepy. It was only six-thirty on a Saturday morning, but, back home, there was always someone outside at any time of night. Without all the beach-goers and tourists bustling around, it was simply a small, sleepy town and almost intrusive to be out this early in the morning. When things were too quiet, I'd usually become agitated since I was so accustomed to noise all around me, but I enjoyed the peace, another thing that had eluded me until I'd come here.

I reached into my purse to dig out my phone and text Joe when the creak of his door startled me.

"Want to come inside before people think you're casing the place?" Joe leaned against the doorjamb with his arms linked across his bare chest, in nothing but a pair of sweat-shorts. I'd seen him naked most of this week, but standing like that, lean muscle everywhere and a blinding smile stretching his lips, my pulse still surged, and my body still ached. I kept expecting us to burn out, but Joe did more to me with those crystal blue eyes than the other men I'd been with could do with their hands.

Joe was beautiful and belonged to me—now. Everything else faded into the distance.

"Do you always come to the door without a shirt?" My eyes traveled up and down his body.

"When a pretty girl comes over, usually." He grabbed me by the waist and kissed me. Close-mouthed but slow and full of intention. "And this pretty girl is going to stay." His hand weaved into my hair before he kissed me again. He tasted like coffee and toothpaste, and when his tongue collided with mine, I was hungry for more. Joe pulled back on a throaty groan.

"Let's get upstairs before we put on a show. This street may look sleepy, but more people are around than you may think." He took the suitcase and lifted my laptop bag from my shoulder. "Come on." He beamed at me before grabbing my hand.

I followed Joe up the stairs to his apartment. "This place is yours. Feel free to sleep or whatever you want to do while I'm working."

I nodded, scanning his living room as if I were seeing it for the first time. It was quaint and cozy. Joe didn't have much in the way of pictures, but I spotted a few family photos under his huge mounted TV. I recognized his parents and figured the girl in the picture was probably his older sister. I guessed my focus was always on his bedroom, so I'd never taken in many details.

"I could open with you. If that's okay, I don't want to bother you or anything, but—"

He pressed a finger to my lips. "What did I say about not bothering me? I asked you to stay because I want you here, and, since I own the place, you can stay there all day if you'd like. I just didn't want you to be bored."

He wrapped his arms around me and pressed a kiss to my forehead.

"I'm never bored with you." I let my hands drift down his torso, tracing the hard planes and ridges I'd memorized at this point. "Watching you in action is sexy."

"Is that so?" His finger wandered down my spine and left goose bumps in its path. "Come with me." He grabbed my hand and pulled me toward the bathroom. "I tried to remember what shampoo you used." He nodded toward the shower caddy in the corner. "When we were in the tub, I wasn't paying all that much attention." He flashed a devious grin over his shoulder. "And didn't know which of you it was for, so hopefully I picked all right. You have towels behind the door, and I don't know if you wanted to unpack anything, but I cleaned out a couple of drawers in my dresser. It's only a few days, but…"

Joe trailed off, his smile now shy as his eyes darted around the bathroom.

"You did all that for me?" I wrapped my arms around his waist. For a man who described himself as aloof when it came to women, he sure knew how to pay attention. I liked to think that was because he only paid attention to me.

"Of course, I did. I told you I want you here. I can make you breakfast, and you can sit at the bar with me this morning. How does that sound?"

Joe was all man but had this adorable vulnerability. The sweet sincerity in his eyes was disarming and irresistible.

"Being with you sounds amazing, and you make a fantastic breakfast." I kissed his chin. "I'm ready when you are."

"I've been ready all morning, waiting for you, baby." He ground his hips into mine with a devious grin. A tiny gasp escaped me at how *ready* he was.

"What time do you have to open?" I whispered against his neck as I peppered kisses along his jaw, giving his Adam's apple a lick when I saw it bob along his throat.

"We open early today." His voice was strained as I moved my lips down his chest and dropped to my knees.

"Well, not like we have to worry about traffic to get there, right?" I gazed up at him with hooded eyes. "Only a quick walk downstairs." I licked my lips and met his heated gaze. "I'll wear my glasses next time." I pulled down the waistband of his shorts, and Joe grunted a curse when I took him in my mouth the second he sprang free.

Joe made me feel beautiful, sexy, and brazen in a way I never thought I could be. I was high off the groans erupting from his throat and the way he gripped the back of my head, twisting his fingers around a fistful of my hair and pulling hard when his length poked the back of my throat.

There was no time to get creative on a time limit, but I sucked and licked and enjoyed every inch of him until he pulsed down my throat.

Joe's darkened gaze slid to mine as his chest heaved up and down. His hand cupped my chin, his features a mix of shock and elation, as if I'd just given him the greatest present of his life.

He lifted me up from the floor, devouring my lips with a passion that made my head spin and my heart pound. I was breathless and dizzy when we broke apart.

"I may trap you here."

I cupped his cheek and gave him a soft kiss.

"And I wouldn't fight you."

"Hey, Joe, who's the new girl?" Mr. Milano, a long-time resident of Ocean Cove and regular since I'd opened The Beach Pub, nodded his head to where Caterina pounded on the keys of her laptop at a table next to the bar. For the past couple of mornings, she'd planted herself there while Dominic and I set up, and she hung around most of the day.

"Her name is Caterina, and she's staying with me." I didn't add 'for a few days' because I hated remembering it. When he'd asked me about her, I realized I had no idea what to call her. We weren't friends. I guessed we were dating, but calling her my girlfriend didn't seem right, even though the thought of her with someone else made me want to crush the glass I was drying into tiny shards. I watched her brow crinkle, her eyes fixed on the screen and nothing else. My girl in my place. Maybe girlfriend wasn't completely inappropriate. Our time together since she'd come to stay with me was the happiest I'd ever been, if a bit bittersweet. I wanted her and wanted *us* enough to figure out some kind of plan for what would happen after she left. But no matter what happened when she went home, our bubble would be broken, and things wouldn't be this easy again.

"Hmm. I see." I turned to Mr. Milano's snicker.

I set the glass back on the shelf behind the bar. "What do you see?"

"You got it bad. Whatever you're doing, your eyes follow her. Can't say I blame you. I wasn't always this old. The beauties don't come for me like they used to." He chomped on a piece of toast, his wistful gaze fixed on Caterina. "She's a knockout. Good for you, kid."

"Thanks." My gaze once again gravitated toward Caterina. She looked away from the screen for a moment and caught my gaze. A smile ghosted her lips before she turned back to the screen. "Yes, she is."

I motioned for one of the waitresses to come over and refill his coffee. Mr. Milano liked to sit by the bar and chat up Dominic and me whenever he came in. He'd regale us with his glory days and what the shore had been like back when he was our age. He was a lifelong bachelor but often had nieces and nephews visit him during the summers. Whenever my mother got on my case about being alone, my mind always wandered to him. If that was my path, I was all right with it. I never thought I was missing out on much—until a week and a half ago.

"Excuse me," I told him before I made my way over to Caterina's booth and sat down next to her.

"I thought you were only working on Sunday night, catching up on emails." I stretched my arm along the back of the seat. "You're on an extended vacation, remember?"

"I'm not working for me, I'm working for *you,* right now." She turned to me with a raised brow before going back to the screen.

"Is this role play?"

She dropped her fingers from the keys and swiveled her head toward me.

"Role play? Seriously, Joe?"

"Oh, come on. You said, 'working for me'." I crept closer. "Are you trying to sell me something? I could be *so* into this." I squeezed her thigh under the table. "Come into my office," I whispered in her ear and nuzzled her cheek. "Peel your clothes off, and show me what you've got."

She jabbed my arm before squirming away. "I told you before, no going into your office when there are so many people here. We're too loud." She'd dropped her voice to a whisper at the end.

I choked out a laugh before coming closer.

"You mean, *you're* too loud." And she was. I'd made her come enough times to know she couldn't help screaming, except that time on my porch when she bit her lip so hard she almost drew blood.

"All right, just look at this." She turned her laptop so I could see the screen. "You mentioned that you sponsor local events in the winter and fall, but this is a Halloween tour. Almost like part of a scavenger hunt. They do it across towns around the area. The Beach Pub could be a stop along the way."

I scanned the online sign up form. "Yes, but this is for pumpkin patches. I don't have any plants—only sand in the back."

"Not all of them, and they're not all real ones. Some establishments conjure them up. What if you buried a few in the sand? You could have the very first beach pumpkin patch. That could be cool. We could decorate the place a little, maybe have some photo ops and food specials. This tour seems to be gaining popularity, and you'd be Ocean Cove's first vendor to sign up. Maybe boost other surrounding businesses, too, like Maria's."

"I think the zeppoles and rainbow cookies I've bought since you've been here gave her a nice boost already." I laughed when she elbowed my side. "Is it expensive to sign up?" I tried to keep this place alive in the off-season, but it was a challenge. I'd still have to worry about winter, but a flutter of activity in October would be a godsend.

"Not really. They offer this cash prize at the end, and the participants have to visit each stop. It's not big enough that they all would do it, but it's good promotion to get your name out there, and I bet gets others to stop by, too. We just need to make the blurb for this place sound as awesome as it really is. I can take care of that if you'd like. What do you think?"

"I think let's do it. Wow, this is..." I was distracted by her beaming smile as she clicked to the next page. "Fantastic," I continued. "I've been trying to do something to attract people but never knew where to look."

She wrapped her arms around my neck and planted a kiss on my lips. "I think this is going to be great. I've looked up this tour in a few places, and I think this could be exactly what you need in the fall. Stick with me."

"Always," I whispered before I kissed her, close-mouthed but slow enough to draw a couple of glances in my periphery from staff passing by.

I'd stick with her as long as I could.

## CATERINA

"Why are you always so secretive?" I asked Joe, trying in vain to be indignant as I stood before him naked and dripping.

"Because that's how you plan a surprise. Why can't you just go with it?" He turned to hand me a towel with a raised brow, his sandy brown hair now almost black from the water and stuck to his forehead.

"Can't you give me a little hint?" I peered at him with doe eyes and a tiny pout.

"No, and stop being nosy." Even without contacts or glasses, I spotted Joe's snide grin.

I lost any words for a snappy comeback as my eyes roamed over his body. I followed the towel as he rubbed it down his arms, then back and forth along his back and...lower. The muscles along his shoulders rippled as his body moved, sucking all the coherent thought right out of my head. I'd never win an argument with him if he distracted me like this.

Since I'd arrived at his apartment on Saturday, we'd done everything together: eating, sleeping, showering. Not that I minded, by any means. In fact, we hadn't spent more than a couple of hours apart at a time, and he hadn't annoyed me once. I even missed him when he wasn't around, which didn't bode well for me when I pulled out of his driveway tomorrow morning. There was no denying we'd both let ourselves grow attached, which was wonderful, other than the fact we'd inevitably have to *de*tach. And soon.

"You can't ever stop staring at my ass, can you?"

I rolled my eyes and looked away, cinching my towel between my breasts as I tried to pretend I didn't get caught ogling.

"Hey, we have a little time." He turned around, backing me against the sink.

"Not that much, and I don't only stare at your ass." I narrowed my eyes at his crooked grin. "I stare at all of it," I whispered.

A heat flashed in his eyes. "I know. You're not exactly subtle." Instead of wrapping his towel around his waist, he let it almost fall as he turned and rubbed himself against me.

"Oh my God, Joe...are you giving me a lap dance at 6:30 in the morning?" I brought my hands to my heated cheeks, all of me flushed and hot even though I'd just taken a shower. I leaned against the counter as he turned to face me, cracking up as he gyrated his hips, his abs rippling as he ground against the terrycloth, letting it fall just enough to tease everything but stay covered.

A dirty grin split his mouth as he pinned me in place. "What's wrong, not enjoying the show?"

I skated my hand down his still damp chest before our mouths crashed together. Our lips and tongues tangled as if this were the last time we'd kiss. He was ridiculous, and *mine*.

It didn't feel right to claim him, but I hated the thought of him with anyone else. He wasn't the type of guy who enjoyed a string of mindless hookups, even before we'd met, so I wasn't concerned about that. But was it fair to be committed to someone you only saw once a month? For either of us? The joy from only moments ago evaporated like the droplets rolling down Joe's chest.

"Stop it," he whispered against my lips. "None of that yet, all right?"

"If not now, then when?" I raked my fingers through his wet hair, hating the same strain of despair reflected in his blue eyes.

He didn't reply before he unfastened my towel and let it pool at my feet. His gaze held mine as he leaned in for another kiss. This one slow but hungry, his tongue making long sweeps into my mouth as his hand moved between my legs.

Avoidance wouldn't help us, but I enjoyed every second.

JOE LEFT the restaurant in the early afternoon, and we spent the rest of the day traipsing around town, talking about everything except where I'd be tomorrow.

"This town is really nice," I said while getting lost in the crashing of the waves as we strolled up and down the beach. "It's going to be hard going back to city noise. It's all so peaceful here."

"It is. That's probably why I came here. I grew up in the city, but I knew, even then, it wasn't for me. This is where I belong." He cast a quick glance toward me, words unsaid dangling between us. He belonged here, that was obvious. The city was all I'd ever known, and I'd never considered the possibility of leaving. It was where I'd grown up and where my family was. As a child, I even dreamed about working in Manhattan and remembered how thrilled I'd been when I'd gotten my first job in Midtown. The world beyond the five boroughs had never occurred to me.

"You're lucky. Not many know without a doubt they're where they're supposed to be."

"True," he said, staring out into the distance. "But I never hated knowing that until this week."

When his gaze stumbled to mine, all I could do was nod.

"I want you with me every fucking day. And I know you can't be because you have a life and a job that you can't just leave, but I wish you could. I'm a selfish asshole, but I..." His Adam's apple bobbed as he swallowed. "I want you, and I'll take whatever I can get."

My eyes clenched shut when his hands framed my face. The conversation he kept putting off was here, but I wished I could run away from it like Joe had been doing until this point. He pressed a kiss to my forehead then my eyelids and cheeks before returning to my mouth. I felt every ounce of his affection and desperation as his mouth moved against mine, and I gave it right back to him. I hated knowing he belonged here, too. Because I didn't.

"Don't give up on us. Please. I want you; I want this. We can make it work. Please, Caterina."

I nodded, my words trapped behind the lump in my throat.

"Yes?" he asked as he gripped my face tighter.

My voice was sandpaper as I tried to keep it together. "I want this, too." I reached up to grip his wrists. "I'm not sure how it will work, but yes."

"We'll *make* it work. And you have to come back in October for all that Halloween stuff you have planned." Joe searched my face, hope illuminating his features and making him seem much younger than his thirty years. His gaze was expectant, almost pleading, and it felt like I'd already started to leave him. Things were changing between us before I'd even gotten into my car.

"That's true. Wouldn't be right if I didn't come back and make sure it all went off without a hitch."

The Beach Pub wasn't the only merchant I convinced to sign up for the Halloween Scavenger Hunt. Maria's Bakery, Boozy Spoons—the ice cream shop that pushed my inebriation over the edge at the festival—and even a couple of the hotels had been interested. I'd been searching for more opportunities like this one for the winter and found a few Christmas events. But I wanted to see how this all went first before I got ahead of myself. I'd started researching for Joe's sake, but getting the whole town involved for initiatives like this would not only help them in the off-season but maybe even increase their profits in the summer. I took what I'd learned about social media for my clients at work and tried to use it to Ocean Cove's advantage.

"There's no doubt it will. You're smart. And beautiful." He ran his thumb along my bottom lip. "And I want you to stay mine."

He'd never called me his outside of his bed before. I didn't want anyone but Joe, no matter where he was. I'd take whatever I could get, too.

"Because if another man in Brooklyn makes you mozzarella sticks, I'll lose my shit."

Raising my gaze to the playful yet determined scowl on his face, I brushed his lips with mine. "I promise; no one but you."

"Ready?" I called down my short hallway. I'd tried to plan the perfect last night for us, but, now, I wished we'd just stayed in my apartment under the covers. We weren't over, but I didn't know when she'd be in my bed again. That made me never want to let her out of it, but I wanted to do something special for her tonight, for us, to make tomorrow less awful.

"Well ..." Her heels clicked closer on the wood floor. "If I knew where I was going, I could get ready faster." I held back a laugh at her frustration. It would have been easy to just tell her, but watching her get so flustered as she attempted to figure it out was half the fun.

When she came into view, my greedy eyes drank up every perfect inch: her strapless black dress and matching heels, cherry red lips, and, *fuck me,* those glasses. I ran my hand along my jaw as my eyes shamelessly roamed her body.

Her glare softened as she climbed onto my lap. "I'm guessing this is okay?"

"You're so gorgeous, it hurts." That wasn't an exaggeration. My heart seized in my chest at how beautiful she was.

"You aren't so bad, either," she whispered before brushing her lips against my cheek. "I like you in a button-down." She pinched one of the buttons between her fingers. "You look like the hot businessman you are." She tilted her head, still circling the button with the pad of her thumb. "You didn't have to go to all this trouble just because I leave tomorrow. I would have been thrilled with the Shrimp Scampi from the pub and staying in for the rest of the night."

"I'm not taking you out because you're leaving. We're celebrating the best almost two weeks I've ever had." I tucked a lock of hair behind her ear. "And because it's a beginning, not an end. Understand?" I lifted a brow.

Her mouth flattened before she nodded. I still hated to see her go, but I meant every word I said. Even though she was leaving, we were only getting started.

Madeline's was the closest thing Ocean Cove had to an upscale restaurant and was known for the best seafood on the South shore. Since Caterina loved anything raised from the sea, I thought it would be perfect.

"Would you split oysters with me?" she pleaded when she lifted her gaze from the menu. "No one usually likes them but me, but I'm sure they're amazing here."

"I'll split them with you, but you know what they say about oysters." I took a long pull from my IPA.

She shook her head. "That's a myth."

"You'd better hope so. We're already one scream away from someone calling the cops." The corner of my mouth tipped into a smirk when I spied the twitch of her lips.

"Is it weird being in a restaurant when you own one?" She leaned her elbows onto the table and rested her head on her hand. "I would think it would be hard to just enjoy it."

"Not really." I swept my gaze around the room. "This place is about as different from the pub as you can get. We're pretty strict with kitchen hygiene, so I can spot when things are off easier, which, yes, I hate. But overall, I can detach. It's always been good whenever I come here."

"You mean your dates usually went well here?" Caterina teased as her eyebrows shot up.

"I've never been on a date here. This is where you take a girlfriend, and I never officially had one of those." I scooted my chair closer to the table and draped my hand over hers, sliding my thumb back and forth along the top of her wrist. "You have me in a way no one else ever has. You should know that by now."

"I do." She turned her hand over and laced our fingers together. "I haven't been myself since I arrived here. I'm different, and I like who I am when I'm with you. You have me in a way no one else ever has, too."

Things had been so natural with Caterina from the beginning. From the second we'd met, I'd had this odd urge to know everything about her and for her to know me. It wasn't just the insane chemistry, although we had plenty of that. After spending my entire life holding in or hiding what I thought made me weak, I could tell *her*. I could *show* her. Instead of the embarrassment I thought I'd feel, she'd lifted the weight off my chest enough for me to breathe. I was different around her, too. And I liked this better version of myself.

After dinner, we went for a walk around the restaurant. The dining area was surrounded by a large patio. There was an outdoor party with a DJ, and the closer we came, the louder the pulse of the base was under our feet. We couldn't talk much over the music, but I didn't mind the silence. I held her hand and led her around like we'd been a couple for years, not weeks.

The tempo slowed with the next song, and I stopped. Caterina turned to me with a wrinkled brow.

"What's wrong?"

"Dance with me."

"Here?" She scanned the area around us. "We're in the middle of nowhere."

I pulled her by the waist and grabbed her hand, threading our fingers before I brought our joined hands to my chest. We swayed back and forth to oddly poignant lyrics about fighting and not giving up. Whenever I wanted something, I didn't stop until I got it. And I'd never wanted anything or anyone more than the woman in my arms. I didn't doubt things were about to get complicated, and I'd have to fight, but I wouldn't give up. I couldn't.

"Doesn't matter where we are, Caterina." I ran a finger along her jaw. "Remember that."

## 32

## CATERINA

AFTER WE LEFT THE RESTAURANT, we ended up at the same beach he'd taken me to on our first date. As much as I tried to relax and have a nice time, a stopwatch ticked in my ears and echoed so loudly through my troubled brain, it was hard to concentrate on anything else.

"Did you have your people drop off food for us?" I asked him as I noticed a large bag resting on one of the blankets. The area was almost pitch black with only the light of the moon and the stars in the distance, but there were a couple of lanterns planted in the sand.

"It's nice to have people." He winked as he dug into the bag. "I thought we'd have dessert here."

"Dessert? I can't eat anything else." I rubbed a hand over my stomach, thankful for the stretchy material of my dress. "But I wouldn't refuse taking them on the road tomorrow." I cringed when Joe's face fell.

He nodded without lifting his head. "I can pack it for you. I'd planned on packing food for you anyway." My heart squeezed at his sad smile.

"Are there any rainbow cookies in there?" I sat up on my knees and sifted through the bag in an effort to shift the mood.

"Maybe." The corners of his mouth twitched. "Like I don't know my girl has a sweet tooth."

I stopped searching through the bag and lifted my head, not able to tell him how I felt at that moment but compelled with the burning need to show him. I tumbled back on the blanket and pulled him on top of me, my legs parting as Joe settled himself between them. This felt a lot more like home than my apartment would tomorrow. I threaded my hands into his hair and brought his lips to mine, savoring him for a second before dragging my tongue along the seam of his lips. They parted on a groan, and I let my tongue swirl around his mouth, memorizing his taste and the deep noises erupting from his throat when my nails dug into his back.

I whimpered when he broke the kiss and buried his head in the crook of my shoulder, trailing kisses down my neck and across my collarbone as his hand fisted the hem of my dress.

I dug my heels into the sand as his lips traveled all over my body, crying out when he dipped his tongue into my cleavage and licked along the swell of my breast.

"I told you oysters were a bad idea." His laugh vibrated against my cheek as he tugged my dress over my waist.

He kissed along the inside of my thigh, almost where I wanted him but far enough away to draw out a whimper of frustration.

"Joe," I croaked out and rolled up on my elbows, needing to do something with all the dread and frustration swirling around inside me.

"Caterina," he answered with a half-smile, his eyes hooded and dark.

"I need you." The words fell from my lips in a plea. This time, I couldn't wait until we got back to his apartment. I needed him inside me, filling the empty parts that I'd leave behind tomorrow.

Joe dragged my panties down my legs, flinging them somewhere behind him. I was already so wet, the warm breeze cooled my core. He ran his finger up and down my slit before he gave me one, long, and torturous lick, swirling his tongue around my clit before pulling it between his teeth. I spread my legs and pushed the back of his head closer. He lifted my hips and devoured me, his mouth relentless and rough as his hands traveled back up my body, yanking down my dress and cupping my breasts. It was as if I were Joe's last meal, and he wanted every last bite.

When the tremors started rippling up my legs, I tapped Joe on the shoulder for him to look up. When he met my eyes with swollen, wet lips and a hazy stare, I almost came from that sight alone.

"Please. I can't wait." My breaths were quick and shallow as I begged.

Joe straightened to dig his wallet out of his pants pocket and grabbed the foil packet inside. He dropped his pants and rolled on the condom before plunging inside me.

His thrusts were hard and shallow at first, working off the buildup from before, but then they slowed to a languid, torturous pace. He kissed me, deep and slow with his hand cradling the back of my head. Joe was making love to me. He had been all along, but the sadness and fear made the longing between us so strong it scratched at my throat. We'd been having sex since we'd met, but once he pulled out of me this time, I wouldn't be the same.

"No giving up, right?" he panted as he moved faster. I nodded as tremors rocked the lower half of my body. My mouth fell open as I fell over the edge. Joe muffled my screams with his mouth until he stiffened above me, grunting through his release until he slumped onto the blanket beside me.

"I like dessert on the beach," I whispered before kissing the top of his head.

He chuckled as he turned toward me, resting his chin on my shoulder. His eyes were glassy and distant, maybe feeling the same shift that I did.

"Want to stay for a while or go back home—to my apartment?" He winced at his slip. The word "home" now carried an unexpected sting.

"Let's go back. This is nice, but if I'm going to spend tonight naked and eating cookies, I'd rather have a little privacy." I crinkled my nose at Joe.

"You can eat cookies in my bed anytime you want. Especially naked." He leaned over to give me a soft kiss, his lips lingering on mine and saying so many things without any words.

You're supposed to feel a little sad when vacation ends, but it's not supposed to break your heart.

## 33

## CATERINA

I STUFFED the last of my clothes into my suitcase and took one last glance around his apartment. It was funny how my stay here felt so normal. I'd almost had a little hope that we'd get sick of each other, and my long drive home wouldn't feel this ... heavy. I'd been dragging from the time I'd gotten up this morning and doing everything in slow motion because I couldn't find it in me to go any faster.

Joe was up and already at the restaurant when I'd awoke. Dominic couldn't open today, and no one else had keys. I trudged down the stairs with my suitcase, trying, with no success, to go any faster. I opened the front door and found Joe packing something into my back seat.

"What are you doing?" I asked as I came closer.

"Good morning." He pecked my lips as if it were just any other day. "You should have texted me when you were ready. I would have come up to carry your suitcase down."

"I'm fine. I carried it up three flights of stairs at the Anchor. No worries." Joe took the suitcase from my arms and slipped it into my trunk.

"I didn't know The Beach Pub had porter service." I crossed my arms and leaned against the back of my car.

Joe rubbed his neck and came closer. "We're *full* service, Ms. Longo. Complete with take-out window." He motioned inside my car. "I packed some food for you and slipped an iced coffee in the cup holder, so you don't have to stop on the road."

"That was very thoughtful. Thank you." My voice cracked as I closed the tiny distance between us and ran my finger along the collar of his polo shirt, blinking away the tears threatening to spill from my eyes.

"I told you, no tearful goodbyes. It's not like we won't talk later on or see each other soon, right?"

"Then why do I feel like we're Danny and Sandy from *Grease*?" My gaze slid to his, and I waved my hand at him. "You're a guy, so you probably have no idea what I'm talking about."

"I'm a guy with a mother and sister who watched that damn movie on a loop. I think my father still has a video of me at my kindergarten graduation singing a cleaned-up version of 'Greased Lightning'."

"Please find that video for me." I cupped his cheek as he laughed, turning his head to kiss my palm.

"I'll see what I can do. So, you're about to tell me this was the best summer ever and how it's not fair you have to go away."

"Not bad. And you're going to say how this isn't an end."

"And I'd be right." He grabbed me by the waist and pressed a kiss to my forehead.

"If you remember, it wasn't so easy when summer was over. Their *beginning* didn't start until almost halfway into the movie."

"Because Danny Zuko was a dumb kid who didn't know

what he wanted or how to fight for it. I know exactly what I want." He framed my face, his thumbs gliding over my cheekbones. "I want *you*. I want you more than I've ever wanted anyone else, and bridges and highways won't get in my way."

I bit the inside of my cheek and nodded. I wanted him, too, but was afraid if I tried to speak, I'd lose the battle with the tears threatening to spill down my cheeks. I covered his mouth with mine instead, our lips crashing together in a bruising kiss. I fisted his T-shirt before our kiss slowed, dropping my head into his chest to breathe him in one more time.

"I'd better get going," I whispered, hating that I couldn't delay the inevitable anymore.

Joe cupped my chin and eased my gaze to his before reaching behind me to open my door.

"See ya," he whispered with a sad smile.

I kissed him one more time before slowly pulling away and sliding into the driver's seat.

"See ya, Zuko."

His shoulders jerked with a sad chuckle. "Drive safe."

I nodded before he shut the door. After I started the engine and took off, I spied Joe in my rearview mirror, his hands stuffed into his pockets as he watched me go. I blinked away an errant tear and focused on the road ahead, not what I was leaving behind, no matter how I wanted to stop the car and make a U-turn.

I took the long way out of town, remembering all the side streets Joe had showed me. I grew more agitated as I headed closer to the highway and farther away from him. One of the older hotels at the last traffic light before the entrance caught my eye. It reminded me of the Anchor with the vibrantly loud outdated colors and flashing neon "no vacancy" sign.

A shiver skated along my limbs as an all too poetic realization hit me. Joe and I had "no vacancy" for anything. We were already booked to capacity. How would there be room for one more commitment? Especially a commitment that lived three hours away.

Joe and I were perfect together in Ocean Cove, in his apartment, living carefree on the sand. But once I went back home, was there room for each other in our lives? Our *real* lives—not the fantasy we'd lived out for the past couple of weeks.

We'd try. We'd hurt, and possibly never get back the magic we enjoyed all this time. But the rotten feeling that filtered through me from my head down to my toes didn't feel like fleeting magic. It felt a lot like fate. And like my car was headed in the wrong direction.

I PULLED into my assigned parking spot at my apartment complex after three and a half hours with no stops. Exhausted, cranky, and bone-sad, I balanced my suitcase, laptop bag, and the large insulated bag Joe packed for me until I unlocked my apartment door. I put the food in the fridge first, all five tins plus a box of cookies, and headed to the scene of the crime.

Scanning the living room for the first time after I flew out of here two weeks ago, everything looked the same but unfamiliar. I glared at my once beloved couch, angry I couldn't lie on it without being disgusted.

"Well, look who decided to come home."

I swiveled my head toward Trent, leaning against my living room wall.

"Ugh, I'd forgotten about you." I kicked off my sandals and plopped into the recliner. The furniture needed a good cleaning, followed by some holy water. Thanks to Trent, I had a long afternoon of tossing sheets and scrubbing, and just looking in his direction exhausted me.

"Well, that's pretty obvious. I've been ready to talk, and you've been gallivanting at the shore."

A humorless laugh tumbled from my lips. "Ready to talk? Not entertaining more houseguests?" I raised an eyebrow and leaned back. "I told you to get out. I gave you plenty of time to pack your stuff and leave by the time I got back."

"I said I was sorry."

"No." I shook my head slowly. "You didn't."

"That's because you didn't give me a chance."

Rage boiled in my gut at how, even now, he was blowing off what he'd done as a flippant mistake, not a deliberate act of blatant disrespect.

"Look, Cat, we can make this work. I'm headed to the Mets game tonight with some clients, but we can talk about this when I get back later." He grabbed his keys off the rack before pausing to search my gaze. "What were you doing there after your friends came back? I figured you went to your mother's house, but she said you were still on vacation."

He didn't believe me when I'd left or when I'd stayed or that I'd really meant to get the hell out of my apartment. To him, I was good old reliable Cat. The woman who'd never push him or make a fuss about anything. I was a doormat and an easy means to an end.

I replied with a shrug as he looked me over. Little did he know about the glorious loophole I'd found, thanks to his indifference. His name was on the lease, but he'd never made it to the landlord's office to sign it. With the absence of a signature or security deposit on his behalf, I could legally throw him out.

I was almost glad he wouldn't leave on his own. For the first time, being underestimated was fun.

"I enjoyed myself so much, I decided to use my mountain of earned vacation time and stay for a few days longer. Nothing like a little ocean air and sand to give you clarity." Or a beautiful man with a huge heart to open your eyes to all that was missing—and wrong—in your life. But I wouldn't give Trent the satisfaction of knowing about Joe. Like everything else about me now, it was none of his business.

"Knowing you, a vacation by yourself would be a dream." I swore I caught an eye roll as he unlocked the door. How long had he been a dick, and how stupid had I been to stay?

"It was. Have fun at the game." I crossed my legs and waved. Trent shut the door behind him without another word.

I pulled my phone out of my purse and dialed my cousin.

"Cat? You have some explaining to do, little cuz!"

"What the hell are you talking about, Pete?" He owned a hardware store down the block from my apartment and worked as a locksmith after hours. All of my family was scattered around Brooklyn, mostly in Bay Ridge, which had its great points and its awful points. For the quick favor I needed, it was great, but the way extended family immersed themselves in my business, not so much.

"Running away on vacation by yourself was enough of a shock, but I saw Claire in the store the other day, and she told me you shacked up with some guy you met over there. No one could believe it. Did you get drugged or something?" I bristled at his hearty laughter.

I cringed at the universal reputation I had for a boring existence. This also meant my mother had found out I'd been staying with a strange man before I'd had the chance to explain. She couldn't ground me in my thirties, but I was still in a load of trouble. None of us in this family ever grew up to the point of escaping our crazy parents' rage.

Claire and her loose lips were dead.

"I promise, I'll tell you all about it, but I need you to do me a solid first. How fast can you come over and change the locks?"

"What's wrong? Did that douche hurt you?" Pete roared so loud I had to stretch the phone away from my ear. My family had never been crazy about Trent. He had this dry sense of humor that sometimes came off as arrogance, but I used to think he was cute and funny. How long ago that was, I couldn't recall, but I'd beat myself up about it later. I had more pressing matters at hand.

"Before I left for the shore, I caught him with another woman in our apartment. I told him it was over and to get out, but he won't leave. He just went out for the night, and I'm stuffing his clothes and whatever else he has into garbage bags to leave in the lobby. While he's out, I need a quick—"

"Say no more. I'll be there in twenty."

"Wait, can you ask Aunt Nancy if she has any of that homemade industrial strength cleaner and an extra pair of gloves? I need to scrub down my furniture." I peeked into the hallway closet and thanked God for the new bedding I'd bought last month that was still in the packaging. The sheets were going down the trash compactor, but I would salvage my furniture.

"You got it. And you better start talking when I get there." Pete hung up. For a forty-three-year-old married man with two young kids, he loved gossip a little too much.

I made my way into the kitchen to gather some garbage bags when my phone buzzed in my hand.

**Joe:** *Just wanted to see if you got home yet. And tell you that I miss you like fucking crazy already.*

After a shitty welcome home, seeing Joe's name flash

across my screen was like having a cozy, sexy blanket draped over me.

> **Caterina:** *I'm home. And I miss you like crazy, too. I'm disinfecting my apartment now, but what time do you get off work tonight? I'll call you.*

> **Joe:** *Probably late. The place is packed today. But call me whenever you want. And I mean it. Whenever.*

> **Caterina:** *Four a.m. it is ;)*

> **Joe:** *I'd still answer if it was you.*

A smile curved my lips as I stretched my arms over my head. Things would change now that I was home, and I'd start by taking out the trash.

## 34

## CATERINA

"Someone came in this morning and told me the video in our story was cool. I had no clue what the hell they were talking about until they showed me their Instagram." The deep rumble of Joe's laugh echoed in my ear.

I cringed and drew back in my office chair.

"Sorry about that. I logged on and posted something last night before I went to bed and forgot to tell you. But hey, it worked!"

"Of course, it did. My girl is a marketing genius. It's the last weeks of summer, and we need all the business we can get. Still can't come out on Labor Day?"

In the month since I'd been back, getting into a normal groove was kicking my ass. We had a campaign launch coming up the first week in September that took up most of my days, and, as we got closer, my nights and weekends too. The timing of the launch barred anyone on my team from making Labor Day vacation plans. I knew that at the beginning of the summer, but now that it cost me three days with Joe, I wasn't so okay with it.

"No, I can't. I'm hoping not to work the whole weekend, but it's going to be a bitch. I would if I could."

"I'm sorry you're going to miss the Labor Day party we're having. And my bed is lonely as hell. I'm not used to having all the covers anymore."

"I don't steal the covers."

"Please, you almost hog the whole bed. I never minded since you were always on top of me, anyway. Like I wish you were right now."

"Joe," I groaned, my eyes clenching shut as I wished the same thing. "Don't get all sexy when I'm spending the afternoon going through spreadsheets."

"Don't get all sexy?" His husky laugh made my heart squeeze. "I'm not sure if I could help it. Just comes out, you know?"

"Don't I know it." I rubbed away the ache in my chest, missing him so much it was painful. "Try to save it for later." Joe still had moves across the distance, but phone sex depressed me. It only made me yearn for the real thing and pissed me off about a wasted long weekend even more.

"Come on, Cat. I'm starving and not eating at my desk again." My friend Amy tapped me on the shoulder. "Let's get some air for a change."

I turned to her with a nod and held up a finger. She nodded as she mouthed *boyfriend*. Not wanting to explain the semantics, I nodded.

"Listen, I'm going to get something for lunch. My friend is forcing me out of my office. Talk later?"

"Of course. I'll hold in the sexy until then."

"I'm sure all the women still notice."

"Doesn't matter if they do or if they don't. I don't notice anyone but you." His voice dipped low as the air shifted between us, even across the miles. Even though I was plagued with daily doubts of how we'd get this to work, the one thing I never questioned was how Joe felt about me and about us. He was all in, and so was I. Figuring out how to be all in yet so far apart was the taxing part. "Get out of the office and eat."

I held the phone for a couple of seconds after he hung up. He kept asking when I could come out to see him, but I never had an answer. I hated the hope followed by disappointment laced in his tone whenever he'd ask.

"It's been almost a month, and you haven't told me anything except that you broke up with Trent and met someone at the shore," Amy told me as she popped open her container of salad. We sat at a table in Pershing Square near Grand Central Station. Eating outside in the sunshine reminded me of Joe's outdoor patio. *Everything* reminded me of Joe. I'd sworn I'd spotted him on the train three times this week. A guy with the same light brown hair and profile made my heart jump, although, my head knew it wasn't him. It sank when he'd turned around and confirmed it.

"Trent and I broke up right before I left. It's why I left early," I explained as I dug through my salad for the two pieces of avocado I'd asked for but couldn't find. "He did something I couldn't forgive, so I told him to get out by the time I got back home. But he wouldn't leave."

"Was he sorry and wanting to work it out?" Amy frowned. She didn't know Trent as the douche he really was. She only knew the cordial, yet aloof man, I'd taken to the company holiday party.

I choked out a laugh as I twisted the cap off of my bottle of water.

"Sorry that he was losing a two-bedroom apartment in walking distance of the subway station? Yes, very sorry. Hurting me? He couldn't have cared less. While he was out, I stuffed all his belongings in garbage bags and had my cousin change the locks."

Her jaw dropped. "I'm in awe. Good for you, Cat."

"Don't be in awe. Things should have ended long before he—" I skipped over the blow job on my couch. My hands were raw from scrubbing that damn thing every day, and it still seemed tainted.

"I left the bags in the lobby with the building's security guard, who ended up calling the cops to have him removed from the premises. I was able to watch the whole thing on my intercom camera feed." Still, I wished I'd asked the landlord for a copy of the tape. That was great TV.

"Anyway, Joe owns a restaurant in Ocean Cove. We met the night I arrived, and, long story short, we've been together ever since. I stayed with him an extra few days after my friends went home."

Amy grinned. "Judging by the hazy look in your eyes, I guess things are still hot and heavy."

"Well, we said we'd give long-distance a try, but I have no clue when we'll be able to see each other."

"Why can't you go see him this weekend and work from there? All the other managers do it."

"That's why the other managers are hated," I said before taking a long swig of water.

"Some, yes, but that's not why. Plus, I know you'd work from a gas station if you had to and still get more done than all of us. You could make it a long weekend whenever you wanted."

I nodded. That did sound amazing. It was hard to reconcile the fun-loving Caterina from the shore and the nailed-to-her-office-chair Cat. I used to think I was working toward a goal; now, it just seemed as if I was missing out on all the important things.

"Anyway, show me a picture." She propped her elbow on the table and held out her hand.

I unlocked my phone and swiped past the picture of the selfie Joe took of the both of us in bed before I handed it to Amy. We were covered by the sheets, but that one was only for my eyes.

Amy gasped as she scrolled though the pictures. "You spent two weeks with *him* and still came back? He's *hot*, Cat. You guys look amazing together."

A smile touched my lips. We were amazing together when we were actually together.

I snapped out of my trance when Amy dropped my phone on the table.

"What? Oh, the one of us in bed?" I cringed and took back my phone.

"No." She giggled and covered her eyes. "The video."

"The video?" I snatched back my phone and glanced at the still of the video on my screen. It was Joe, in a towel, mid-lap dance encore. When did he do this?

"You didn't know it was there?" She gaped at me as I shook my head in disbelief.

"Absolutely not."

She was still laughing when I punched out a text.

**Caterina:** *I'm going to kill you.*

**Joe:** *??*

**Caterina:** *Don't play dumb, Magic Mike. When did you do that?*

**Joe:** *You just found it now?*

**Caterina:** *No, my friend did. She wanted to scroll through my vacation pictures and stumbled upon my naked boyfriend dancing with a towel. So, thanks. Now I can't look her in the eye for the rest of the day.*

**Joe:** *Your BOYFRIEND misses the shit out of you, right now. You must be seven shades of red.*

It wasn't until he capped the word *boyfriend* that I realized my slip. I didn't want anyone else, and I didn't want *him* with anyone else, but neither of us had used the words before. In fact, I avoided them when I could because I was afraid of getting my own hopes up. Or, if I was honest with myself, referring to any kind of commitment between us upset me because it wasn't the commitment I wanted. I was in love, plain and simple. The timing made it all sound crazy, and that's exactly what we were—crazy in love with separate lives too far away to be shared.

"Cat, are you all right? You looked a little distant, just now."

I nodded, going back to the still of the video with a smile creeping on my lips.

"Yeah, I'm okay. It was a great two weeks, but we're having a hard time extending vacation to real life."

"As sad as you look right now, I'm jealous as *hell* of you." Amy chuckled. "The way he was looking at you in some of those pictures... I've never seen you so lit up before." She patted my hand. "I'm sure you guys will work it out."

I shrugged, not nearly as sure but hoping she was right.

I JERKED out of a restless sleep around two o'clock in the morning when my phone buzzed under my pillow.

"Hi, Joe." My mouth stretched with a yawn.

"I'm sorry. I shouldn't have called you so late."

"Or early, I get up at five, so it's all relative." My voice was hoarse and full of sleep even though I couldn't get any. "I don't care what time it is when you call."

"What's wrong?"

"Nothing." I answered a bit too quickly to be convincing.

"Come on, baby. Talk to me."

"I'm okay," I lied. I was weak. I promised I'd try, but I was failing in every way. I still couldn't shake my obligations at work right now. All I wanted was to take off for the weekend and be with Joe, causing my frustration to rise. I was overdramatic even in my own head, but I still felt hopeless and helpless.

"I just...I really miss you."

"I miss you too, beautiful. So much, you can't imagine. My pillow still smells a little like you, so I pretend you're still in bed with me."

"You haven't changed the sheets since I left? That's gross, Joe."

His laugh boomed in my ear. "I changed the sheets. They got too much of a workout when you were here, so I didn't have a choice. But I left the pillowcase."

"Does it work?"

"Eh, not really. My pillow doesn't hog three quarters of the bed."

"Again, I do *not* hog the bed."

"*Again*, yes, you do. But having those warm and naked curves all over me makes it worth it." His playful, gruff voice triggered a hot shiver. "Why I always ... woke you up."

"I remember." I never got much sleep in Joe's bed, but I'd still had a hard time sleeping in my own since I'd come back.

"And I can bury my head in the pillow, but it's not the same as when I bury my head between your legs. So, it's a pretty subpar substitute."

"Is that so? I'm sorry to hear that."

"Without you coming in my mouth, it sucks."

My cheeks heated as I shook my head. Sweet and dirty, that was the Joe I knew, and the Joe I wanted so much it hurt.

"You have such a filthy mouth. And I miss it so much."

"Pretend you're here with me."

"What like phone sex, again? I don't know how good I'd be this tired. The FaceTime with me in the shower this morning wasn't enough?"

That involved a wall mount for my phone and a lot of maneuvering to get everything into the right spot, but it was worth every bit of hassle and then some.

"That was amazing," he rasped. "But I don't think phone sex is what we need right now. Lay your head on my chest."

I turned on my side, imagining resting my cheek on Joe's hard chest instead of my therapeutic neck pillow.

"My finger is running up and down your back. Do you know you fall asleep in less than five minutes when I do that?"

"I do?" I lifted my head off of the pillow.

"Yes. That and playing with your hair but, sometimes, after ... you have a lot of tangles." I grinned, nodding in agreement although I was alone in the dark of my bedroom. "But the tip of my finger up and down your back always does the trick. You slump against me, and you're out like a light."

"I wish you could do that now." My heavy eyes welled up before I sucked in a breath and blinked it away. "I can't sleep very well these days."

"I wish I could, too. I wish … I wish for a lot of things. And you're at the top of my list."

"So are you." I relaxed, picturing Joe's finger moving up and down my back in my mind's eye, almost feeling his chest rise and fall under mine. I thought of strong arms, a crooked grin, and the sexiest blue eyes I'd ever seen. If I tried hard enough, I could see the man who knew me for only a short time but better than I knew myself—the man I wanted to be mine.

## 35

## CATERINA

"Is it tomorrow yet? Are you sure you just can't call out sick or something early?"

I giggled into my pillow, shaking my head at Joe's adorable impatience. Deciding to try not to be the office doormat anymore, I told my boss that I would work remotely for Labor Day weekend. She was fine with it, but Sharon, the other manager on my team was not and didn't hold back showing it. While I put in all those needlessly long hours, Sharon made sure to never linger past six and took our new remote policy a bit too far at times, going "dark" as we all liked to joke for the day while she was supposed to be working from home. We were both on the same level, but she had five years seniority and wasn't afraid to use it whenever she could.

"Do you know me at all, Joe? I've never called in sick unless I had no choice. I would have had perfect attendance in high school had it not been for my stupid appendix almost bursting in senior year," I whined. That's always bothered me.

"Sometimes, I feel so bad for you when you were a kid. I can see you crying to your mother to be allowed to go to school like my sister would even though she had a fever."

"I can't help the way I'm wired." I rolled out of bed and rubbed my eyes. Joe's hours were getting later, and his phone calls came right around the time I had to start getting ready for work. He might have been miles away, but he was still part of my everyday life. The excitement over seeing him for the first time in over a month sparked a glimmer of hope in my chest that maybe, just maybe, we could make this work. "Love me or leave me."

My sleepy eyes bulged when I realized what I'd said. Yes, I loved him, but I didn't want us to say it over the phone at five o'clock in the morning. It seemed cheap, and even though we both had whiplash from how fast we were going, that, at least, shouldn't be rushed.

The long beat of silence between us unnerved me a little.

"I'm definitely not leaving you." The familiar creak of his bed as he settled in made me impatient, too. I should be there, and, in only a couple of days, I would be. "I haven't tasted your pussy in so long," Joe groaned. "I think I'm going to do that the second I see you."

"Really? I'm meeting you at the restaurant. You'll do that with all your customers there?" I crossed my legs, wishing that second was now.

"I have an office, remember? With a couch. There's no way I'm waiting until we close. I can almost taste you right now." His gravelly whisper took me back weeks ago, to those few wonderful days that were probably the best of my entire life.

"Is that all you want me for? A Labor Day sex marathon?" I laughed, expecting to hear him laugh with me but was met with another long minute of nothing.

"I want you for everything, and you should know that. I miss you more than I've ever missed anyone. It's like a limb is missing or something. You were only here for a short time, but I can't remember what it was like before you." Joe yawned, and my lips tingled to kiss him goodnight.

"I know the feeling well. Crazy, isn't it?"

"That's the thing. It's not crazy at all. Go to work. I'll text when I get up."

He was right, the crazy part was that it *wasn't* crazy. In fact, nothing ever seemed more right.

"YOU'VE GOT to be kidding me." I glared at Amy, not wanting to believe what she said.

"Nope, Sharon called Emma this morning to say that she's so sorry, but she had to leave on a family emergency for the weekend. Who calls their boss on a Thursday to call out for an entire weekend? Want to bet the emergency is on Long Beach Island? Emma is pissed beyond belief, but now we have to come in Friday and maybe Saturday to split the work she would have done for the weekend."

"And we have to all be in on Monday, so any Labor Day plans we had ..." I couldn't say it out loud.

"Gone." She plopped into my office chair as her head fell back. "She's a sneak. Why can't anyone see this? You've been picking up her slack for months."

I was partially responsible for Sharon. I'd made it too easy for her to come and go with as little effort as possible because what else did I have to do but work? I had a relationship I didn't care enough about at the time to worry if I had to stay late. Now, I wanted to spit nails right after I spit at her.

I'd thought about what Joe said this morning all day, how he didn't remember how life was before I came into The

Beach Pub. Things were complicated like I knew they would be, but sitting here at my desk, I wasn't as satisfied as before I'd left. I loved my job and my clients, and, while this launch was a lot of work, it was exciting. But, unlike before I made the hasty drive to Ocean Cove, I wanted more now and couldn't go back.

## 36

# JOE

"CATERINA, it's okay. I mean, it sucks—a lot—but I understand. Just makes the next time we see each other that much better." I tried to mask how disappointed I really was and not make her feel even worse. After a month without her, I was ready to lose it but would keep myself in check until we hung up. Then, I'd take it out on the punching bag in the makeshift gym we'd made in the corner of the restaurant basement or have an extra shot of something at closing time when her absence always gnawed at me the most.

"I'm sorry, Joe. I miss you so damn much. I hate that I—"

"Stop it. I miss you too. We knew with the jobs we have this would happen sometimes. It's just life, is all. The important thing is that we keep trying, right? Maybe it's better you didn't come."

"Why?" I smiled, thinking of her stiffening in her office chair as her guard went up. *Fuck, I missed her.*

"Because I wouldn't have let you out of my bed. You wouldn't have gotten any work done, and poor Dom would have dealt with one of our busiest weekends all by himself.

Once I got between your legs, there would be zero chance of me coming up for air."

"I actually believe you." She laughed before groaning in frustration. "But I still can't see anything good about not being with you. I miss you so much, it's making me crazy."

"The way I look at it, being this miserable about not seeing each other may not feel all that lucky right now, but it is."

"So both of us feeling like shit right now is lucky?" I pictured her full lips drooping in a frown. I hadn't tasted them in a month, but they were unforgettable.

"Yes, it is."

"Did you just use your *boss* voice on me?" She always teased me about my stern tone when I spoke to my employees but loved it when I used it on her in private.

"It means what we have is worth fighting for." A long silence hovered between us. I knew when she left, it would be tough, but we were too good together to give up.

"I better get back. I still have a mountain of work to go back to."

"Yeah, this place is crazy right now, too. But hey, don't be upset. We hit our first bump in the road, that's all this is."

"Yep, just a bump," she halfheartedly agreed, making me wish I could jump through the phone and pull her into my arms to make her believe it.

"I'll call you tonight. It may be late, or early tomorrow." We already had customers waiting to be seated today, and last night, the bar was packed. I wished I could drop everything and go see her, but it wasn't possible. Still, the itch to do it in the first place spoke volumes about how I felt about her.

"Don't work too hard." I heard the smile in her voice.

"Right back at you." We said goodbye and hung up. I left my office and headed to the dining area, even more crowded now since I'd stepped away to take Caterina's call. This was what I wanted and what I'd been working toward for the past two years. I should've been happy, and I was, but the sour pang in my gut wouldn't let me fully enjoy it.

"Hey." Dom smacked my arm, startling me out of my trance. "When does Caterina get here tomorrow?"

"She doesn't. I just spoke to her, and she can't get away from the office this weekend, after all." I lifted a sad shoulder. Pretending to be upbeat for Caterina was taxing, and it almost felt good to wallow in front of Dominic. I nodded a hello to a regular customer over his shoulder and tried to get my head back to where it was supposed to be, but my heart wasn't in it today. It was stuck in Brooklyn with Caterina.

"Sorry, man. Maybe you can go see her next week. I could handle the straggler rush."

"Maybe, but I've taken advantage enough already. I can't keep leaving this place with you on a whim."

"A whim?" An incredulous laugh fell from his lips. "You look like someone killed your puppy right now. Caterina isn't a whim to you, that's pretty obvious. I'm happy to help you when I can."

"Because you know I'm going to owe you big in the off-season." I forced out a chuckle, but Dominic only shook his head.

"When you're that sick over someone, you need to make it work." He turned to head back into the kitchen.

I *was* sick over her because I loved her. It was a first, and, if this month had taught me anything, she would be the last. Whatever I had planned, for myself or for this place, I always imagined it with her by my side, or else it was hollow, exactly like I felt today.

## 37

# CATERINA

*A WEEK LATER*

**Caterina:** *Thank you. That was very sweet but you didn't have to do that.*

**Joe:** *Do what? Send soup to my sick girlfriend? Even though she wouldn't let me drive up and take care of her.*

**Caterina:** *I'm fine, Joe. Weak and a little woozy but fine.*

All week long, Joe and I planned for what I hoped would be a romantic weekend in my apartment. I couldn't wait for him to get here until I started throwing up on Thursday, and Friday. Today was the first time in three days I'd managed to swallow anything without the threat of it coming back up.

**Joe:** *I still don't see why I couldn't come see you this*

*weekend. I haven't seen you in so fucking long. I don't
care if you're throwing up.*

**Caterina:** *I care. For two reasons.*

**Joe:** *I can't wait to hear what they are.*

**Caterina:** *One, I don't want you catch this stomach
plague I have. And two, I kinda don't want to ruin the
image of me tan and naked on the beach with you on
the night before I left. The putrid way I look now
would totally erase that from your memory.*

**Joe:** *A lobotomy wouldn't erase that, baby. I hate that
I'm not with you this weekend.*

**Caterina:** *Trust me. I hate that, too.*

**Joe:** *Dominic's uncle lives in Bay Ridge and swears
by the soup at Rino's. I thought you could use that
more than a flower delivery.*

**Caterina:** *They do have good soup. I usually get
minestrone, but the chicken soup is perfect. I still have
to go slow on the noodles.*

**Joe:** *My chicken soup is better.*

**Caterina:** *I'm sure it is.*

**Joe:** *I'd make it for you right now if I was there.*

**Joe:** *I'd give anything to be there.*

**Caterina:** *I know, baby.*

**Joe:** *Baby??*

**Caterina:** *Yeah, so? You call me that all the time.*

**Joe:** *But, you never called ME that before ;)*

**Caterina:** *I'm dehydrated and, like I said, woozy.*

**Joe:** *You like me, don't you?*

I loved him, but wouldn't tell him until he was in front of me. Although, when the soup delivery arrived, enough emotion swept over my weak self to want to call him and blurt it out. Texting was safer in the condition I was in.

**Caterina:** *I hate that you aren't here, too. But the soup makes it feel like you are.*

**Joe:** *Eat, and get some rest.*

**Caterina:** *I will. And I do like you. There, I admit it.*

**Joe:** *Good, because I like you, too. I like you so damn much.*

ANOTHER WEEK *LATER*

**Caterina:** *I hate hurricanes. Are you guys okay?*

**Joe:** *We're fine. I doubt it's going to get as bad as they're saying. We're all boarded up, generators charged.*

**Caterina:** *Maybe I should have attempted the trip?*

**Joe:** *No, I don't want you driving in this. I wish you were here with me, though. Storms can be fun with the right company.*

**Caterina:** *Oh really, who's your company now?*

**Joe:** *Dom. Not fun.*

**Caterina:** *We need to start decorating for the tour soon.*

**Joe:** *Can you come in next week?*

**Caterina:** *I may have a work event on Saturday, but I'll see if I can get out of it.*

**Joe:** *We have to run out of bad luck sooner or later, right?*

**Caterina:** *I can take my phone and run in the shower for FaceTime, that would cheer us both up.*
**Joe:** *It would, but I want to see you in person. I want my mouth and my hands all over you. The longer I have to wait the more you better brace yourself.*

Rain pelted my window as I stared at the blackened sky. At least Joe and I were both in the same storm together. The straws I grasped at to feel close to him were becoming more pathetic as time went on.

## ANOTHER WEEK *LATER*

**Caterina:** *This blows.*

**Joe:** *You're in a suite at Yankee Stadium fully loaded with food and booze. That drop you hear is my heart bleeding for you.*

**Caterina:** *It's a client outing. And maybe it doesn't blow that much, but I'd rather be with you.*

If I had a dollar for every time one of us said "I wish you were here" or "I'd rather be with you" during all the weekends since I've been back, I wouldn't have to work because I'd be rich. The changing leaves taunted me. They were a marker of how long it had been since the summer and how long I'd gone without seeing Joe. We still spoke all the time, but nothing was good enough except seeing Joe in the flesh. And neither of us could figure out how to make that happen.

**Joe:** *I know. I'd rather be with you than do anything else. We'll work it out.*

**Caterina:** *You're always so sure.*

**Joe:** *About you? Always.*

As ridiculous as it was considering the time we'd spent together and the time we'd spent apart, I was sure about him, too. It was the whole bridging the separate lives thing dragging me down with uncertainty.

**Caterina:** *As long as we keep trying, right?*

**Joe:** *I'm never going to stop trying.*

**Joe:** *And neither are you.*

## CATERINA

"You're in a good mood today," Amy said after our last conference call of the day ended. "Is Joe coming this weekend?"

"No, I'm going to see him. Only he doesn't know it yet." I grinned, almost feeling my cheeks crack from the excitement. After all the anguish of another month of failed plans, this time, I wasn't giving the universe the opportunity to screw us over again. In fact, my car was already loaded with Halloween decorations I'd picked out for the tour. My plan was to take the subway home, grab the bag I'd already packed, and drive to Ocean Cove. Three hours of traffic alone didn't bother me in the least, especially since this time, I wouldn't be running away in a rage. Knowing where I was heading, and who I was headed to, excited me so much my knee bobbed like I was an impatient kid on Christmas.

"Oh, sorry," Amy gasped when she knocked over my shopping bag from this afternoon. "Wait a minute." She laughed as she picked up the spilled contents of the bag. "What is *this*?"

Covering my eyes, I yanked the purchase I'd made on my

lunch hour out of Amy's hands. It'd been two long months without Joe, and I wanted to give him the best reunion I could. After sifting through a sea of lace and G-strings, I settled on a crotchless, barely-there one piece. He could appreciate the whole package without having to worry about peeling anything off to get inside me.

"Now, that's what I call good weekend plans!" She dropped the shopping bag on my desk and turned to leave. "See you on Monday." She stilled and glanced at me over her shoulder. "Maybe."

A laugh, carefree for a change, bubbled out of me when I noticed my phone buzzing across the desk. Smiling at Joe's photo on my screen, I snatched it up and pressed the green button, so giddy that in only a few hours I'd see him for real that it was pathetic.

"Hey, Joe. What's—"

"Hey, baby. I didn't know if you were still at work, so I called your cell. I have to leave tonight, and I'm not sure when I'll get the chance to call you."

I stilled as my stomach sank to the floor under my desk. Aside from the crushing disappointment, Joe's short and flustered tone had me frozen with worry. "What's wrong?"

"My grandmother took a bad fall. She's fine, only a few stitches, but I'm the closest one since she lives in New Jersey. My mother and sister are coming down late tomorrow afternoon, but someone needs to keep an eye on her until then. We're all staying until Sunday night. Eighty-five-years-old and still lives alone. She's stubborn as hell."

"So, that's where you get it from." I tried to make my voice sound light, but I was sure Joe could hear the crack at the end. Hopefully, he was too distracted to notice.

"Like you should talk," he teased. "Are you okay? You sound a little off."

"Nope," I answered shrilly, my effort to sound cheery unsuccessful. "All is fine. You're a good grandson." My eyes landed on the bag of fancy underwear on my desk, and, although this cancellation was no one's fault, I still wanted to put my fist through the shiny material and tissue paper and forget how all my joy had disintegrated in a matter of minutes.

"When she's settled, I'll call you. We need to talk about what we have to do for the tour."

I fought the urge to scream as I was reminded of all the pumpkins and light up spider webs I'd piled into my trunk last night. I wanted to do this with him. I wanted to *be* with him. Yes, I knew long-distance would be difficult but not impossible.

"Sure." My gaze wandered around my empty office, feeling more alone than I had in months.

"Caterina, what's going on? You don't sound like—"

"I'm fine. I just really miss you."

"You have no idea how much I miss you. I'll call you as soon as I can."

I ended the call, my face falling into my hands as hot tears of frustration pricked my eyes. Grabbing my phone again, I scrolled my contacts for Megan's name.

"Hey, girl! Did you get on the road yet?"

"He's not there, so I'm not going. But I don't want to go home. It's still warm enough for the rooftop bar on 51st street. Can you meet me there?"

"Sure, sweetie." The genuine sympathy dripping off her voice made me feel even worse. "I'll meet you there at 5:30."

"Thank you." I stuffed the bag into my desk drawer and headed out, hoping a drink and a friendly ear would fill the gaping feeling in the pit of my stomach.

"You've had some bad luck," Megan reasoned as she pinched the stem of her happy hour wineglass. "It happens."

"Two and a half months of bad luck. How long can we keep this up? This is exactly what I was afraid of."

"I grant you, you've gone longer than I thought you'd have to without seeing each other, but I still like the effect Joe has on you."

"What effect is that?" I slammed my glass down on the table. "He's reduced me to a mopey, sad girl who keeps listening to eighties ballads on a continuous loop and wastes money on expensive underwear she'll never use."

"Aw, babe." She patted my hand. "Give the underwear a chance before you throw it out." An unexpected giggle slipped out at her arched brow. "He's still supposed to come to Brooklyn for your cousin's engagement party in a couple of weeks, right?"

I took a long pull of my fruity half-priced cocktail and nodded. "So far."

"Anyway, he made you realize you want more out of life than working all the damn time. Other than the month you came back, you haven't worked a late night since. I see you once a week instead of every other month. He opened your eyes to all the life going on around you that you didn't know you were missing."

"I'm missing *him*. What am I supposed to do about that?"

"Not much you can do, but have patience."

Megan was right. Joe did make me want things, but I wanted them all with him. The extended time apart wasn't my fault or his, but that didn't make it hurt less. My patience was hanging on a fraying thread of frustration, and the only thing I was sure of in that moment was that it was about to run out.

I spent the rest of the weekend alone. Joe was busy with his family, so we spoke in sporadic texts back and forth. More than a painful goodbye, I was afraid of fading away even more.

After the back-to-back months of disappointments we'd had, and the obligations that kept pulling us away from each other, it was hard to shake that fear.

Joe had been on my mind all morning, and, as if I'd conjured him up, my cell phone lit up with his picture right after I settled into my office.

"God, I miss you so much." I smiled at his exasperated greeting even before I had the chance to say hello.

"Well, less than two weeks, you'll be here. So, you won't have to miss me for much longer."

There went the familiar stomach drop at Joe's long pause.

"I can't come to Brooklyn in two weeks. Dom's father is getting out of a rehab facility, and Dom is heading home to stay with him for a while. There's no one else to watch the restaurant, and we're still getting a good amount of customers. I'm so sorry. Maybe you could come the weekend after?"

"I'm godmother to my cousin's baby the week after." The frustration I'd been fighting came to a boil, hitting me hard and obliterating what was left of my patience.

"Why are we doing this, Joe?" My voice cracked as I finally broke. "Are you really happy like this? I'm just a voice on the phone to you—"

"Stop it right there. You are *not* just a voice on the phone. We knew it would be tough, but we said we wouldn't give up. You promised me you wouldn't give up."

"Do you think I don't want to be with you? It's all I think about. *You're* all I think about. But how long can we go on like this? How could we even say we're together now? Plans that always fall through, always disappointing each other, maybe we should have just left this at the beach."

"You don't mean that. Caterina. I love you. I didn't want to tell you over the phone but, yes, I fucking love you. And I'm not running away because it's not easy. Why are you?"

"Joe, I can't do this right now. I need to think. I'm sorry." I ended the call and pulled at my hair by the roots, trying like hell to hold it together enough to finish work for the day. When the man you love tells you he loves you, and not only do you *not* say it back but hang up on him right after, what future do you really have? As I snuck to the ladies room to attempt to get myself together, it seemed as if we never had one at all.

**Joe:** *We need to talk about this.*

**Caterina:** *I can't right now. I'm sorry.*

I THREW my phone down on the bar, frustrated as fuck and wanting to dig my fist into something so it would feel as badly as I did. The distance between us was wearing on me, too, but not having her in my life at all wasn't an option. For the past couple of days, we'd only spoken in spotty texts as she wouldn't answer my usual early morning calls. Even though she'd never said it back, I knew she loved me. So, why was she so willing to give up? It had me twisted in all kinds of knots and snapping at anyone who had the bad luck of crossing my path.

I turned around and leaned back on the counter, taking a deep breath before I faced everyone, attempting to at least pretend to be a professional business owner. I could nurse my broken heart on my own time.

"Have you seen the owner of this place? I'd like to speak to him." I stilled at the sound of my father's voice behind me.

When I turned, I found him perched on a bar stool. Despite the way we'd left off at dinner all those months ago, a smile pulled at my lips.

"That's me." I turned and rested my elbows on the counter. "What can I do for you?"

His eyes, the same ones I saw reflected back at me in the mirror, bored into me before he took in a deep breath. "Did I fuck up with you, Joey?"

A rush of shame made my shoulders droop. "Dad, I—"

"Do you know how I felt when I heard about the money Owen gave you to open this place?" He splayed his hands on the bar, appearing more unnerved than I could recall ever seeing him.

"Disappointed, annoyed I opened a business without the collateral I needed and worried I took a stupid risk?" I shrugged, my gaze darting everywhere but his.

"Jealous. So jealous, I didn't know what to do with myself. My son was building a dream and didn't want me to have any part in it."

"It's not that I didn't want you to have a part in it, it's ..." I let out a long breath as I figured out how to voice the issue that had plagued me for what felt like my entire life.

"It's what?" Dad whispered, his voice laced with both anger and a little sadness. I never wanted to hurt my father but didn't realize how much I'd been doing it while trying to impress him. I was making us both crazy and needed to stop.

"I'm not you, Dad. I'm not the great Lucas Hunter, and I never will be." My eyes darted from his.

"First of all, I'm not the great Lucas Hunter. I struggle and screw up as much as anyone, and second, you don't have to be. Is that what this is all about?"

"I never wanted the corporate life you and Bella love." *And Caterina.* I never connected her relentless drive to succeed with my father and sister's and didn't think it was possible to feel worse than I did five minutes ago, but here I was. Maybe she didn't want to be tied to a restaurant owner in a beach town. The rational part of me knew that wasn't the reason things were strained between us, but the insecurities I'd fought against with my family made it all too easy to believe.

"And that's fine." He scanned the busy dining room and patio with a slow smile pulling at his lips. "You've done an amazing job. You did things your own way, and I'm nothing but proud. I just wish you'd let me in. Did you think I'd judge you if this place didn't take off? Hell, I never would have the guts to buy my own business and build it from the ground up. I'm in awe of you."

A lump grew in the back of my throat, making it hard to speak. "I didn't want you to see me fail." My voice sounded small, like the kid I'd always feel like in my father's presence. "I didn't want you to think I was weak. This is where I'm supposed to be, and I'm happy here, but part of me always wished I was like you and hated that I wasn't."

His features relaxed as he patted the stool beside him. "Sit and have a cup of coffee with your old man."

The corners of my mouth twitched as I made my way from behind the bar to the seat next to him. I called one of the waitresses over to fill our cups but didn't glance my father's way.

"Look at me."

I slid my gaze to his raised brow.

"I would never see you as weak. Sometimes, businesses flourish and fail for reasons you can't control, but I know anything you could do to be a success, you would." He dropped his hand to my shoulder. "Don't ever think you're my disappointment. You're my prize."

He pulled me in for a hug and kissed my cheek, just like he used to when I was little and would race to the door to greet him after work. I laughed as I pulled away, feeling lighter than I had in years, other than the one pang in my gut that wouldn't go away.

"Now that that's settled." He smiled around his coffee cup. "How are things going with Caterina?" He spotted the wince I tried to hold in. "What happened? Did you break up when she went home?"

"No. Yes." I groaned and rubbed my eyes. "I honestly don't know. We said we'd try and it's been three months. Our plans keep falling through, and, this last time, she got upset. She said maybe we're just torturing ourselves." I ran my finger around the handle of the mug. "Maybe she's right. Maybe we don't work in real life."

"I saw the way you were looking at each other at dinner like I told you. That looked pretty real to me. How do you feel about her?"

I let my head fall back on a groan. "I'm crazy about her. We fit. I can't explain it. It doesn't make sense to love someone after only two weeks."

"I loved your mother that quick. It happens." He shrugged before draining his coffee and motioning to Jordan for a refill.

"No, you didn't. You knew Mom in college."

"I was a stupid asshole back then who didn't notice anything, so all that time doesn't count." He nodded a thank you to Jordan when she filled his cup. "When I saw her ten years later, I couldn't explain it either. It was like I was hit with something. I couldn't stay away from her, even though it was wrong at the time. From that night on, I couldn't remember what life was like before her. All I knew was that I couldn't go back."

"That's exactly how I feel." I dropped my head to the counter and groaned.

I heard his sad laugh next to me. "So, tell her."

"I did. What else am I supposed to do?"

"I know!" Jordan interrupted as she served other customers at the bar. "My boyfriend sent me a playlist when we had a fight. It was so sweet; you should do that!" Jordan's widened eyes danced.

"Like a mixtape?" Dad squinted at her.

"I don't know what that is." Her nose scrunched before she fluttered back to the dining area.

"That didn't hurt at all." I cracked up at Dad's grimace. "But something like that isn't a bad idea."

I barked out a humorless laugh. "I already told her I loved her and that I wasn't giving up and then got total silence. I can't see how a song would make her believe it anymore than I could."

"What if ..." Jordan came back, bouncing up and down with her hands folded under her chin. "You had the songs delivered to her. Like on a jump drive. My boyfriend did it through an app, but that way would be *so* much sweeter."

"And then what?" I frowned and crossed my arms. "I have it sent to her office?"

"Or delivered," Dad said, tapping his fingers on the counter. "Bella works in the same area Caterina told us her office is in. And she feels pretty awful about mentioning Owen's contribution to me. I'm sure she'd deliver it to her. I can give it to her tomorrow when they stop by. Abuse her guilt a little." We shared a laugh before I nodded.

"Is Mom with you? I didn't even ask when you got here, sorry." I pushed off the stool, realizing I hadn't done a walk through in a bit to see what was going on.

"No, I came alone. I needed to speak to you and couldn't

take it anymore, so I woke up and drove three hours, no big deal." His lips twitched as he rose to stand. "Go do what you have to do. I can man your post until you're done. Dominic!" He called out to where Dom was speaking to one of the busboys. "I'm filling in for Joey for a bit. What does he do?"

"A lot of whining." Dominic chuckled as he came closer. "Usually, at this time of morning, he walks around, makes sure people are happy, I'm more grunt work." Dominic slapped my arm before he ventured out to the patio.

"Thanks, Dad. And I'm sorry—"

"Don't be. All is good now." He squeezed my shoulder.

"When I get back, maybe we can talk about those investments you were suggesting? I'm doing more in the off-season to keep the place alive, but a more reliable stream of income would be a big help."

He nodded, all the tension between us now gone. I felt the relief from both of us in his easy smile. "Sure, we can do that." He patted my cheek. "Go. Grand gestures take time and a little thought. I got this."

"I'm sure you do." I grinned and made my way back to my office. After digging through my desk drawer for the drive I hoped I had left, I settled into my desk chair and plugged it into my computer. This wouldn't take long because I knew exactly what to upload and what I wanted to say.

I only prayed she was still willing to hear it.

## 40

## CATERINA

"I DIDN'T EXPECT you here so late." My mother regarded me with a furrowed brow after I unlocked her door and stepped inside the apartment I'd grown up in.

"I wasn't doing anything at home, so I figured I'd come by." And I couldn't take being alone one more second.

Mom motioned to the kitchen table for me to sit. "I'll heat up some macaroni. What's wrong?"

I sank my teeth into my bottom lip and shrugged, not wanting to answer as my mother grabbed a wooden spoon and turned on the burner. Her apartment hadn't changed much since I'd moved out. In fact, my room was more or less the same, just overloaded with storage. This apartment was the one constant in my life, and although I didn't live here anymore, it was home.

"Joe can't come to Ashley's party, and we got into an argument, I guess." I didn't know what to call it. The more I reflected back on my last conversation with Joe, it seemed more like an adult tantrum on my part than an argument.

Mom didn't reply or turn around. Like Joe, I was my parent's twin. I had a few inches of height on my mother, but we shared the same big dark eyes and chestnut hair. I prided myself on being her mini-me as a little girl, always wanting to be just like her, and doing everything I could to make her happy, even when she wasn't the most reasonable.

When I came home from Ocean Cove and confessed where I was after the girls came home, I braced myself for how my mother would react, but all I'd gotten was a nod. No "what was I thinking staying with a guy I hardly knew?" or alluding to what I was doing with him during those extra days. She only asked his name and what he did for a living. I was relieved if a bit unnerved.

"I guess we aren't exactly on great terms."

Mom set the bowl on the table. I picked off a rigatoni at the top with my fingers like I'd always done as a kid before anyone was looking. A big plate of my mother's macaroni always soothed me, but when I swallowed, the ache in my stomach didn't ease. My insides were too sad and raw to absorb any kind of comfort.

"What happened?" She handed me a plate and fork before digging a big spoon into the bowl.

"I told him maybe we should have left what we had at the beach." I blew out a long breath before rising from my seat to get something to drink. "Maybe it's for the best. This isn't fair to either of us." I reached into the fridge and pulled out a bottle of water, letting out a slow breath as I leaned against the sink.

"Really? You don't look like you believe it's for the best. Sit down, Cat."

I came back to the table and plopped back into my seat.

"So, you panicked." She crossed her arms and drew back in her chair. "Is that right?"

"You *want* me with Joe?" I coughed out a laugh. "You want me traveling back and forth all the time, three hours from home to see a man who can never move from where he is?"

"If that's what makes you happy, yes. I wouldn't be thrilled about you in the car all those hours alone all the time, but if that's what you wanted." She shook her head. "You worry me, Caterina."

"I always worry you, Mom." I pushed a couple of pieces back and forth on my plate, not wanting to meet my mother's gaze.

"You make yourself so miserable, at such a young age. You're supposed to be happy now. Maybe you should move to where Joe is."

I dropped my fork along with my jaw. "You're serious? You're suggesting I quit a stable job I enjoy to move to a sleepy beach town for a man I've only known for three months?"

She leaned her elbows onto the table before lifting her gaze. "When you're an old woman like me, I want you to look back at this time of your life and see good memories, not have it all be a blur of nothing because you ran away scared. When you came home and told me about Joe, it was the happiest I'd ever seen you. I never saw even a tiny bit of that when you were with Trent."

I narrowed my eyes at my mother. "Who are you? Are you the same woman who told me the minute I turned sixteen that I needed a job that summer so I could see what the world was really like? Who was on me my entire senior year of high school to go to college in Manhattan so I could stay home because I was too young to be so far away from home and family?" My other friends were my age and traveled all over the country for school, so that logic never made any sense even back then.

"That was me trying to keep you grounded, and, because I'm a selfish woman, keep you close. You were all I had." She regarded me with a sad smile. "Still are. I'm probably to blame for how you are now."

"And how is that?" I pursed my lips and tilted my head.

"Scared to take chances, even when it makes you miserable."

"No, you're not ... well, maybe a little." I laughed for the first time in days. Mom scowled but couldn't help a tiny smile.

"What do I do now?" I whispered, more to myself than my mother.

"What do you want to do?"

My reply came quick without a second of thought.

"I want to be with Joe. By trying to put a stop to the constant disappointment, I ended up hurting the both of us. The distance is still not ideal, but I can't not have him at all."

"Then call him and tell him."

Since he'd texted yesterday, I hadn't heard another word from Joe. I wouldn't be surprised if he'd thrown his hands up and said enough. And I wouldn't blame him at all if he did.

"Or you could sit here and play with your food like a sad little puppy. Choice is yours, cookie."

## 41

## CATERINA

"Good morning. How are you today?" Emma peeked in my doorway.

I turned around with a shrug. "Fine," I lied. Sleep eluded me, no matter what time I tried to close my eyes. I'd almost called Joe a dozen times, but I chickened out, too afraid of what he'd say. Mom was right. I was afraid to take chances. If he brushed me off, at least I'd know. This not knowing was killing me, but I couldn't bring myself to find out.

"I have some news." She stepped inside and leaned against the edge of my desk. "I fired Sharon today. She's clearing out her office now."

"Wow." I first cringed over the extra work I'd have, but, in reality, I'd done her job *and* mine all these months. There wouldn't be much of a difference as far as workload. Only now, the extra work I took on wouldn't be optional.

"I didn't realize how much you were pulling her weight. Let's talk after lunch. I have a one o'clock meeting, so I'll find you after. Sound good?"

I nodded, unsure of what this meeting meant, but glad Emma knew the truth. "Sure, we can talk then."

"Great." She pushed off my desk, her gaze still on mine. "The launch went off without a hitch with talk of even more work. And that's, in large part, because of your efforts. You have a bright future here, and I'd like to talk about all that could entail."

Going back to my computer screen, I tried my best to focus. What I missed the most was something to look forward to. The texting back and forth, some of it sweet, a lot of it dirty. The long phone calls that still always seemed too short. I'd complained about not having him the way I'd wanted, but not having him at all was a new and painful kind of torture.

I'd be thirty-four this November, and it felt as if I'd wasted most of those years. The only time I didn't consider a waste were the weeks I'd spent in Ocean Cove. I even counted the time after. As I allowed myself to finally take in the letdown of it all, the loneliness hit me hard, now that I finally had a chance to let myself think about it.

"Cat," Amy called, startling me out of my haze. "Someone's here to see you. She's waiting by reception. Are you okay? You seem a little wiped."

"I'm good," I lied as I followed Amy to the reception area. I found a tall, slim woman with long dark hair sitting on one of the leather chairs. She looked familiar, but I couldn't place her.

When her dark eyes met mine, she rose from the seat and rushed over to me.

"Caterina? I'm so sorry to surprise you at work like this. I'm Bella. Joe's sister." She extended her hand with a sincere and easy smile.

"Oh, nice to meet you." I took her hand and studied her gaze, trying to figure out why Joe's sister would pay me a visit.

"I know you're probably busy, but do you have time for a quick cup of coffee?"

If only I was busy, it would give me the distraction I needed from missing Joe so much I ached.

"I do. Is the Starbucks downstairs okay?"

Bella nodded and followed me to the elevator. We traveled down in a weird silence. From what Joe had told me about Bella, she looked every bit the financial executive in a black pencil skirt, sky-high heels, and button-down white blouse. Advertising and marketing was a casual industry unless we had a client meeting scheduled for the day. I felt like a college kid standing next to her in my dark jeans and sleeveless blouse. She had a strong resemblance to her mother, which was why I thought I recognized her.

She insisted on treating and led me to a table in the corner.

"I won't take up too much of your time, I promise." She reached into her bag and pulled out a flash drive and an envelope. "This is for you. From my brother."

I eyed the tiny device after she slid it across the table.

"It's probably the photos I asked him to get of the restaurant so we could figure out fall decorations. Not sure why he sent you all this way and didn't email them to me, but thank you." I stuffed it into my wallet, feeling the weight of her stare in a way that made me uncomfortable.

"My office is only around the corner; I didn't have far to go." She leaned closer and tilted her head. "Long distance is hard. Owen and I did it for years. My husband, Owen, he's Joe's idol, so I'm sure he mentioned him a time or two." She chuckled and took her coffee cup in both hands. "It's tough and frustrating. As much as I always loved him, sometimes, it was too much. Especially after long periods of time when we had no choice but to be apart."

I nodded and took a sip of coffee. "It is. Your brother deserves better than a part-time girlfriend."

"What do *you* deserve, Caterina?" She arched a brow.

After what I blurted out to Joe ruined everything, I was tempted to say not much.

"Let me tell you something about my baby brother. He has more passion and heart than anyone I've ever known. We all worried when he moved away to run his own restaurant, but we shouldn't have. He knows what he wants and is smart enough to know how to get it." She leaned back in her chair and held my gaze. "But before he mentioned you, I'd only ever heard him so passionate about a goal—not another person. He loves you. It's pretty obvious."

I swallowed the lump in the back of my throat, too overwhelmed to reply.

"Judging by the way he sounded when he asked me for this favor, he's as miserable as you look." As much as it should've relieved me that Joe was as miserable as I was, I hated it.

"Have you ... spoken to him recently?" I stammered.

"This week, when he asked me to deliver this to you. I won't tell you what to do, but he wants you to look at whatever is on that drive. At least, give him that." She patted my hand. "I better go. I have a meeting in a few. I'm glad I got to meet you." I stood from my chair when she rose from her seat.

"You too. Thank you."

After Bella left, I drained the last of my coffee and rushed back to my desk. I shut my door and plugged in the thumb drive, clicking the first folder open, I found a bunch of pictures of us Joe had taken with his phone.

My eyes clouded as I sorted through the images. Happiness radiated off both of us in each shot: one of us on the beach on my last day there, one of me sleeping with a sloppy "See? The entire bed!" in handwritten scrawl across the image. A sad laugh escaped my lips before I clicked open a folder with audio files.

The first song was "Summer Nights" from *Grease*. I laughed and paused it after recognizing the opening chords. When I played the next song, the air drained from my lungs once I realized it was the same one we danced to after dinner on my last night. The lyrics punched me in the gut in the very same way now as they had then. The singer pleaded not to give up on him because he wasn't giving up. That was exactly what I'd done after I'd promised Joe I wouldn't.

I stopped the song and unplugged the drive before opening the small, plain white envelope.

*We knew it would be hard, but it's too good to give up.*

*So don't. Love, Joe*

I stared at the letter in my hand for a few minutes before popping off my chair and heading into my boss's office. After days of moping and afraid to do something about it, once my decision was made, I couldn't wait another minute. I'd already wasted enough time.

"Emma?" I knocked on her door. "If you're free now, can we talk?"

She motioned to the chair in front of her. "Absolutely. My next meeting was just cancelled. Let's talk about what we can offer you."

"Before we do that, I'd like to ask about the new remote policy."

"Busy is good, but it's nice to be able to breathe just for a moment." Dominic shut his eyes as he leaned against the wall, letting out an exaggerated breath.

"That it is. Now starts the creative part of the year," I told Dom. Customers rolled in all summer with little effort on our part. In fact, according to the numbers I'd run last night, this was our best season on record. I'd answered a few emails this week about the Halloween scavenger hunt, and, before Caterina and I were ... whatever we were now, she'd found similar opportunities for Thanksgiving and Christmas. She was brilliant and beautiful, and still not speaking to me.

Bella confirmed that she'd dropped off the drive and letter to Caterina yesterday and made sure to stress how sad she seemed. While I didn't doubt she felt as terrible as I did, at least I'd done something about it. When she let herself go for a little while and gave into what we had without worrying about logistics or what would go wrong, she was perfect. *We* were perfect. If only she stopped being so damn stubborn. I loved her enough to wait and fight, but if she'd already given up, what was I really fighting for?

In an effort to distract myself, I surveyed the lunch crowd. For October, on a weekday, it was still a healthy amount of people. Dad started an investment account for me, and the numbers were in good shape. That used to be all I needed to be happy until a gorgeous Italian girl from Brooklyn strolled into my restaurant looking for something to eat and upended my priorities. Now I needed *her*, and the more time passed without some kind of a reply, the more of a lost cause it became.

"Joe?" Tommy, one of our waiters, tapped me on the shoulder. "I tried taking a customer's order, but she's insisting on speaking to you. She's at the booth in the corner." He tilted his chin toward the back and hustled to the next table before I could ask why. I blew out a slow breath and shook my head as I made my way to the corner, stopping in my tracks when I recognized the woman sitting in the booth.

"I'm dying for some *mutzadalle* sticks. Think you could hook me up?" Caterina's lips spread in a slow smile.

I blinked a couple of times, wondering if this was an illusion brought on by wishful thinking. In the days following her departure, I saw her everywhere, and it had driven me mad. But as I stared at her head on, this wasn't a sadness-induced mirage. She was here, sitting at the same table as she had that first night she'd stumbled in here looking for an escape. It seemed both like yesterday and a lifetime ago.

She rose from her seat and walked toward where I stood, trying to will my heart back into my chest. She was so beautiful, it was unfair. I'd never stood a chance.

I wanted to scoop her in my arms and kiss the hell out of her, not giving even one fuck about the bustle of customers around me, but we needed to talk first.

She reached out to place her hand on my chest, stilling before her palm settled over my racing heart. "I'm sorry, Joe. I

panicked, and I hurt you, and I never, *ever* wanted to do that."
She swallowed and darted her eyes away for a moment. "How
I feel about you...it scares me. The two weeks I spent with you
were the happiest I've ever been, and I was afraid of never
having that again."

She took a deep breath and grabbed my wrist. "I love you.
And I don't care how hard it is. Whether or not I see you once
a week or once every six months, I'm yours." A watery smile
stretched her lips before she laced our fingers together and
squeezed my hand. "All yours, baby." Her features hardened
before she clicked her tongue against her teeth. "Again, if you
could just blink or—"

She squealed as I lifted her by the waist and crushed my
lips against hers. I dug my fingers into her hair as I kept my
other arm around her waist. After the past few days, afraid I'd
lost her, she was back in my arms, and I couldn't put her down
until I was convinced this was really happening, not some
dream my lonely mind had conjured because I missed her so
damn much. We belonged together, and, now that she was
back in my arms, I'd be damn sure to never let her go again.

"Hey, lover boy!" We broke apart as we turned to
Dominic's voice. "Customers, dude."

Caterina giggled into my neck before I set her down.

"So, you love me?" I whispered before tucking a lock of
hair behind her ear.

"So, so much, Joe." Her chin quivered as she nodded.
"You have no idea how—"

I grabbed her hand and weaved through the tables, pulling
her behind me.

"Sorry," I muttered to a few patrons I recognized. "I
haven't seen my girlfriend in a long time." I turned my head,
searching for a wince at my use of the word girlfriend, but she
didn't flinch.

"Where are we going?" Caterina asked as she tried to keep up with my swift pace out of the restaurant.

"My apartment," I told her before taking her mouth in another sloppy but grateful-as-all-hell kiss. "I won't be able to hold back or be quiet." The corners of my lips twitched when her eyes darkened. "And we both know you can't." I looped my thumbs into the waistband of her jeans and yanked her closer, right into the bulge in my pants that was about to break my zipper. "I need inside you...a few times. I'll owe Dominic for taking the lunch rush." I nipped at her jaw, loving the way she slumped against me. "And part of the dinner one, too, most likely." I leaned my forehead against hers. "I love you so much. I'm afraid if I stop touching you, you'll disappear."

"Nope." She blinked away a tear and tried to cover it up with a swipe of the back of her hand. "I'm right here, and I'm not going anywhere."

"Well," I slid my hand to the nape of her neck, "you did say you loved me, and that you're mine. You even called me baby." I covered her mouth with mine again and grazed my teeth along her bottom lip as I pulled away.

"Get upstairs before I get arrested in front of my own restaurant." My hand came down on her ass with a loud smack before I opened my front door and pulled her up the stairs with me.

Maybe we didn't have it all figured out yet. But I knew, without a doubt, nothing would ever be better than this. Better than *us*.

## CATERINA

### ONE MONTH LATER

"HE FITS IN REALLY WELL!" My cousin Rosa whispered behind me as we peered at the zoo that was our family from the doorway of my mother's kitchen. Thanksgiving was always a chaotic madhouse, and adding my family chomping at the bit to meet Joe for the first time, the energy had somehow intensified. Although the taste of *anisette* made me want to puke, I let my aunt pour a drop in my coffee to ease my anxiety.

"He's a tolerant man." I sipped my coffee, cringing as the taste of licorice assaulted my taste buds each time I swallowed.

"And hot as hell." She nudged my side. "Nice work. I know I wouldn't have come home if I'd had a taste of that on vacation."

"That's enough, Rosa," my Aunt Renee scolded from across the kitchen. "Make yourself useful and put these out before we do Cat's cake." She handed my cousin a tray of cookies. This was why you never wore pants with buttons on an Italian holiday. We had a round of antipasto before dinner, which consisted of a large tray of lasagna in addition to the turkey, and seven different kinds of dessert, including my plain yellow birthday cake with chocolate frosting.

"Is Phil still chewing his ear off about his restaurant?" Aunt Renee *tsk*ed as she swept her gaze over the couch, where my uncle droned on, and Joe sat in rapt attention. "You're right, he is a tolerant man."

I grinned, loving having Joe here with my family. He was too good of a person to be anything but friendly and respectful when they all swarmed us the second we stepped foot in the door. Having Joe in my life was a gift I'd never expected to get, and I enjoyed every second.

"Where the hell are the candles?" My mother rummaged through one of her many junk drawers before I tried to wave her off.

"I'm thirty-four, candles aren't necessary."

"Of course, they are." My mother banged the box of old, reused-God-knows-how-many-times candles on her kitchen counter.

"You didn't lie about your age, did you?" Rosa dropped a hand on my arm, her brow furrowed in concern.

I tried to hide my eye roll before shooting my cousin a glare. "No, I did not. Thirty-four isn't old. In fact," I said before catching Joe's gaze ."I feel younger all the time." He wore a dark blue sweater molded to his torso and dark jeans. His lips spread into a wide grin, and I wished we could move along with dessert so he could spread *me* back at my apartment. Something about having Joe in my apartment and in my bed excited the hell out of me. I'd been visiting him the past three weekends, thanks to my new work schedule, but this was the first time he was able to come in to see me.

The Halloween Scavenger Hunt had been a success, and, next week, I'd be helping Joe and Dominic decorate for the Christmas tour I'd discovered online. The Beach Pub didn't quite see the summer volume of business, but it had a lot more activity than usual after their busy season ended. My chest swelled with pride that I was able to help Joe and that I didn't have to keep ungodly long hours to feel good about what I did for a living.

I went out into the living room and made my way over to Joe. There was no room on the couch, and I'd never hear the end of it if I planted myself on his lap. I stood next to him, rubbing his back in slow, hopefully, soothing circles.

"Thank you for your patience," I whispered as he rested his head on my hip.

"I'm happy to be here. No need for thank you." He nodded toward the dining room table. "Now, I see why you love dessert so much. I own a restaurant, and I don't think I've ever seen this much food in one day."

"We like to eat." I shrugged. "And on holidays, we eat a lot." My aunt fluttered around the cake, fussing with the lighter.

"Where did you find a three and a four?" I groaned as I made my way over to the table after spotting two mint green number candles shoved into the cake.

My mother shrugged. "I saved them from when you were little and just found them now. Easier than counting them out."

"Who knew candles lasted that long?" My Uncle Zaro snickered before elbowing my side.

Joe snaked his arm around my waist from behind.

"Can we leave after the cake?" His words fanning hot against my neck triggered goose bumps down my shoulder. "I need to wish a hot cougar a *very* happy birthday."

My mouth fell open before I turned my head. "I am *not* that much older than you are. Three years does not make a cougar."

His lips twisted as his head cocked from side to side. "Technically, now, it's almost four. But—"

Joe was cut off by the off-key rendition of "Happy Birthday" my family bellowed out. My icy glare only made him laugh harder.

As a kid, I'd put a lot of effort into my wish each year. My family would yell to blow out the candles already, but I took my time because I refused to waste my wish. Yet, I'd never really expected anything I'd wished for to come true. Today, I blew the candles right out.

After years of being afraid to go outside the lines, and only doing what I thought I was supposed to do, this was the year I realized all it had cost me and all I'd missed. I finally believed I deserved more than the tiresome life I'd allowed myself to have, and on one lowly Thursday night, I jumped in my car and decided to do something about it. After a lifetime of making excuses out of fear, I'd learned there was always room for the important things in life, and how important it was to fight for them, even when they seemed impossible.

Joe buried his head into my neck and brushed a kiss behind my ear.

"I love you," he whispered. "Happy early birthday, baby."

I didn't need my wish, because this was the year they all came true.

# EPILOGUE
## ONE YEAR LATER

### Joe

"Nervous?" Dominic asked as we closed out the register for the day.

"Nope. What's there to be nervous about? We pretty much live together now. That's like being married already. This is just sealing the deal, right?"

Dom arched a brow. "You're scared shitless, aren't you?" He studied me as he filled the bank deposit envelope.

"Terrified," I finally admitted before letting my head drop into my hands. "This woman is my whole damn life. I don't think I can handle it if she says no." I'd had the ring for weeks already, but each time I thought of asking Caterina to marry me, I broke out into a cold sweat. It wasn't because I was unsure. In fact, I'd never wanted anything more, which is why the thought of her saying no scared the shit out of me.

She still traveled back and forth between Ocean Cove and Brooklyn, but sublet her apartment when she started working remotely from here most of the time. Thanks to her, The Beach Pub was now profitable all year long. Summer was still when most of the cash flowed in, but through events and social media, the off months weren't dead anymore, and that was all Caterina.

I'd offered to give her some kind of salary hundreds of times for all she put into promotion, but she'd refused. She insisted helping me was its own reward, and she loved finding new ways to get our name out there. We were even able to keep half the staff instead of just getting by on two waitresses and a bus boy until Memorial Day. Combined with the invest-ments my father made on our behalf, we were in a great place —the best place since I'd first opened.

"She won't say no. You guys are still attached at the hip after a year. Just don't fuck it up tonight." He smirked before handing the envelope back to me to put into the safe.

"Thanks for the vote of confidence." I barked out a laugh as I looked over the numbers before locking the envelope away. "If she doesn't hit any traffic, she should be here in another hour or so. Plenty of time to set up what I need to."

"You aren't taking her on the beach to propose, are you? It's like twenty degrees out there." He narrowed his eyes as he shrugged on his jacket.

"I have a plan, no worries. What about you?"

"What do you mean, what about me?" Dom had a defen-sive edge to his voice, as he always did whenever I asked him about his life outside of this place. He pushed me about Cate-rina but was tight-lipped about his own personal life.

"You were the first one to tell me there's more to life than working. I haven't seen you with anyone since—"

"I'm fine." His answer was curt and not sarcastic like he usually was. "We just got you a life. Next year, maybe we'll work on mine." He slapped my arm before heading toward the door. "Good luck, man."

"Thanks, Dom. For everything."

IIe lifted his gaze to mine and rolled his eyes. "Save the sappiness for your woman. And thanks aren't needed. You deserve this. You both do." He reached for the door handle before glancing back at me. "Just don't fuck it up." His lip curled into a smirk.

"I'll do my best." The door shut behind him, and I was alone. I sucked in a long breath before I got to work, first shoving the velvet box I'd hidden in the safe in my back pocket. My worries finally started to dissipate as I realized there was no way I could mess this up. From the very beginning, she'd been the one.

## CATERINA

"JOE?" I knocked on the locked door of The Beach Pub, shivering and praying Joe would put me out of my misery and let me in. This was the worst cold snap I ever remembered in November, and it made me dread the winter to come. Beaches might have been an oasis during the summer, but living so close to one during the cold months chilled me to the bone.

I let out a white puff of relief when I spotted him on the other side of the glass door and heard the locks click open.

"Thank God!" I pecked him on the lips and hurried inside. "It's like Antarctica out there." I pulled off my coat and gloves, rubbing my hands together in an attempt to get some of the feeling back. "I think you should invest in a fireplace." I blew at my hands to defrost them, but it was no use.

Joe took my hands in both of his before bringing them to his mouth and planting a kiss on both of my palms. I stopped shaking from the cold and shivered for a whole different reason. Even after being together for over a year, this man still had the power to melt my extremities to jelly.

"We're on the water, baby. It's always colder here. I can warm you up, though." He pulled me to him and brushed my lips with his.

"That sounds great, but can you feed me first? I left right after the meeting to get a head start on the road, and I'm starving."

"I'll make you something. Go sit down, and I'll be right out." He pressed a kiss to my forehead before heading into the kitchen.

I plopped into the booth I always used, exhaling in relief after finally getting here after sitting in traffic for almost four hours. I could have slept at my mother's house, but I didn't like to spend a night without Joe if I could help it. The closer I got to Ocean Cove, the more I'd relaxed. Brooklyn would always be my home, but this was where my heart was.

"You love that table, don't you?" Joe came out of the kitchen and set a plate in front of me, along with a cup of tea.

"I do," I answered, chuckling when I realized he made me mozzarella sticks. "Still have a lot of these on hand, I see?"

He nodded. "This table is where I first saw you. I bet you don't even realize."

I crinkled my nose before taking a sip of tea. "Actually, I do. But how did you remember that?"

"I remember when I came over to ask if I could help you, and you looked up at me with dark eyes and long lashes and the most kissable lips I'd ever seen."

I crossed my arms and leaned them on the table. "You didn't know that yet."

He arched an eyebrow. "I found out soon enough, didn't I?"

"You did." I held his gaze as I swirled a stick in marinara sauce.

"I loved you from the second I saw you. Confused the shit out of me, but I couldn't ignore it." His lips curved as he leaned back.

"Ignoring it didn't work for me, either. I tried, but ..." I shrugged. "No use."

"I remember that, too." His eyes darted around the room. He seemed jumpy and impatient for some reason. "Grab your coat. I want to show you something."

"Ugh, Joe." I groaned. "Can I finish my tea first before I freeze up again?"

"Come on, it's just for a minute." He stood and grabbed my coat from where it was draped over the seat.

"Fine." I shrugged it on and stuffed my hands into my pockets as I followed Joe outside. "Where did you get all these?" I eyed the lanterns half buried in the sand around the patio. "Is this for the Christmas promo? I can't believe I didn't think of it last year. Maybe we could get a couple of space heaters? How much would it be to rent a few or maybe we could buy—"

I trailed off when I turned and couldn't find Joe behind me, my breath catching in my throat when I realized he was down on one knee.

"Joe, I ..." A sob choked my words before I could say anything. Joe was it for me. I'd known that for longer than I wanted to admit to myself, but now that the moment was here, my head spun as a ton of emotions swirled through me. Tears streamed down my cold cheeks as I remained totally speechless.

"I meant what I said. I loved you from the second I saw you, and I never stopped. What we have is something I'd never expected. I never thought I had room for anyone else in my life, but I can't live without you. You *are* my life. I know we're together in all the ways it matters, but I want us to be permanent. Forever. Because that's how long I'm going to love you. Will you marry me?"

He dug into his back pocket and opened a black velvet box. I couldn't see too much detail from the dim light of the lanterns or the tears clouding my eyes, but my breathing quickened at the sparkle in the middle of the box.

"Yes," I managed to croak out. "All I want is forever with you. Yes." I grabbed his face and crashed my lips into his. "Can you put the ring on my finger before it freezes off?"

He laughed against my lips as he slid it on, pulling me down to kneel before he kissed me, long and deep enough to forget about the icy wind surrounding us.

"When do you want to start forever?" he asked before rolling me onto my back. The sand was frigid, but I didn't care. I was too lit up inside.

"How does now sound?"

# BONUS EPILOGUE

## CATERINA

"I still don't get why you couldn't stay with me tonight."

A smile stretched my lips at Joe's exasperation, picturing him laying on our bed with his lips jutted into a pout. I slipped under the covers, my lids so heavy that I was about to doze off in the middle of our argument.

"Because it's tradition. We aren't supposed to spend the night together before we get married," I told him on a yawn with the phone cradled until my ear.

"We've been living together for months. Tradition is stupid." His words were stunted, like a little kid having a tantrum. When I didn't think I could love him more, Joe always proved me wrong. I hated being without him, too—even for only a night. But staying at The Anchor again brought it all into full circle. The last time I was here, I was so lost I wasn't even sure who I was. Now, I had everything I wanted and more than I could have imagined possible.

"You're so sexy when you pout. Growl for me, baby," I teased, loving the grumble reverberating in my ear.

"I guess if you'd rather spend the night, alone, on those scratchy sheets instead of our bed, there's nothing I could say."

"It's fun reliving the memories. I'd rather get ready for tomorrow where I could keep my family more or less contained."

Lou gave us an awesome rate for any family traveling in for our wedding this weekend. I loved my family but would rather have them stay in a hotel than our small apartment. We'd talked about getting a bigger place but the convenience of living right over the restaurant halted any real motivation for us to look elsewhere.

Soon, we'd have no choice.

"Did they give you the same room?"

"Almost. Third floor, 324 this time. Although I have the same sailboat painting to stare at for the night." My head sunk into the pillow as my exhaustion overpowered any anxiety for tomorrow. The wedding was more for our families than us. We would have been happy at City Hall, but my mother had a fit. Even Samantha, who was always so easy going gave Joe the world's most heartbreaking guilt trip. Although not having a church wedding and saying our vows on the beach behind the restaurant didn't exactly sit well with my side of the family, everyone was satisfied, mostly, to at least be celebrating with us.

"Baby, I'm so tired. I'll talk to you in the—" My eyes popped open at the loud knock on my door. "Hold on, Joe. Someone is at the door." Who the hell would be knocking on my door now? I already said no to a late-night swim with my cousins and just wanted to sleep. I'd forgotten how taxing it was to have so much family around. I rose from the bed, yanking my hoodie off the back of the chair by the door and pulling it over my head to cover up my barely-there nightshirt. I squinted through the tiny peephole but couldn't make out a damn thing without contacts or glasses.

"Who is it?"

"Since you're getting married tomorrow, someone ordered you a stripper," Joe bellowed from the other side of the door.

I unlocked the door and pulled him in.

"Are you crazy?" I slapped his chest as it shook with a laugh.

"Are you naked under that hoodie?" Joe framed my waist and pulled me flush to his body. "Not sure I like my fiancée answering the door like that. This," he hissed as his hand wandered under the hem of my shirt, "is for my eyes only." He dipped his head to kiss me, nipping my bottom lip before he pulled away.

"I only opened the door when I realized it was you. You act like I never lived alone in New York City." I peered up at him, narrowing my eyes. "The only weirdos around here tonight are all related to me. I can take care of myself."

"I know you can." My eyes fluttered as he cradled my face, skating his thumbs back and forth along my cheekbones. His touch always relaxed me. Maybe I was a little nervous, but not unsure. This man was my home, and there was nothing I wanted more than to be with him for the rest of my life.

"Hey," he crooned. "What's wrong?"

"Nothing," I shook my head and averted my gaze, still feeling the weight of his concerned stare. "Just tired."

"You've been tired for a while. I told you if this wedding planning got to be too much to let me know. Our mothers would get over it if we eloped." He pulled me into his chest and rubbed my back.

"Maybe yours would." I wrapped my arms around his waist. "Do you know how long it takes for an Italian woman to let go of a grudge?" I lifted my head and kissed the corner of his mouth.

"No." His lips curled up into a sexy smile. "How long?"

"Not sure. Because I've never seen it happen. Besides, it's not a big event in a hall. It's another party in the restaurant. Business as usual except I'll be in a fancy dress and you in a dark suit." I feathered my hand down the soft cotton of his T-shirt. "I hope."

He laughed before his smile faded. "I needed to see you before tomorrow. I'm so damn ready to marry you."

"I'm so damn ready to marry *you*." I looped my arms around his neck. "You're right. Tradition is stupid. Stay with me." I pulled back and chuckled at his pinched brow. "You'd just have to leave early. I have hair and makeup at eight." I rolled my eyes. "Please. I need to sleep next to you."

"You don't have to convince me. You had me at stay." He pecked my lips before kicking off his sneakers and pulling me by the hand toward the bed. Now, we really *were* full circle.

"Are you sure nothing is wrong?" Joe asked as we climbed into bed. "You'd tell me, right?"

I shook my head against his chest. "No, nothing is wrong." *Technically.* Maybe planning such a complicated wedding gift for my soon to be husband wasn't a good idea, but I was too tired to ponder it for very long. "Good night, baby," I murmured into his neck.

"Good night, Mrs. Hunter."

I groaned as I settled into his side. "Thanks to you, no one can call me Cat after tomorrow. I'll be *Cat Hunter*."

His laugh rumbled against my cheek. "Well, technically that could be my name since I always hunting for your p—"

I put my hand over his mouth and felt his smile against

my palm. He peeled my fingers away and kissed my wrist. "Your real name is too beautiful not to use anyway."

"Dirty to sweet in 0.6 seconds." I yawned again, the fatigue knocking me over. "Don't ever change, baby."

"Go to sleep." His finger trailed up and down my spine, and I never stayed away longer than minutes when he did that. When it came to Joe, resistance was always a waste of time.

## Joe

"I think the rock band we had last week drew a less rowdy crowd than this one." Dominic stuffed his hands in the pockets and scanned the beach outside. There were only about twenty guests who made the trip, but what they didn't have in quantity, they made up for in sound. "Someone snapped at me for it being too warm outside for October." His shoulders bunched before they dropped on a dramatic sigh. "It made me a little misty for the old neighborhood."

"Once things get going and everyone is eating and drinking, it'll be fine."

I wasn't the usual hands-on host today. All I cared about was watching Caterina walk down the aisle to me. I hoped she wasn't getting sick from all the pre-wedding bullshit we had to deal with, but it was almost over. Then, I got to keep the most beautiful woman in the world for the rest of my life. Whatever happened today other than that was just a tiny detail I didn't give a shit about.

"I think everyone is here." My father came over to us. "Let's get this show on the road before we lose control of the crowd out there." He nodded outside with his lips tipped into a smirk.

"Sounds like a plan to me." I took a quick gander outside. Everyone was seated, the speakers were working. I planned to marry the love of my life in less than fifteen minutes. There was no bridal party other than two co-maids of honor and a best man. My goal was to get in and out as quickly as possible.

"All right. I'll go outside to tell them to start the music." Dom shook his head as he studied my face. "I don't think I've ever seen you this calm. It's freaking me out."

"What's there to freak out about?" I lifted a shoulder and adjusted my cuff links. "I'm where I'm supposed to be."

"You really are calm," Dad said, dropping a hand on my shoulder. "And happy. You both are going to have a great life together."

"We already do. This is just a formality."

Dad choked out a laugh. "We'll see how much a formality it is when you watch the woman you love walk down the aisle to you. It's going to hit you then, so don't get cocky."

"Oh my God!" My mother's voice cracked behind us. We turned around as she brought her hand to her quivering mouth.

"You've seen me in a suit before, Mom. You don't have to get all choked up." I smirked at Dad.

She rushed over to me and swatted my chest. "It's not the suit. You're getting married today. I guess it all just got real." She smoothed the lapels of my jacket as her eyes filled with tears. I grabbed her hands and squeezed.

"I'm happy, Mom. Tears aren't necessary."

"And you're going to ruin your makeup. Waterproof mascara only holds up so far." My sister came up behind her and grabbed our mother's shoulders. Bella smiled at me, but her eyes were just as glossy. "Baby Joey is getting married today."

I pulled them both into a hug and rolled my eyes at Dad. He looked us all over with a laugh and shake of his head.

"He's getting married, not heading off to war," Owen drawled as he peeled them both away from me. "The music is starting. You'd better get out there, Joseph." He smiled, big and bright but his eyes were wet, too.

Once they were gone, I exhaled a long breath. "Sorry to make you do double duty today, Dad."

His eyes narrowed as he came closer. "My son asked me to be his best man." He swallowed before putting his hands on my shoulders, something he always did when I was a kid but was a little weird now as we were the same height. "It's the greatest honor of my life, not a hassle."

"Please don't start crying, too," I begged as my lips twitched into a smile.

He laughed and slapped my back. "Let's go. Caterina is going to expect you to be waiting for her, not the other way around."

I'd been waiting for Caterina all my life, just didn't know it until I met her.

Dad and I made our way outside and I took my place at the end of the aisle, waiting for a glimpse of my future wife. When I spotted her at the end of the aisle, my jaw went slack and all I could do was whisper a *wow*. Her hair was down in dark waves spilling down her shoulders. Her white lacy dress hung off her shoulders and hugged all my favorite places, but it was the dark eyes that got me right in the chest as they met mine. I was hers from the second I saw her but today, she officially owned me body and soul. My gaze clouded as she came closer. She was so damn gorgeous I couldn't take it.

"Told you," Dad said in my ear.

"You're always right," I answered without turning around. It was impossible to take my eyes off the woman coming toward me.

"Not bad," she whispered, her hand sliding down the front of my jacket. "You're kinda cute." She bit her bottom lip when she caught my gaze.

"You're gorgeous. Please marry me."

She handed her bouquet to Megan behind her and cradled my face.

"How fast can we do this?" she asked. "I suddenly can't wait another second."

"What kind of menu is this, Joe?" Caterina's Uncle Ricky came up to me at the bar. The menu was everything I served Caterina the night we met. Mozzarella sticks, wings, nachos, and the shrimp and oysters she loved so much from Madeline's. The party was for my wife, and while I wouldn't be disrespectful, I didn't care too much about who did or didn't approve.

"They're all your niece's favorites. Happy wife, happy life, right?" I smiled even though I got a scowl back.

"Someone just offered her an oyster and she said no before running toward the bathroom. You should check on your happy wife." He snickered and made his way back into the dining area.

I rushed past him and found Claire standing by the single bathroom toward the front of the restaurant.

"Is Caterina okay? I just heard she was sick."

"I'm not sure. One of her cousins offered her an oyster and she looked like she was about to puke. She asked me to stand guard outside. Can't say I blame her, I never understood how she liked those." Her mouth twisted in a grimace.

"Caterina," I yelled as I knocked on the door. "Are you all right, baby?"

The lock clicked before she opened the door a crack.

"I'm fine." Her eyes were heavy as she averted my gaze. "Don't worry, just go back inside."

"If you're sick, I'm taking you home." I pushed inside and closed the door behind me. "The important part is over, they can all stay for as long as they want. No one cares as long as I keep the bar open and food coming."

"I'm okay, really. Go back outside and I'll be there in a minute."

I draped my hand over the nape of her neck. "You haven't been feeling well for a while, did you think I didn't notice? If you're sick, you don't have to stay. Like I said everything is done—"

"I'm not sick, Joe. I'm pregnant."

"You're—" The room spun as shock filtered through me. It was a good shock, but one I never saw coming. "How long ... when did you ... why didn't you tell me sooner?" I stammered, a myriad of emotions robbing my ability to speak.

"I made a box." She plucked a tissue from the box on the counter and dabbed under her eyes. "I had a feeling but I didn't see the doctor until yesterday. I bought a rattle, a tiny spatula—I thought of you and the restaurant and it made sense at the time—and a Yankee onesie I found in town. I didn't want to blurt it out to you like this. The nausea didn't hit me until just now."

She sniffled into the tissue as her chest heaved up and down. "I had a whole thing planned. I was going to tell you how you were my every dream come true and when I found out I was having your baby I actually felt a little scared. Like how my life could possibly be this amazing." Another sniffle. "I love you so much and I hope we have a boy. I hope he has the same beautiful blue eyes and amazing heart as you. I'm greedy and I want another Joe." She choked out a laugh and lifted her gaze to mine. "That was my wedding gift and now it's all ruined because one of my relatives probably had a big mouth and told you I looked sick."

I stepped toward her and cradled her face. "You didn't need the box, baby. You were already the best gift I'd ever received. This," I swallowed, a sudden lump in my throat making it hard to breathe. "You're right, it's a little scary to have everything you've ever wanted." I splayed my fingers over her still flat stomach and squeezed. "I hope it's a girl. I hope she has dark eyes and fire, and loves cookies as much as her beautiful mother." She giggled as she rested her forehead on my chin. "I'll spend the rest of my life spoiling the shit out of both of you and I'll love every minute of it."

"It's a little unexpected, and soon."

"So are we." I shrugged. "This means we need to finally figure out..." I motioned upstairs to our one-bedroom apartment.

"Yes, sooner rather than later. But let's not worry about that today." She cinched her arms around my waist. "It's a relief that you know. But let's not tell anyone else, yet."

I kissed the top of her head. "Fine with me. Are you still feeling sick?"

"No, not at all. I didn't even throw up, I just felt this awful wave of nausea and ran inside before I puked on the sand. Once I came in here I was fine."

I reached behind me and turned the lock on the door. Caterina's eyes widened as she shook her head. "Joe, we have family crawling over the restaurant. Nosy family who probably saw you run in here."

"And?" I asked as I backed her against the counter. "I have never seen you more gorgeous than you are today." I kissed her jaw and moved my lips down her neck. "You have the sexiest shoulders, did I ever tell you that?" I ran my tongue along her collarbone and she slumped in my arms. I grinned in victory. "So beautiful." My fingers skated down her dress and until they found the slit on the side. "My beautiful wife is having my baby." I ran my hand up the inside of her thigh and dipped into her panties. "You're fighting me, but you're already soaked."

"You're in a suit, Joe." She rocked against my hand as my thumb circled her clit. "I've been wet for hours."

I dropped to my knees and tugged her dress above her waist. "Something else you should have told me sooner. Hold on to the counter and spread your legs."

She leaned back with a loud moan, doing as she was told.

"Such a good girl." I licked across her hip as I pulled her panties down. My cock was ready to burst through the zipper of my suit pants when I heard a knock at the door.

"Hey guys?" I heard Claire and a voice I didn't recognize chuckle. "Sorry to bother you when you're ... but people are asking about cake, and keep looking this way, and Cat didn't sound so sick just now."

Caterina's head fell into her hands on a groan. "Ugh, Joe."

"I'm not the loud one, sweetheart." I pulled her panties back up and smoothed her dress over her legs.

"Cake means it's almost over, right?" Her lips lifted into a crooked smile.

"It does, now. I may have other stuff out there for you, too."

"Like what?" Her eyes danced when I stood.

"The baby likes sugar, I see." I caressed her stomach and

gave her a soft kiss. "I'll load you both up with sweets and get us out of here."

"Sounds perfect." She framed my face. "I love you."

"I love you, too." I kissed her hand and unlocked the door, ignoring all the smirks thrown our way as we headed back inside.

I knew it on the night I'd met Caterina and was one hundred percent certain of it now.

I was the luckiest bastard on the planet.

# ACKNOWLEDGMENTS

For once in my writing career, I will try to keep this brief. After a tough year, writing *No Vacancy* gave me back my joy of writing, and I am over the moon to finally get this published.

To my husband and son, you both say I'm the nucleus of our family, but you're the ones who keep me going every single day. I love you more than you could ever imagine.

To my betas: Amie, Becca, Bianca, Jaimee, Jeannine (all *Grease* references are dedicated to you) Jodi, Julia, Kristy, Lara, Laura, and Lisa. Thank you for pushing me to make this story something I'm proud of. I'm lucky to have such amazing and brilliant women to call my friends.

To Christine, you kicked my ass again, and I adore you for it. I've learned so much from you, and although I doubted my ability to write, or speak, English for a little bit, I'm a better writer because of you, and I can't thank you enough for it.

To Mitzi, thank you for always polishing my words and making them shine, and thank you for your constant support of my books. You teach me something every time.

To Najla, brilliant, professional, amazing, any other awesome words I can't think of Najla. Thank you for this gorgeous cover and always being so fantastic to work with.

To Regina, thank you for this beautiful photo that is so Joe and Caterina, I want to cry whenever I look at it because it's so damn perfect.

To Tracey, Kaitie, and Tabitha, thank you so much for

being my final checking eyes and ensuring Joe and Cat enter the world as perfect as they can be.

To Becca, thank you for expressing your love of Joe and Caterina with beautiful teasers.

To Beth, always my Oracle. Thank you for organizing a flawless promo with Panda & Boodle and for still not blocking me and my neurotic ways. You're a gem, and I'm happy to call you a friend.

To Jodi, I don't know what I would do without you, and I hope I never have to find out. You're an amazing PA, friend, and human. Thank you for all you do for me and all that you are.

To all my good author friends I've found in this crazy journey, thank you for your guidance and for giving me something to aspire to.

To my beloved Rose Garden, who has stuck with me from the beginning and continues to grow, thank you for giving me the love and support to keep going. Your excitement fuels mine, and you're my favorite place on Facebook.

To all the bloggers and readers who took a chance on me. I strive to give you my best in every book, and I pray I delivered. Thank you for reading Joe and Caterina's story. I hope you loved them as much as I do. Stay tuned in 2020 for Dominic's story!

# ABOUT THE AUTHOR

Stephanie Rose is a badass New Yorker, a wife, a mother, a former blogger and lover of all things chocolate. Most days you'll find her trying to avoid standing on discarded LEGO or deciding which book to read next. Her debut novel, Always You, released in 2015 and since then she's written several more—some of which will never see completion—and has ideas for hundred to come.

Stay in touch!
Join Stephanie's Rose Garden on Facebook and sign up for Stephanie Rose's newsletter at www.authorstephanierose.com

Follow Me on Book+Main @stephanierose

facebook.com/authorstephanierose

instagram.com/authorstephanierose

bookbub.com/profile/stephanie-rose

twitter.com/StephRoseAuthor

# BOOKS BY STEPHANIE

**The Second Chances Series**
Always You
Only You
Always Us, A Second Chances Novella
After You
**Second Chances Standalone Spinoffs**
Finding Me
Think Twice
**The Ocean Cove Series**
No Vacancy
No Reservations
**The Never Too Late Series**
Rewrite
Simmer
Pining
**Standalones**
Safeguard
Just One Favor

Made in United States
Orlando, FL
25 November 2022

24991916R00176